QUEEN
OF THE
STRIP

QUEEN OF THE STRIP

by

L. J. BROOKSBY

CREATIVE ARTS BOOK COMPANY
Berkeley • California 2000

Queen of the Strip is published by Donald S. Ellis
and distributed by Creative Arts Book Company

For Information contact:
Creative Arts Book Company
833 Bancroft Way
Berkeley, California 94710

ISBN 0-88739-234-2
Library of Congress Catalog Number 98-89794

Printed in the United States of America

To all those brave folks who lived on the Arizona Strip
in the late 1800s and early 1900s.
Their heroic examples made this book possible.

QUEEN
OF THE
STRIP

One

An expression of weariness crossed her youthful face as the man's cigar slid from one side of his mouth to the other. "I understand the express car is carrying a lot of cash this trip." His rough voice carried to the man sitting across the aisle from them as the swaying passenger car pushed his body more firmly against her.

"Yup, that's what they say. Wouldn't surprise me none if the Kid stuck his face into the picture before long," the slim cowboy across the aisle drawled.

His stubby fingers lifted the cigar from his mouth as he squinted past her at the grime-coated window of the locomotive passenger car. The brazen sun shone hot through the smoke, highlighting a light film of dust that lay over the worn leather seats and those occupying them. Several hard-eyed men, most of them wearing six-shooters strapped to their thighs, were seated among others dressed in business suits. The noise of the wheels rushing along the tracks made normal conversation almost impossible, which accounted for the lack of talk and the glazed look on the other occupants' faces. The four women passengers sat in seats next to windows, trying vainly to see through the soot and smoke to catch a glimpse of the passing countryside; not that it was so interesting, but they had been on the train since it left Salt Lake City early this morning, talking little during brief stops, and now just wanted the trip to end.

He shuttled his glance to her face, seeing a young girl in her late teens or early twenties, with long chestnut hair that flowed over slim shoulders. A fashionable bonnet perched on her head, shading weary hazel eyes from the incoming rays of the sun. She wore a modern dress, definitely of eastern make, with a matching handbag resting on her lap. Sweat slowly made its way from her hairline, trickling down the sides of her lovely face.

"You gettin off the train at St. George, Ma'am, or continuing on to Mesquite?" His foul-smelling breath hit her with a vengeance. She had been traveling for a week now and looked forward to getting off the train in St. George to rest for a day before continuing on. It would feel like heaven to be in a hotel room where she could take a leisurely bath, stretch out on a bed, and not hear, see, or smell this dirty old passenger car.

Her voice barely reached him, even though he still pressed against her side. "I'm leaving the train in St. George."

Suddenly there came the squeal of brakes, the grinding sound of iron wheels on iron rails, and the passengers were thrown violently forward. He was a huge man and he fell heavily against her, pressing her against the window and knocking the breath from her chest. The men who were standing in the aisle found themselves sprawled on the floor, while screaming and cursing from the other passengers filled the air. When the train slowed and came to a sudden stop, the jolt threw the passengers back against their seats. The young girl gasped with relief when the huge man's weight shifted off her. She breathed deeply and gratefully as the pressure on her chest decreased. The air filled with dust, which caused her to cough and choke; it seemed she would never be able to breathe normally again.

The rear door of the car burst open to reveal a tall slim man with a bandana covering the lower part of his face and a forty-four six-shooter pointed at the passengers.

"Just sit quietly, folks. It'll only take a minute for my friends to relieve you of your valuable possessions and empty the safe in the baggage car."

He stood easily, his hat pushed back slightly, revealing the sandy hair evident under its brim. The western shirt he wore was opened at the throat, worn but clean Levi's dressed his long legs, a full cartridge belt slanted across his waist, and the forty-four's open-topped holster hung low, tied to his upper right thigh. Only his gunmetal gray eyes were visible above the bandana; there were small lines running out from each corner, giving the impression that he smiled a lot. He appeared to be in his early twenties, and his carefree attitude said there was nothing in life worth worrying about.

Two other men, their faces also covered, shoved into the car carrying small gunnysacks. Moving quickly among the passengers, they collected money, watches, jewelry, and anything else that looked valuable. Opening the women's purses as they came to them, they dumped the contents into the sacks. The tall robber standing in the door spoke softly as one outlaw approached the young girl. "Don't bother with her. She's too young to be carrying anything valuable."

The thief glanced at him, scowled, then shrugged and continued on to the next passenger. It was plain to everyone that this slim man in the door bossed the outlaws.

When the thieves were almost finished, a loud explosion from the baggage car rocked the train. Everyone knew the safe had been blown. The tall slim man smiled at the passengers. Tipping his hat towards the young girl, he gave a slight bow and said: "Have a pleasant trip to your destination, Ma'am."

The two men with the gunnysacks passed out the rear door as he whirled and disappeared over the back railing of the car. It wasn't long before the passengers saw eight horses with riders leave the train and gallop away through the trees.

Cursing that had been interrupted began again, aided by crying women and general confusion as packages, hats, purses, and wallets were collected from the filthy floor.

The young girl relaxed in her seat, clutching her handbag which contained two hundred dollars. Gladness filled her heart.

The outlaw thought her too young to be carrying anything important, so she still had the money her father sent to pay her way back from school. She hadn't needed it because she had held a part-time job as bookkeeper for the railroad headquarters in New York. This provided her with enough to travel on, and since she worked for the railroad, her travel expenses were few.

The conductor came through the car, trying to bring some order to the chaos, a bloody bandage tied around his head.

"Show's over, folks. That Arizona Kid's gang relieved Wells Fargo of another thirty thousand dollars. They didn't kill anyone, just busted a few heads, one of 'em mine.... I didn't move fast enough to suit them."

A stout, sweating man, dressed in an expensive eastern suit, said bitterly, "That isn't all he got! I had two thousand dollars in my billfold. The rings he took cost plenty too."

Another man shouted angrily, "Why doesn't the railroad do something? The Kid robs a train or stagecoach at least once a month, and no one knows how to stop him."

The conductor shrugged his shoulders. "The railroad has tried, believe me. The Kid just disappears into thin air after pulling a job. There were six armed guards in the express car this trip, but by the time they picked themselves up off the floor, the Kid's gang had them covered." Then he sighed. "The train's disabled, and we'll be sitting here till another one comes to get us. The telegraph wires are cut somewhere down the line-that means no help till we don't show up at St. George and they send someone out to look for us. You might as well get out and stretch-it'll be dark before help arrives."

The young girl was the last to leave the car. She stepped down, walking beside the tracks to the front of the train. A large tree had been cut down, and now rested on top of the locomotive. The timing of the falling tree looked perfect: the engineer and fireman saw it starting to fall, tried to stop the train, and then, seeing they were too late, jumped before being hit. The tree had pushed the train off the tracks and bent the engine; this locomotive would not be pulling anything for some time. Whoever the Arizona Kid was, he planned things well. It would probably be two days before anyone went hunting for him, and by then he and his gang would be so far away or well hidden, no one could catch them.

The young girl heard some of the train crew discussing the wreck and saying how lucky they were. From her point of view, she didn't see much luck, except no one was seriously hurt. Then she overheard one of them say, "Yeah, I was on the old ninety-seven when they got 'er...Dan West was the fireman. Remember him? Well, that engine cracked and this superheated steam came rushing outta there like a rifle bullet—cut off his foot and cauterized it all at the same time. Didn't even have time to scream."

Uneasy crewmen gazed at the ground pensively...it was painful to hear, even worse to know such things could happen to them. The young girl felt her skin crawl, then turned to watch the flagman set up the flares-they surely didn't need another train plowing into them. She decided to take the engineer's advice and go find a place to rest.

It was a beautiful spot to wait for help. There were tall pines close to the tracks, gamma grass covered the ground, the air smelled fresh and clean, and the shade felt especially welcome after the hot passenger car. People were already lounging around, sitting under the shady trees, and several card games sprang up among the men. She didn't know what they were using for money, but their lack of funds didn't seem to dampen the spirit of the games. The other three ladies had found a secluded spot under a large blue spruce and were talking excitedly to each other.

When the young girl passed close by, she heard the name of

the Arizona Kid mentioned. Apparently, he was very well known in this part of the country. She had been gone for four years, with only her father's letters to keep her posted on what happened on the Arizona Strip, and he never mentioned depressing events.

Those years had been filled with school; now she wondered why she had really gone back East. Her father said it was to become a lady, but what would a lady do on the Arizona Strip? It was important to her father, however, and he often reminded her of this in his letters. She wondered if, because he'd raised her alone, he felt inadequate when it came to "female" things.

Well, she had learned it all, but it still didn't take the wildness out of her. She would rather be riding on her father's ranch with a six-gun strapped to her side than learning how to carry on a conversation with men and women who didn't care about anything other than who was going with whom and where the next big party would be. Yes, she learned how to manage a business and do the books of a large corporation by working for the railroad, but she really wanted to tame a bucking bronc and shoot dollars out of the air with a six-gun. If any of her friends at school had known what she could do with a horse and six-gun, they would have been shocked.

She continued walking up the slope of the hill. Just below the summit, a large evergreen tree stood with spreading branches. It was an ideal place to rest while waiting. She spread her skirts neatly under her as she sat down, leaning against the tree. The train and all its passengers were still visible, yet they were far enough away that she couldn't hear any sound from them. The peace and quiet was wonderful after the noisy train. Her eyes closed and her thoughts centered on the man responsible for the delay.

She was startled when a soft, now familiar voice came from the other side of the tree. "Did you really have anything of value in your handbag, miss?"

Her eyes widened. That voice belonged to the leader of the outlaws. Why would he be here? He should be miles away by now. She started to stand up.

The concealed man cautioned: "Just relax, miss. If you make a fuss, I'll have to take you with me—I'm sure you wouldn't like that. Besides, someone might get hurt, and I don't think it would be me."

"Of all the nerve! Why are you hanging around here? Surely someone will see you, then you might try to kill them."

Her voice rose slightly as she spoke. It seemed impossible that she was having a conversation with the outlaw who just robbed the train. And the audacity of him! Putting the responsibility of the passengers safety onto her, when he should've ridden off with the rest of his gang and left them in peace. She felt really annoyed.

His voice came softly to her again. "I just wanted to know if I'd missed anything valuable by not letting Randy search your handbag. If something was there, and word got out that the Arizona Kid had missed it, I'd be the laughingstock of the whole country. So you see, I have to know."

She was dumbfounded, angry, and, at the same time, scared. If she told him about the two hundred dollars, he would take it. What should she do? She couldn't lie, even to an outlaw. Her father's training had been to always tell the truth, no matter what the consequences. She sat there thinking, hoping this was a dream. No such luck. There was the wrecked train and its passengers down below. Why in the world had she wanted to get this far away from the others? And what possessed the Kid to stay around here where he might be seen? It was probably just a game to him. The more danger involved, the happier he'd be. Well, there was no use lying. He might as well know what she had in the handbag. After all, that's what he wanted.

Disgustedly, she answered him. "There's two hundred dollars in it."

Muted laughter floated out from behind the tree. "Miss, you sure put one over on me. You sure look like an eastern girl. I didn't know they had enough spunk to admit something like that."

She answered huffily, "I'm not an eastern girl! I've been away to school for four years. I grew up on the Arizona Strip, then my father sent me East so I could become a real lady." Unconsciously, her back straightened and her chin came up, taking on the pose that had been drilled into her.

Still angry, she spoke with contempt: "If you'd been taught to be a gentleman, people wouldn't be robbed of their money and valuables."

The Kid chuckled. "You sure are a wild one. Maybe I should take you with me, you'd fit right in with my ornery men. Besides, it would be nice having a pretty girl like you around."

The minutes passed as they each sat with their thoughts. She was afraid to speak since it might cause him to really take her with him. She wouldn't put it past him to do just that. The time to shut up was now.

His voice drifted again to her: "Who's your father, miss?"

Uh-oh, this wasn't what she had expected. She hesitated, not wanting to answer. Why did he want to know? Would he harm her father? Did he think they had a lot of money and planned on robbing them? Or was this a part of his game? But he'd be able to find out anyway, so what did she have to lose? After all, it wasn't every day that a young girl like her carried on a conversation with a famous outlaw while they sat under a pine tree. When she wrote to her friends back East, they'd be horrified. Imagining their reaction, she began to smile, which made her voice warmer than she'd intended.

"My father is Bert Jackson. He runs the Lazy B-J ranch on the western part of the Arizona Strip."

There was another chuckle from the Kid. "That certainly explains you, then. So you're old Bert's daughter, a chip off the old block. No wonder you're so feisty. Old Bert was a real he-hound; yes sir, he was quite a man in his younger days. They say he could shoot your right eye out at five hundred yards. It was a shame when he got all crippled up. Now all he does is tend bar and tell windy stories."

Startled to hear this, the young girl tensed. Her father wasn't a cripple, at least not when she left for school. "You sure we're talking about the same man?" she asked, fear beginning to cloud her mind. Her father certainly never mentioned any accident; the Kid must be talking about someone else.

The Kid sensed he'd made a terrible mistake. He remembered now that she said she had been gone for some time. Maybe her father hadn't wanted her to know of his troubles; she would've insisted on coming home if she'd known.

The Kid spoke cautiously: "Miss, I'm sorry if I've mentioned something you weren't aware of. The Bert Jackson I know got trampled badly by a wild bull about two years ago."

Silence surrounded the young girl as her thoughts raced. Her father was the only Bert Jackson on the Strip, but he didn't own a bar he owned a ranch. Clinging to this, she asked hesitantly, "Is the man you're talking about the owner of the Lazy B-J ranch?"

Reluctantly, the Kid answered, "He was the owner till the accident. Now he's owner of the Golden Palace saloon in Pine Wood, Arizona."

Her father a saloon owner? Things were happening too fast for her. This outlaw sat telling her facts she knew nothing about. Why hadn't someone in Pine Wood let her know what had happened to her father? She was coming back home expecting to live on the ranch, and now the ranch belonged to someone else. She didn't know what to do. She wanted to get to her father as fast as she could to see how he was and what she could do to help him.

"Kid, my name is Rita Jackson. I'm Bert Jackson's only daughter. Is there any way I can get to Pine Wood without waiting for the train to be repaired?"

"Well, miss, my men and I always stake another bunch of fresh horses down the trail before pulling a job. If you want, you can ride behind me on my horse till we get to where the other horses are stashed. My men will already be gone. I'll pick up my other horse and rendezvous with them later. You can ride this horse on to Pine Wood, leave him at the livery stable, and I'll pick him up one of these days."

Rita thought fast. If she took his horse, the posse trailing his gang would follow her tracks into town and find out she had brought the horse there. Since the Kid had not taken the money from her handbag during the robbery, it would look like she was an accomplice in the holdup. Her father had enough trouble without her bringing any more down on him.

The Kid must have read her thoughts, since he asked: "How well do you know this country?"

"I know my way around, so I could get to Pine Wood without any problem."

"Then the thing for me to do is take you to Joe Weitzel's place, just this side of the Utah line. It's only about five miles from here. I'll let you off close to his ranch, then you can walk in and tell him about the train wreck. He'll let you borrow a horse to go on to Pine Wood. I'll backtrack to wipe out my horse's hoof prints and then head out to meet my men."

This had to be the weirdest day Rita had ever experienced. This famous outlaw wanted to help her when he could be miles away and safe. He probably thought it would make the game that much more exciting.

She said, "If you really mean it, I accept. I know Joe; he'll be glad to loan me a horse. And he could send one of his men into St. George to let them know of the train wreck and get help to those poor people sooner. Besides, that gives me a good excuse for leaving the train."

No answer came from behind the tree. Her heart beat wildly. Rita stood up and slowly walked around the tall pine. The Kid was gone. She hadn't heard him leave, yet no one was there. She gazed around uneasily, then heard a low whistle from over the crest of the hill. Hurrying up to the top, she saw the Kid on a palomino horse, the mask still covering his face. She ran to him as fast as her dress would let her. He reached down, took her arm, and swung her onto the back of his saddle. The horse immediately broke into a lope, carrying them towards Joe's ranch.

It was not a pleasant ride for Rita because her dress kept riding up on her legs. She tried to pull it down, but it was impossible to keep it where it should be, so she gave up. She would probably never see the Kid again anyway, so why worry about her bare legs showing?

As for the Kid, he was rather enjoying the ride. The beautiful scenery plus the feel of Rita's body pressed against his back pleased him. All in all, this had been a very interesting holdup. He could not recall a more exciting one....he began to wonder if he could end all his robberies this way. As he recalled, though, he had never seen a young girl as beautiful as Rita at any of his past robberies. He knew he'd have to spend more time in Pine Wood from now on.

The Kid finally drew the horse to a stop. "This is where you get off. It's been a very pleasant visit. Tell old man Bert hello from the Arizona Kid." He took hold of her arm as she slipped from the saddle. "Hope to see you again someday, Rita." He saluted her, then pulled his horse around and vanished into the trees.

Rita had not even thanked him, and for some reason she felt all alone as the dust from his horse settled. With a big sigh, she turned and started down the pine-covered knoll towards Joe's ranch. She had to admit it had been quite an experience so far. She could see the Weitzels ranch house nestled in the valley below. There were men working in the corral; dust boiled up from what appeared to be a branding operation.

While she walked, her mind reeled in turmoil. Would her father believe such a fantastic story? She'd been in a train wreck caused by the Arizona Kid, then carried on a conversation under a pine tree with said Kid, who gave her a ride to a ranch close by so she could get to her father quicker, thereby cutting down his time to get away. It was hard to believe it herself. Maybe she had dreamed it all. But these trees were real, and that really was Joe's place below. She shook her head ruefully. It would certainly be a different homecoming than she'd planned.

Two

As Rita came down the hill, one of the cowboys at the corral saw her. He pointed in her direction and the branding stopped. They watched as she walked towards the ranch house. How often did they see a young pretty girl walk out of the woods and onto the ranch. Where could she have come from? Dressed like she was, it couldn't have been far, but there wasn't another place close by.

Then Joe, who had been leaning against the corral fence, jerked upright. This girl looked familiar. As he squinted at her, he suddenly let out a shout: "Well swallow my beard, if it ain't Rita Jackson. What in tarnation are you doin' here, girl?"

Rita stopped in front of Joe. "Hello, pardner," she said, laughing. "You look like the cat's got your tongue, Joe."

"Well, honey, it causes a mite of excitement when you come walkin' into my ranch dressed like a city girl." He repeated the question again. "What in blue blazes brought you here?"

Rita's face grew serious. "The Arizona Kid wrecked and robbed the train I was on; the wreckage is about five miles due west. I walked here to get help from you. Would it be possible for me to borrow a horse to continue on to Pine Wood? I understand my father has been injured, and I'd like to get there as fast as I can. And if you could send a man to St. George to alert the railroad people of the train wreck, I'm sure those stranded passengers would appreciate it."

The men were hanging on her every word by this time. Amazement lay on all their faces. Joe looked dumbfounded, then worried. His face was pale as he stared at her. "You been gone a long time, honey."

Then he turned to his men. "Ed, you catch and saddle, then ride to St. George as fast as possible. Bill, saddle a fast horse for Rita." He turned back to her. "You come in the house with me. We need to talk while Bill is saddlin' your horse. Walkin' all that way, you must be thirsty as well as hungry."

"Thanks, Joe, I'm both. But I'm awfully worried about my father and want to get to Pine Wood as soon as possible," she said as they started to the house.

Joe gave her a steady stare as they walked. "How long since you heard from your pa?" he asked.

Rita sensed something wrong in Joe's question. When they stepped through the kitchen door, she said: "About three weeks; he sent me some money for traveling expenses." She paused as Mrs. Weitzel came forward, surprise on her face.

"Rita Jackson! For heaven's sake! What are you doing out here, and all dressed up like a New York lady." She hugged Rita as she talked. "My land, it's good to see you. It's been a long time since you visited Joe and me."

She started to say something else when she caught Joe's eye. He shook his head slightly. Suddenly she realized Rita probably didn't know about her father.

Rita smiled at Joe's hearty wife, a large woman in her fifties with a big bosom and ample stomach. Her face seemed to have a perpetual smile on it. She'd been like a mother to Rita after Rita's mother died when Rita was ten.

"I'm back to be a cowgirl again. You can have the East. You never see the sun or the stars, and the people aren't friendly by a mighty long ways. I'm so homesick for the ranch I could almost cry. I missed all the openness and all the wide space between the mountains of the Strip. After being on that train for a week, and back East for four years, the smell of pine and sage is just wonderful."

Joe explained to his wife: "The train was wrecked by the Arizona Kid. Rita walked here to get help and to borrow a horse to go on to Pine Wood."

Steering Rita to a chair at the table, he said gently: "Sit down, honey, there's a few things you should know before you go into town."

Rita could tell by Joe's expression that he wasn't comfortable with what he had to say. She told him, "If it's about Dad's accident with the wild bull, I heard about that on the train. I also heard he sold the ranch and bought a saloon in Pine Wood."

Neither Joe nor his wife would meet her eyes. They stood close to each other, strangely solid in their oneness, as if each gathered strength from the other's presence.

"You didn't already know those things, Rita?" Mrs. Weitzel asked, hoping she was wrong. "Your daddy didn't write and tell you?"

"I guess he was afraid I'd leave school and come home if he told me. I hadn't heard anything about his trouble till I was talking to-" Here Rita hesitated a moment, then went on. "A man on the train told me about the accident with the bull."

Joe sent his wife a veiled look, full of hidden meaning. "She hasn't heard from her pa in three weeks."

"Oh my goodness!" Mrs. Weitzel exclaimed, breaking her connection to her husband to come over and place a comforting arm on Rita's shoulder, whose need would be greater.

By now Rita knew something was definitely wrong, something they were very reluctant to tell her. She stared straight at Joe. Her voice broke as she cried: "What's happened? Is it more bad news about my father?" What else could happen this day? She wondered, almost ready to scream. Turning from one to the other, she implored: "Won't one of you tell me what you're talking about?"

Sadly, Joe looked at her anxious young face. "Yes, Rita, there is more bad news." He paused, wishing with all his heart he didn't have to do this, then gave a big sigh and with great reluctance told her. "Your pa got shot and killed a week ago. With this heat, they held the burial the next day."

For a moment Rita sat frozen: couldn't move, couldn't think, couldn't talk...then her face crumpled, and tears rolled down her cheeks. She buried her face in her hands, great sobs shaking her body while Mrs. Weitzel hugged her close. Patting Rita's back, she murmured unhappily: "Now now, honey, I know it's quite a shock. I wish we weren't the ones to tell you, but it's better you hear it here than when you get to town. We're truly sorry about it."

Getting a measure of control over her emotions, Rita asked pitifully: "How did it happen?"

Joe, standing around feeling useless and wanting to help, felt glad to tell the story. "He was gettin' ready to close up the saloon one night, when a gunfight broke out between two men playin' cards. One accused the other of cheatin', both went for their guns. A stray bullet took your pa in the chest. He died within minutes."

Wiping away the tears with her handkerchief, Rita folded it in her lap. "I guess I'm not as tough as I thought. Dad always taught me to take setbacks in stride, but too many things have happened today. This last shock was a real corker. I haven't seen him for four years, then for him to be killed when I was coming home." She let out a sobbing sigh. "I didn't even get a chance to say goodbye at his burial." A new thought took hold of her mind. "Where was he buried? Since the ranch belongs to someone else, he couldn't be buried by Mother."

Mrs. Weitzel spoke quietly: "The new owner is a very nice man; he and his wife requested the burial be on the ranch by your mother's grave. The preacher did a nice service; almost everyone from the surrounding area was there. Your pa made a lot of friends while tending bar these last few years. People who'd traveled through in the past and met him came to the service. The ranch owner fed everyone afterwards. His men barbequed a steer; it was a good thing since over three hundred people were there."

Staring off into space, Rita said sadly: "That's nice. I'll have to thank him sometime for all he's done."

"Your pa built a small house for you at the edge of town; he looked forward to surprising you. All his spare time for the last year went into building that house, fixing it to be comfortable, and putting in a lovely yard." Mrs. Weitzel tried to sound cheerful, but her voice betrayed her. Tears crept slowly down the time-worn furrows in her cheeks.

As the room grew quiet, Joe and his wife held their breath, waiting for what this bereft girl would do or say next. "If you don't mind, I'd like to walk up in the trees for a little while. I guess there's no need for me to hurry to Pine Wood now."

Rita pushed up from her chair; she wasn't hungry anymore. She gave a weak smile to her two friends as she went despondently out the door. The big sorrel horse Bill had saddled for her stood tied to the hitching post, standing patiently. She had a sudden wild urge to jump into the saddle and ride off to anywhere, and had even taken a step to do this, when she realized that, dressed as she was, it wasn't possible. She patted the horse on the neck and trudged around to the back of the house, where there was a small stream running through the trees.

Walking slowly along the mossy bank, a light breeze lifted her hair, and she began to feel better. She found a flat rock and sat down, then took off her shoes and socks, letting her feet dangle in the clear water.

For a while her mind drifted, trying to repair the damage caused by sudden pain. She noticed that the tamaracks were in bloom, with dutiful bees rushing to do their work. The lone willow tree had a few branches caressing the water, as if thanking it for the life it gave. The smell of greenness was everywhere, filling her senses with the promise of new growth and hope. She wiggled her toes in the water and felt that the earth was giving comfort. With an aching but recovering heart, she came back to the present. What was she to do now? Perhaps it would have been better if the Arizona Kid had taken her with him-then she wouldn't have to face the bad news about her father, at least for a while. Here she was, coming back to be a cowgirl on her dad's ranch, and now she probably owned a saloon.

She tried to remember what the Golden Palace looked like, but too much time had flowed under the bridge, with too many new impressions flitting by. She did remember that there was always someone shooting up the place. Her father would never let her near it when they were in town. There were also some fancy-dressed ladies living upstairs; she thought some of them were very beautiful and often wished she could dress like they did. But she knew instinctively that telling that to her folks would have merited a sound thrashing. With sadness she thought: Never again will my father have to teach me a lesson.

Her mind drifted back in time to when she was a little girl. She had frequently bounced on his knee and would put her small hand in his big rough one when they went for a walk. He'd been both mother and father to her after her mom died. She remembered when he gave her first horse to her, and when he taught her to use a six-gun, how to draw fast, and shoot from the hip. He said she was a natural with a six-gun: anything he threw in the air she could hit, no matter how small.

It had been such a sad time for both of them the day she went away to school. It was all she could do to step up on the train. He reminded her then that some things hard to do were worth the effort. Trying to hold back the tears, she had boarded the train. Not till she was safely inside, where her father couldn't see her, did she cry.

Those years at school had been difficult at first. Eastern girls walked, talked, and looked like nothing she'd ever imagined. She tried her darndest to be as they were—only because that's what her father wanted—but she could never completely scrub off the West. Many times she purchased a ticket back home, only to turn it in a short time later. That's probably what got her the job doing books at the railroad: being there so often, the ticket agent recommended her for the job. It became easier after that; the time left until she finished was short, and with school plus work, her free time was limited. When she quit her job to catch the train home, her boss said she could come back anytime, but she knew she wouldn't ever go back East again. That day was the happiest one she had after leaving the Lazy B-J. Now it had all turned to sorrow.

If there were only someone she could turn to for help, someone strong and carefree like the Arizona Kid. She envied him, no cares in the world, just living to play a game. What game should she be playing now? How could she run a saloon? There were undoubtedly girls there plying their trade; how was she to react to them? They were probably only doing what was necessary to make a living, but could she respect that? Would she need to tend the bar, listening to the rough talk of the patrons, seeing men killed in shoot-outs? Well, the Kid had said she was a wild one, so maybe she'd fit right in.

With her thoughts drifting all over the place, she began to

relax. The cool water running over her tired feet felt good. Searching around, she saw she was well hidden from the ranch house. The Weitzels would see that she got her privacy. She'd been looking forward to a good bath at a hotel tonight, so why not now? A deep pool upstream a little ways beckoned; she could take off her clothes and swim for a while. That would be much better than a bath in a dinky tub.

The thought brought action, and in minutes she was in the water, swimming with strong strokes, feeling the cool water flow over her body. Tense muscles relaxed with the exercise and her head began to clear. A good hour passed before she climbed out and lay on a large rock to dry off.

After a time she got up, dressed, and started the inevitable walk back towards the ranch house and reality. When she passed a bunched group of scrub oaks, a big palomino quarter horse pulled out in front of her, blocking her path. She had been staring at the ground...when she looked up, she recognized the horse, then the rider. Sitting easily in the saddle with his bandana still over his lower face and a worried look in his eyes was the Arizona Kid. "You didn't start right away for Pine Wood, so there must be something wrong. I intended to follow and make sure you got to town safe. I waited a couple miles down the road, but when you didn't show, I started back to see what was up. Your horse was still tied in front, so I rode to the top of the hill to get a good view of the ranch so's I could tell when you left. Then I spotted you sitting on a rock by the stream."

Rita was beginning to get a funny feeling. "You mean, you watched me take a swim?"

The Kid laughed. "Naw, that part of the stream wasn't visible from where I was. I did climb up a mite higher to see where you went, but when you started to undress, I knew you were going for a swim, so I came back to my original spot. I sure was tempted to come down and join you, but knew if old Bert found out, I'd have to leave the country."

The mention of her father brought Rita's thoughts back to her trouble. "You didn't know my father had been killed over a week ago?"

The Kid's head jerked up and his eyes became ice-cold and steely. His face and body stiffened with anger.

"Who did it?"

His voice was frigid. She knew if he found out, and the man was still alive, he'd go right after him. But she didn't know; she didn't even know if he was alive. Maybe he'd been killed in the shootout. Certainly Joe hadn't mentioned anything about him.

"I don't know. Mr. Weitzel told me about it when I went in the house." She sighed dismally, then explained. "He said there was a card game in progress at the saloon, a gunfight ensued, and a stray bullet hit Dad in the chest. There was no mention of what happened to the two men."

The Kid sat his horse, staring hard at her, wondering how he could kill the man and make things right. Realizing the near impossibility of this, he tried to comfort her, speaking softly, sympathy and regret in his voice.

"I'm sorry, miss. I guess that changes your plans. If I hadn't stopped the train, you'd still be looking forward to seeing your father."

Rita winced slightly. "It was better to hear the word here than in town. At least I have good friends here, and I can get myself together before I arrive in Pine Wood." She paused, and the Kid waited patiently for her to continue. "Kid, what does a person do when their whole world is turned upside down?"

Leaning forward on the pommel in a relaxed pose, he answered her: "Having never taken life too seriously, I'm not the one to say. But it seems to me you're the owner of a saloon now, and that'll be a very big responsibility. I said you had spunk. I think you could make that place really something if you wanted—make your dad proud of you."

Rita gazed into the distance, considering his words. This wasn't what she expected from him. She wanted sympathy, and here he was telling her she'd be a good saloon owner, and probably a madam. Her anger flared and she started to speak, when the scene crossed her mind of a woman running the saloon and parlor house in Pine Wood. That would really be something to write her friends about. Suddenly she felt lighthearted. The Kid had said just the right thing: she could be successful. After all, she had the education, knew how to keep books, and if trouble came, she could shoot with the best of them. A saloon madam wearing a six-shooter on her hip would be the talk of the country.

A smile broke over her face. "Kid, I hope you got what you wanted from holding up the train. I know I shouldn't feel this way, but I'm glad you did. You've given me the courage to take over my father's business, and I know I can make a success of it. Between what Dad taught me and what I learned at school and the railroad, I'll make that saloon the biggest and best place in all of Arizona."

Considering the little he knew about her, the Kid thought so too, but a jot of caution wouldn't hurt. "I'll still ride behind you to make sure you get to Pine Wood safe."

She rubbed under the horse's jawline, smiling. "That won't be necessary. I'm going back to the train. I'll continue into St. George and visit the saloons there. Then I'll have a better idea of what to do when I handle my own. I'll leave for Pine Wood after buying a few things and studying the saloons as much as I need to." She watched him with concern. "You need to get on your way. Already you've wasted time that could have been used in your escape."

The Kid chuckled. "If a posse could follow my tracks, they wouldn't believe them. Why would a train robber hang around for hours, waiting for the posse to catch up? Besides, it's been interesting. Don't be surprised if I walk into that saloon of yours sometime in the future and expect a drink on the house." Smiling behind his mask, he gigged his horse and started off at a run.

Rita called: "You'll get it, Kid."

The dust boiled up from his horse's hooves and surrounded her. She waved to him when she saw him turn in the saddle and give a salute. After a few minutes she sighed, tore her gaze from the trees where he had disappeared, and walked back to the Weitzels ranch. There was a lot to do. She would have Joe ride to the train wreck with her so he could bring back the horse. From now on she would be very busy. She knew her father would want it this way: he'd always taught her to take her lumps and fight on, without wasting time crying over the past. Her head was high and her stride purposeful when she walked back to the ranch yard. Joe and his wife had seen her coming and were waiting for her.

Three

Joe and Rita reached the train wreck to find things pretty much the same as when she'd left: card games still in progress and the women still chatting under the trees. An air of amiability gave the impression of a company picnic. If it hadn't been for the wounded engine lying under the severed ponderosa pine, they would have thought all this was planned. Help had not yet arrived, and none would be expected until evening.

The weary train crew lounged on the other side of the passenger car, in the shade of some pine trees, while the dejected Wells Fargo men sat a little distance away, wishing they had the Arizona Kid's neck in their hands. Joe spoke to one of the railroad men he knew.

"Howdy, Jake. Miss Jackson walked to my place to get help. We sent a man to St. George, so it shouldn't be too long before someone gets here to transport all of you."

All the men pinned their gaze on Rita, surprised that this slip of a girl had thought so logically while they sat around on their duffs. Underneath their dumbfounded expressions, many of them felt a twinge of resentment at being shown up by a female.

"Now why didn't I think of that? I knew where you ranched," Jake muttered to Joe. Turning to Rita, he said admiringly, "You have a head on your pretty shoulders, young lady. Thanks from all of us for what you've done."

Rita smiled and murmured: "It wasn't anything. Joe and his wife are very dear friends, so naturally when I became aware of the closeness of their ranch, I went to them." Her thoughts continued: Wouldn't they all be shocked if they knew how I really got to Joe's ranch?

Joe continued to palaver good-heartedly with the train crew. He didn't get away from the ranch too often and enjoyed talking to men who saw other parts of the country and who made contact with people he considered interesting. Sometimes the stories of those people and their shenanigans were perturbing, but most often they just brought a loud guffaw from the listeners. These God-fearing men knew their way of living was the right way, and all others were slightly tetched in the head. Joe would sift through what he'd heard, then repeat to his wife what he thought was suitable for a woman to hear. She was grateful for even this, since the rough cowhands always clammed up whenever she came near, so her best conversational companion was usually the cat.

Meanwhile, Rita walked off a ways to sit under the fragrant boughs of a pine. She had a purpose to guide her now, thanks to the Kid. What would it be like running a saloon? Surely it would be like any other business, except the merchandise was different, and the customers would all be men. Men. That meant she would have to be tough...the men wouldn't respect a wishy-washy woman running the saloon. Rita's spine stiffened. She could handle it; just let them try anything, and she'd put them in their place. Suddenly she giggled. Here she was, just out of school, perhaps a lady, and ready to take on the whole male population of Pine Wood in a gun battle. Such foolishness. Most of them were probably very nice gentlemen. She had other things to worry about, like the bartender. Was the bartender there able to handle most of the work? And how would she relate to the ladies? Would they resent her and make her job more difficult? Would they all, men and women alike, think her too young to have a sensible brain? Her head swam with questions, but no firm answers. This challenge was becoming interesting. Would the men take to a woman saloon owner? She knew it had occasionally been done in other places, but this was the Strip, and there was no law except what men carried on their hips. All this thinking eventually took its toll: her eyelids became heavy, the shade was cool, and the country peaceful. She drifted off to sleep.

The next thing Rita heard was a train whistle. Help had arrived. It wouldn't take long now for the men to unhook the cars and hook them to the new engine. Later a crew would get the old engine back on the tracks or out of the way, whichever was the most convenient.

All the people stood and cheered as the rescue train pulled to a stop. They collected their belongings and began wending their way down the hill. An energetic bustle pervaded the air, bringing with it jokes and laughter. Workers swarmed everywhere, moving baggage, checking on damage, and helping the ladies onto the train. In only a matter of minutes the passengers were loaded and on their way again to St. George.

Rita sat back in her seat, her mind again very active. She had thanked Joe for his help and promised to keep in touch. Although a part of her was still saddened at the loss of her father, and always would be, she was beginning to feel excited about the future and about how her life would intertwine with those in Pine Wood. Like a child with a mud puddle, she itched to jump in and get started.

As the train gathered speed, the conductor, now with a clean cloth around his wounded head, came into the car and stopped beside her seat.

"Miss Jackson, would you come with me please?" he asked politely.

Amid curious glances from the others, a puzzled Rita stood up and followed him into the special car that had been hooked to the train in Denver. Curiosity and speculation had run rife about who would use that car, conjecture ranging from a governor to a well-known personality. Workers had washed and polished it till it dazzled. And now she was inside. The car was empty, with deep purple velvet drapes covering all the windows. The elaborate interior, with expensive leather furniture, crystal sconces, the finest woods, beautiful gas lamps, and costly china and silver, took her breath away. A wetbar and a small sleeping room stood off in a separate section. As Rita gazed around in awe, the conductor told her, "This is the president's car. We're taking it to California for him. You ride here for the rest of the trip. Make yourself comfortable and fix anything you'd like from the ice chest or bar. One of the crew will be in shortly to make sure everything is satisfactory."

Surprised and thrilled, Rita turned to ask why, but before she could speak, the conductor left. Getting over her shock, she sat in the large soft chair. So this is what luxury was like...it wouldn't take long to get used to it. She knew the railroad owned such cars but had never seen one. The noise from the train wasn't nearly as loud here as in the passenger section, and the air was clean as the smoke from the engine didn't reach this far. She got up and tried the bed in the sleeping room. The soft mattress and feather pillow felt like a cloud from heaven.

Going back to the main compartment, she poured some water into a glass, and putting ice from the chest into it, she tasted the coldest water she'd ever had—at least it seemed that way to her. The swim in the pool had been great, but after the ride back to the train and the nap under the tree, this water was undeniably a pleasure. While savoring its coolness, she wondered why the conductor put her here.

Just then the door opened and Jake, from the train crew, stepped inside. A burly man in his early forties, he stood at least six feet tall, with large forearms and hands. His legs were short, and he looked as strong as an ox. He wore bib overalls with a railroad cap on his head, which he swept off as he spoke.

"Is there anything we can do for you, Miss Jackson?" He paused, giving her a moment of respectful silence, then resumed his more-or-less prepared speech. "We'd like to thank you for your quick action after the train wreck. Help arrived several hours earlier than it ordinarily would have. We want you to know how much we appreciate what you did." Stopping to clear his throat, he went on in a subdued voice. "Joe told us of the shock you received today. We're sure sorry about your Dad."

Smiling sadly, Rita replied: "Thanks for your sympathy, Jake, and please thank the others for me, but you didn't have to go to this much trouble. After all, I'll arrive at my destination sooner too."

"If we'd known you were the one who took care of the railroad books in New York, we'd have put you in here when we picked up the car in Denver."

Looking puzzled, Rita asked: "How did you find that out? And why would I rate traveling in this style?"

"Matt told us about you being the bookkeeper. Since you started keeping the books, our pay arrives on schedule every time. Before that, it could be two to three weeks late. We want you to know how grateful we are." He paused, then said wryly, "I sure hope it doesn't go back to the old way now that you're not working anymore."

Watching the expression on Jake's face change, Rita laughed. "If it does, you let me know in Pine Wood, and I'll fire a letter off to New York for you."

Jake beamed. "Would you really do that?"

"You bet I would." Her mind came back to her immediate problem. Perhaps this man could help her. "Jake, what do you know about saloons?"

The surprise on Jake's face was comical. Then he looked at the floor, and his face began to turn red. Glancing around quickly to see if anyone else was in the car, he lowered his voice.

"Miss, I'm ashamed to admit this to a proper lady like you, but I know more about the inside of a saloon than anyone you've ever met before." He hesitated, then at her expectant look went on. "Joe told us you were the new owner of the Golden Palace in Pine Wood. So since you asked, I'll tell you all I know."

For the next hour Jake filled Rita in on how a saloon works, what the bar girls' jobs were, and how to handle rough customers. Rita asked a lot of questions, which Jake answered as best he could. At one point, one of the crew stepped in to ask Jake something, then nodded and tipped his cap to Rita and left. There was hardly a lull in the conversation. By the time the train pulled into St. George, Rita had a pretty good idea of what she could expect.

When the train came to a stop, Jake opened the door of the president's car and ushered Rita to the station. She noticed the other passengers disembarking, pointing at her and telling their friends about the help she'd given. Jake summoned a hack and took the driver aside. Telling him to take Rita to the best hotel, he gave instructions to get her the nicest room available and bill it to the railroad. Jake told the driver Rita was a very important railroad employee and should be given all the assistance she needed while there. Then Jake explained to Rita where the driver would take her. She tried to object, but Jake wouldn't even consider her request. Her baggage loaded, the driver climbed in and whipped the team to a smart trot for the trip into town.

He pulled up to a magnificent hotel that took Rita's breath away. This must've been built after I left, she thought. At least she hadn't seen it when she stopped here on her way back East. The driver hopped down and held out his hand for her, then escorted her into the hotel to a seat in the luxurious lobby.

"You wait here, miss. I'll take care of registering you and bring in your luggage."

Sitting on a plush velvet settee, Rita noticed that most of the people in the lobby were watching her curiously. The men passing by tipped their hats and spoke kindly to her. The ladies smiled and told her they hoped she would have a pleasant stay, and if they could help her in any way, please call on them.

Rita sat with growing apprehension: everyone treated her as though she were visiting royalty. The hack driver returned with a young man whom he introduced.

"Miss Jackson, Homer will show you to your room. Your bags will come up shortly, and if you want to go anywhere in town, just have the hotel let me know." With that he tipped his hat and left. Smiling at Rita, Homer said: "This way, Miss Jackson."

He started toward the lovely oak staircase that curved up to the second floor and Rita followed. Turning left, he led her to a room at the front of the hotel. He opened the door, stepped back, and politely motioned Rita inside. Moving into the room, she was again met with luxurious surroundings. She couldn't believe this was happening. Walking over to the large beveled-glass front window, she could see all of the city laid out before her, with the red hills to the south in plain view. Turning from the window, Rita opened her purse to find a tip for the young man. He stopped her with a raised hand.

"No thanks, miss. The railroad will take care of everything while you're here. You just let us know how we can be of service to you." Going to the door, he said, "Have a pleasant stay, miss."

The door closed, and Rita was alone. With a sigh, she took off her bonnet, laid it on the dresser, went to the bed, and flopped on it. What a day! There were so many things happening that her mind was all abuzz. How did she ever end up here? It certainly wasn't what she'd anticipated before the train wreck. And who was the Arizona Kid? It occurred to her that if he hadn't held up the train, she would be in the cheapest hotel in town. But here she lay, surrounded by absolute luxury, and it was all his fault. She laughed at the thought; if she ever saw him again, she'd have to do more than buy him a drink.

Someone tapped on her door. When she opened it, Homer stood there with her baggage. He placed it at the foot of the bed, then inquired: "Is there anything else, miss?"

Happily she said: "If you could send up some hot water, I'd like to take a bath."

Smiling at his awed expression, she continued: "My name is Rita, so please don't call me miss anymore. When I've cleaned up, I'll come down to eat."

Homer suddenly put his hand in his vest pocket and drew out an envelope.

"Sorry, miss. I mean Rita, I almost forgot to give you this, and I'll get your water right away."

Rita thanked him and he left the room. She studied the envelope. Miss Rita Jackson was written across the front in bold letters. Opening it, she read: "It would be a pleasure if you would accompany me to dinner in the hotel dining room at eight o'clock this evening. Signed, Mr. Joseph Singer, Proprietor of the Best Saloon and Gambling Parlor in the West.

Rita stood staring at the letter in amazement. People in New York talked of Mr. Singer...some of her friends said he was the richest man in Utah. He traveled extensively throughout the world and owned saloons in many parts of the West. Also, he controlled most of the towns where his saloons were located, but he wasn't a dictator. He was fair and just, and often helped without being asked. Her boss at the railroad had even told her to contact Mr. Singer if she had time and tell him hello. Well, of course she would have dinner with him.

Glancing at the ornate clock on the dresser, Rita realized she would have to hurry to be ready in time. Looking in the mirror, she was aghast at her disheveled hair and rumpled clothes. Then a light knock sounded on the door.

Upon opening it, she found four young men standing there, two carrying buckets of hot water and two carrying a large porcelain tub. They set the tub in the middle of the floor, then poured in the water. Backing away, one of them murmured: "We'll be back with more water in just a few minutes," and they all exited at once, leaving the door open as the steam rose from the tub.

Rita went through her bags to select the best dress she owned. Holding it up, she knew it wouldn't make much of an impression, but it would have to do. Someday she'd have better. As soon as the saloon was going well, she would splurge on some new clothes. Then she stopped thinking along that line; she'd come back to be a cowgirl, and here she was thinking of new dresses and saloons. Disgusted with herself, she turned as the four men returned with more hot water and dumped it into the tub.

When they started to leave, Rita caught Homer's attention and said: "Would you please tell the man who gave you the letter that I'll meet him in the dining room at eight?"

"I sure will, Miss Rita. Is there anything else?" he asked politely.

She thought for a moment, then shook her head. "No, I don't think so. Thanks for all you've done."

"My pleasure," he said, then closed the door and left.

Rita hurriedly removed her clothes and stepped into the hot water. She wished she could just lie back and soak, but there wasn't time. Rushing through the bath, she toweled off and put on clean underwear and the good dress. Combing her hair and piling it on top of her head in a bun, Rita looked in the mirror and decided it wasn't too bad. She wondered what Mr. Singer wanted, and how he knew about her. Well, it didn't matter. He was the largest saloon owner in these parts, and that was who she needed to talk to.

Glancing again at the clock, she read five minutes to eight.

Picking up her handbag, Rita sallied forth, ready for anything, and went down the stairs in her most ladylike manner. The hostess in the dining room saw her descending and met her at the foot of the stairs.

"Good evening, Miss Jackson. Mr. Singer is waiting at his private table. Please come with me."

Rita followed the hostess, a smile of pleasure on her face. At the far side of the dining area she saw a small room with beaded strings acting as a curtain. A table with dinnerware for two waited beyond the beads, and a man was sitting in one of the two chairs. The hostess drew aside the curtain, allowing Rita to pass through.

Mr. Singer rose from his chair, beaming at her. He was rather short, with black hair plastered to his head. His shrewd dark eyes didn't miss a thing. A large cigar rested between his thin lips, and he kept shifting it from one corner of his mouth to the other. His protruding stomach, short arms, stubby legs, and small feet reminded Rita of a penguin she once saw in New York. Rita certainly hadn't expected him to look like this, and she worked hard to suppress a giggle. She had assumed someone with his money and power would look like the Arizona Kid: tall, broad shoulders narrowing to slim hips, long legs, with a kind face and bold eyes. How could such a small man be so important? She hid her surprise behind a smile, taking the hand he offered. It felt puffy and soft and the handshake was limp. The thought went through her mind that this hand probably only signed checks and clipped cigars. Singer lifted Rita's hand and suavely kissed the back.

"Miss Jackson, it's good of you to have dinner with me on such short notice. You are very beautiful, my dear." His high-pitched voice was grating and filled with nervous energy.

Rita curtsied politely. "Thank you for the invitation, Mr. Singer. Mr. Randolph, my boss in New York, asked me to look you up and say hello. This is much more convenient."

Singer's laugh sounded like a parakeet chirp. "Mr. Randolph sent me a telegram saying you were coming and if I needed a good secretary and bookkeeper, to hire you. I met Jake at the saloon earlier and he told me where you were and what you'd done for his crew. He thinks very highly of you, Miss Jackson."

As he held her seat for her, Rita said: "Jake is responsible for my staying at this nice hotel. I don't know why he's being so good to me, but I surely do appreciate it."

The waitress stepped in to take their order. Rita was hungry; she'd had nothing to eat since breakfast. The steak, mashed potatoes and gravy, fresh hot bread with apple pie for dessert would be just right. Singer ordered a small plate of beef stew.

"Would you care for some wine with your meal?" he asked.

"No, thank you," she answered. "I don't like the taste and would much prefer a cool glass of ice water."

Singer gave her a startled look, then said: "You don't drink?" Realizing this was true, he laughed wryly. "Maybe that's the best way to run a saloon. I've seen a lot of saloon owners drink up all their profits, but you won't have a problem."

The waitress left with their orders and Singer got right down to business. She could see that he didn't let anything interfere with his plans, which no doubt explained his success. He kept his concentration on what needed to be done. Resting his arms on the table, he removed the cigar from his mouth and leaned towards her, his face and voice serious.

"As Mr. Randolph said, Miss Jackson, you would be a good employee. Working for me would be a lot better than trying to run a saloon with no prior experience. I know you own your father's saloon, and I'd like to buy you out." He paused, regarding her. "I tried to buy your father out several times but he wouldn't sell. Kept saying you'd come back to this Strip country sometime and would need the business to have something to do."

"You knew my father, Mr. Singer?" Rita asked, surprised.

"Only after he took over the saloon. Being so crippled from the accident, he found it hard to get around, but he wouldn't sell, just kept on working, managing somehow. He hired a bartender to help out, and that relieved some of his load. He'd say he wanted to keep you in school so you could become a lady."

Staring at her intently, he continued: "It looks to me like you succeeded. Your father would be proud of you."

For a moment Rita barely kept back the tears. She looked down at the table while she got control of her emotions, then, returning Singer's gaze, said: "Yes, my father set great store in my becoming a lady; that's the only reason I stayed to finish school. What I really wanted was to be back on the ranch as a cowgirl." Sighing, she continued: "Well, I guess the best laid-plans of mice and men go astray sometimes. With the ranch sold, and me owning a saloon, I'll probably become the lady my father wanted. That, Mr. Singer, is the very reason I cannot sell the saloon. You've told me how hard my father worked to keep it. I'd be very disrespectful if I sold."

A disappointed look came over Singer's face. "I understand your feelings, Miss Jackson, but running a saloon is not the thing for a young lady to do. You should get married and raise a family. I'm sure it's what your father would want."

"I see you didn't know my father very well, Mr. Singer. He'd want me to do just what I plan to do. He taught me to take care of myself, to not depend on anyone else. He would be very proud if I succeeded as a saloon owner, and that's just what I intend to do." Her shoulders were back and her head high as she spoke.

Singer sat watching her, then gave a twisted smile and said: "I can see now why Mr. Randolph spoke so highly of you; you're a determined young woman. I think you'll do whatever you set out to do. Well, if I can't buy you out, I can still be of some assistance in getting you started on the right foot."

His sudden change in manner took her totally by surprise. "Thank you, sir, and I'm obliged for any help you give. By the way, do you know if Jake continued on with the train?"

Now Singer felt startled by the change in the direction of their conversation. "No, Jake stays here at the end of his shift. He uses a room at my saloon when he's in town. That man can drink up a whole paycheck in one night, and when he gets drunk, we have to knock him out by doping his drink to keep him from breaking up the place. He can do more damage in a few minutes than ten men can do in hours. It would take six men to subdue him if we didn't start doping his last drinks."

This news disappointed Rita. She'd considered asking Jake if he would come with her to Pine Wood and help her run the saloon. But if he was that bad, it would never work. Saying nothing of this, she only mentioned to Mr. Singer that she wanted to thank Jake for getting her the hotel room.

When the food came, they both settled into eating. Singer finished first, then excused himself, saying, "I need to get back to business. If you change your mind about selling, let me know. Drop in anytime tomorrow. I'll show you around and help you all I can in your new venture. I wish you luck and will be calling on you frequently in Pine Wood to see how things are going." He stood up, took her hand again, kissed it, then left the dining room.

Rita continued to eat. The waitress came back and said, "That's the great Mr. Singer for you: he never considers the other person's feelings at all. When business is over, he leaves. It happens all the time. His guests are left to finish their meals, and he gets on with his work."

Rita looked up at her and broke into laughter. "I was enjoying the food so much that I didn't even miss him."

This brought a responding laugh from the waitress. "You're all right, Miss Jackson. Most ladies would be mad as all get-out if they were left to eat alone. You look like you're actually happy about it."

Leaning back in her chair, Rita agreed. "Yes, I believe I'm glad he left early. It's nice to talk to someone other than a man for a few minutes."

The waitress continued to chat about Singer and all his businesses. She sat in the chair he vacated and filled Rita in on local gossip. When Rita finished, the waitress got up, saying, "A man by the name of Jake came looking for you some time ago. I told him you were having dinner with Mr. Singer. He didn't seem too happy about that, said he'd wait in the lobby for you."

"From the way Mr. Singer talked, I thought Jake would be drinking up all the liquor in the saloon by now," Rita said with a chuckle.

"You know, I would've thought so too, but he's as sober as a preacher. Come to think of it, I don't remember him ever being in this hotel. I wonder what he wants with you. You don't suppose he's fallen for you, do you?"

Seeing the serious look on the waitress's face, Rita laughed again. "He's old enough to be my father. No, he probably wants to tell me how the crew is coming along with the wrecked engine and about the posse being sent out after the Arizona Kid."

"I can tell you about that," the waitress replied. "The posse won't start till morning, and they won't have any more success catching him than anyone else does." A dreamy look came into her eyes, a subtle smile to her lips. "I'd sure like the Kid to rob me sometime. I'd fall into his arms and make him take me with him."

Rita could see that in the eyes of the ladies of the Strip, the Kid was some kind of a romantic hero. Wouldn't they be surprised if she told how he met her and gave her a ride on the back of his horse? This reminded her of the feel of muscles rippling under his shirt as she held on to him. Maybe she too was beginning to think of the Kid in a romantic way.

Mentally chiding herself for such thoughts, she rose, and saying thanks to the waitress, walked through the beads and out to the lobby. Jake lounged in a big armchair with his head tilted back, snoring. Rita stopped beside him and smiled. He must be tired after today's turmoil. What could be so important he would forgo his drinking and wait in the lobby for her? She hated to rouse him, but if he stayed this way, he would surely wake with a stiff neck. Leaning over him, she put a hand on his shoulder, shaking him gently.

"Jake, wake up."

Jake came out of the chair so suddenly he almost knocked her down. His face showed a wildness and his fists were balled up, ready to strike at whatever woke him. Seeing Rita through bleary eyes, he didn't recognize her at first. Then his vision cleared and he stammered, "Miss Rita, I...I almost clobbered you." He paused, flushing. "You look so grown up and beautiful." Catching himself, he looked down at the floor. "Oh hell, what does an old drunk like me know about beauty? All I ever see is the bottom of a bottle or some fancy-dressed woman in a saloon."

Rita smiled and took him by the arm, leading him out of the hotel. "Let's get some fresh air, Jake. Besides, we can talk outside without all the folks in town flapping their ears."

As they stepped through the hotel doors, the cool evening breeze washed over them. The sky above showed a lovely night with a full moon. They could see the dark mountains to the north. "How kind of you to look for me, Jake. I want to thank you for the hotel room. It's magnificent. I've never been in one so luxurious."

"You deserve the best, Rita," Jake said gruffly. "Nothing is too good for the daughter of old Bert Jackson. He never doped my drinks when I was in his saloon; he just talked quietly to me till I staggered outside to raise Cain." A smile lit his face. "Yes

Ma'ma, I had some real humdinger fights there. But they were all in the street, not in his place. Funny how some men can talk you into doing what they want while others are sneaky doing the same thing." His thoughts must have carried him to those times at Pine Wood, for he became quiet while they walked along the wooden sidewalk.

Rita waited several minutes before speaking. "What did you want to see me about, Jake?"

He started to answer, then hesitated. She looked at him in the moonlight and could tell what he wanted to say made him nervous.

"Is there more trouble, Jake? Is that why you don't want to talk?"

Jake stopped dead in his tracks. "Gosh no, Miss Rita. I didn't mean to make you think there was more trouble. You've had enough bad news for one day." He shuffled his feet, looking uncomfortable, and finally blurted: "I just wanted to see if you could use another hand working the saloon in Pine Wood. I can handle any rough stuff that might happen, and I don't drink when I'm on the job." Relief washed over him at having spoken his piece, and now his eyes were full of hope.

Rita burst out laughing. Taking Jake by the arm again and resuming their stroll, she said: "Great minds run in the same direction, Jake. That's just what I wanted to ask you about. After our talk this afternoon, I wanted to offer you a job working with me at the Golden Palace."

Jake walked beside her like a trusting little boy. Watching him, she felt he'd do anything she asked of him. How could she have been so lucky in finding such a man to fill her father's shoes? She could almost feel her imminent success in the saloon business. One of her major problems, how to control rowdy drinkers, had just been solved. Jake would be perfect, and he'd respected her father. Her thoughts were happy as she anticipated the new adventure she was undertaking. How could one be so sad and then so happy, all in one day? It felt as if her father was still with her, guiding her every action. How could she lose with Jake and her father helping her? She would become the Queen of the Strip. Now that was a weird thought...why did that come into her head?

Four

Rita woke the next morning feeling refreshed. Sunlight peeked around the edges of the blind covering the window. It would be another warm day. Stretching and yawning, she snuggled under the down quilt, then glanced at the clock on the dresser. Nine o'clock! Startled, she began to jump out of bed, then decided there was really no use hurrying. Lying back down, she realized exhaustion had made her sleep so late. A vision of the Arizona Kid popped into her mind, and she remembered all that happened since he robbed the train. Yesterday had been full of experiences, some good, some bad. The ache in her heart for her father was strong and she gave in to grief, sobbing quietly into the pillow. Then, quite unexpectedly, small petals of peace and love seemed to float through her body, as if he were trying to comfort her. Sniffling, she wiped her eyes and said softly: "I won't let you down, Dad."

After a time she got up, dressed, and went downstairs. Jake sat in the same chair in the lobby where she had found him last night. When he saw her, he rose, smiling broadly. Rita walked over to him.

"Howdy, Jake. Is there anywhere we can get some breakfast this late? I don't usually oversleep this way."

"After yesterday's hubbub, it's a wonder you're up this early, Rita," Jake commented. His face bore signs of a recent shave and he wore an ill-fitting business suit that looked new. To all appearances, he hadn't been drinking since she saw him last night. "Yep, there's a hash house down the street that serves a late breakfast." Taking her arm, he ushered her out the door, walking proudly by her side down the dusty boardwalk.

"You look refreshed and ready to go to work this morning," Rita observed. "We'll eat first, then stop in and see Mr. Singer. He wants to show me around the saloon and help me get an idea of what I'm up against. He wanted to buy me out, but I don't want to sell. With your help, I think we can make a go of it."

Jake beamed at the trust she placed in him. "If I had a daughter, that's exactly what I'd want her to do."

While they continued walking, Jake advised: "Mr. Singer is a nice man, but he thinks everyone should do what he wants them to, so he'll try to buy you out again this morning. Just stall him, let him think you might sell sometime in the future. We don't want him totally against us at the very start."

Rita thought about this suggestion. "Isn't that a little deceptive, Jake? He was very straightforward with me, no beating around the bush, all business. I appreciate that and feel we should do the same. I told him last night I wouldn't sell, and he might as well know I still feel that way. Besides, I really don't think he can stop us from being successful, even if he wanted to."

Arriving at the cafe, they took chairs at a table near the front. The place was small but neat and clean. A young lady about Rita's age hurried over. "What would you like this morning, Miss Jackson?"

Her question came as a surprise. It seemed everyone already knew her; the chain of gossip in this town must be extraordinary.

"Just ham and eggs for me." Looking at Jake's big boulder-sized physique, she commented wryly, "Jake probably wants two steaks and four eggs."

Jake laughed, agreeing. "That would be just perfect, Maryann."

They discussed the saloon in Pine Wood while waiting for the food to arrive. Rita was full of questions, which Jake answered rather vaguely. He hadn't been in Pine Wood since Bert Jackson died and wasn't sure who now ran the place.

After eating, Jake thanked Maryann for the good meal, patting his stomach and groaning in mock pain. He paid at the counter and then he and Rita headed for Singer's saloon. They arrived to find Mr. Singer waiting for them in a chair on the front porch. If he was surprised to see Jake with Rita, he concealed it well. Perhaps he saw through her feeble excuse the night before. Greetings were passed around, then Singer ushered them inside, where he proudly showed Rita his saloon.

Card tables and several chairs occupied the downstairs, with a long mahogany bar at the back extending the full length of the room. The furnishings in the saloon were rich and plush. Brass spittoons were placed strategically every few feet and shone as if they had just been polished. A large picture of a half-naked lady reclining on a sofa occupied the very center of the wall behind the bar. On each side of the picture were beautiful gilt mirrors, reflecting the front of the room. Three large wagon wheels, each holding six lamps, hung from the ceiling. A staircase on the east side of the room spiraled up to the second floor. A double door led into Singer's private office on the west side of the room. Two roulette tables stood just in front of this door. The polished wood floor, still damp in spots from a recent mopping, shone in the morning light. A faint smell of whisky, beer, and sweaty bodies pervaded the area; Rita wondered if it ever went away.

Singer led them to his office, where he showed Rita how his books were done and explained. "I keep quite a bit of money to operate on in the large cast iron safe behind my desk."

"Why would you keep money here instead of in the bank?" Rita ask.

"Never trusted banks. If I have the money close at hand I know it's safe. With all the rough men I have on my payroll there isn't any worry about some outlaws trying to take it from me.

Besides, if more is needed, I can always send a runner to the bank for it."

However, Singer explained, they very seldom needed more, since business was so good they sent money to the bank rather than withdrawing it.

After a quick discussion of the book work involved, they tramped upstairs to see where the guests slept. Singer commented that some of the rooms housed the bar girls who lived here. At this hour of the morning most of them still slept in their rooms. Two of the rooms remained empty, so Singer showed Rita what they were like. The rooms were clean, with nice furniture, and the decorations were bright and colorful. He made sure his girls had very good living arrangements. Rita tried to keep her thoughts from what they did to earn this kind of class, but it was difficult, and her face became slightly flushed. Well, she'd just have to get used to it...without the girls, the men would not patronize the saloon as much.

Singer took them back downstairs to his office, where he motioned them to chairs. "Well, Miss Rita, it appears you've convinced Jake to help you out in Pine Wood. It would be a whole lot easier if you'd just sell the place to me. I'll give you more than a fair price since your father was a good friend of mine." He leaned back in his chair, hands clasped across his stomach, waiting for her answer.

Rita hesitated just long enough to collect her thoughts. It wasn't possible the saloon in Pine Wood was as plush and nice as this one, but with the right care it might become so. She knew her father would have liked her to try. There was also the new house he built for her; she could live in it, and with good help, she wouldn't have to be in the saloon all the time. She'd be able to ride the range in order to relax and unwind from business stresses.

"Yes, Mr. Singer, Jake's kindly consented to help me run the saloon. I would be a very ungrateful daughter if I didn't at least attempt to operate it. I'm sure with my training I'll be successful."

Singer sighed. "Well, I wish you good luck. If you come to a point where you want to sell, I'll always buy—not at the price I'm offering now, but I'll buy you out if you eventually decide to quit."

Rita could tell his last statement was meant to put further pressure on her to sell. She rose from her chair, saying: "I really appreciate all you've done, Mr. Singer. You've been so kind and thoughtful. I'll remember your advice and offer. We have to go now, but please come visit us in Pine Wood whenever you can." Signaling to Jake, they shook hands with Singer and left.

Strolling along the boardwalk, Rita asked, "Where is a ladies' apparel shop, Jake? I need to get a few things before we leave. And could you get us seats on the next stage to Pine Wood while I'm shopping? I'll meet you at the hotel for lunch."

"Sure thing, Rita, but the stage doesn't leave for Pine Wood till morning. So take all the time you need for your shopping." He thought a moment. "If you like, I can rent a couple of saddle horses and we could ride to Pine Wood and arrive much sooner."

Thinking of all the shopping she wanted to do, Rita declined. "No, I'll probably have too much to pack on a horse. And if we used a pack horse, it would be awkward, so let's just stay tonight and leave in the morning." Pausing, she changed her mind. "Let's meet at the hotel for dinner instead of lunch; that way I can spend the rest of the day looking around and getting what else we might need."

The two split up, and Rita went to the ladies' shop Jake told her about. The afternoon seemed to fly as she shopped and toured the town. Arriving at the hotel one hour before dinnertime, she ascended the stairs and went into her room, stretching out on the bed, exhausted. It had been a full day, and the coach ride tomorrow would be tiring. A hundred dollars remained of the money she carried in her handbag. Surely there would be more at her saloon in Pine Wood. The thought startled her: here she was, already thinking of it as, hers and she hadn't even seen it yet. Maybe there was a heavy debt on the place that needed to be paid. This thought brought a moment's worry, but it dissipated quickly. Knowing her father, she doubted it. He had always told her not to buy anything unless she could pay for it. That rule had saved her a lot of problems while back east.

Shortly before dinner, she freshened up with the water in the pitcher on the dresser, combed her hair, and put on one of the new dresses she had bought. Looking in the mirror, she wished she could've been dressed this way last night. Oh well, she wasn't entering any beauty contest, so why worry. It seemed most of the people she met today knew her and accepted her as she was. They were all extremely nice, welcoming her to the area.

Going down the stairs, she saw Jake waiting in the lobby. He'd washed, shaved, put on a clean shirt, and dressed in the same business suit. One suit would last a man a long time, whereas a woman was supposed to change clothes almost every day. Rita wondered how this impractical idea got its start.

"I got the tickets for us. The owner at the stage station said your ticket had already been paid for, and since I'm going with you, he provided mine at no cost." Jake beamed at this news. "I'll bet you could get anything in this town you wanted, Rita. Old Bert was so well-liked by everyone that they'd do anything you asked."

Thoughtful, Rita mentioned, "I got the same impression when I talked with folks. It's a nice feeling after being in New York, where no one cares what happens to you. I don't think there's anyplace quite like the West."

The same hostess met them at the door to the dining room. "Good evening Miss Jackson. There's a table over in the corner would you like that?"

Rita looked up at Jake, "That might be a little quieter place for us to talk."

Jake nodded his head and took her arm as the hostess led them to the table. Everything on the menu looked good, and Rita wanted to order it all. She'd been so occupied with buying necessities that she forgot to eat lunch. Finally settling on chicken pot pie, she ordered, and then she and Jake discussed the events of the day while waiting. When the food arrived, they both dug in as though they were starved.

After they finished the rhubarb pie, the waitress came over to sit and talk with Rita for a few minutes. Jake excused himself, saying he would see Rita at the stage station in the morning.

"Are you really the owner of the Golden Palace Saloon in Pine Wood?" The waitress asked.

"Yes, but to be honest, I'm not sure how things will work out since I've been away to school for four years." Rita answered.

"You look so young to be taking on a task like that. And all the rough characters you'll meet would scare me to death."

"Oh, I don't know. You seem to handle all the people that come in here without any problem."

"But this isn't a saloon. There's gunfights and men fighting all the time and what do you do about the girls that work there?"

"Now that does present a problem, but with Jake helping me I'm sure things will stay under control."

Finally ending the idle chitchat, Rita headed to her room. She asked the man behind the hotel desk to wake her at six o'clock in the morning because the stage left at seven. It had been a notable day, and she was glad to snuggle into the comfortable bed for a well-deserved rest.

Jake rose early the next morning. He ate breakfast at the cafe, then went to the stage station to help with harnessing the horses. He was glad to be going to Pine Wood. It had always been a pleasant experience before, even if he did end up dead drunk half the time. He liked Rita and felt sure he would be useful to her in the saloon. Being handy with his fists, and being such a big hulk of a man, he figured he could keep order by his sheer presence. Anyway, he'd traveled enough working for the railroad, and now wanted to settle in one place. He whistled while he worked with the horses...it felt good to be off that noisy train. His anticipation ran high as he waited for Rita.

During the night, Rita dreamed that the Arizona Kid held up the stage she rode on. His men shot the driver and took the strongbox, which contained twenty thousand dollars of Wells Fargo money. Her father was one of the Kid's men. He was pulling her up on his horse to take her with him when a knock on the door woke her. Groggy and disoriented, she took a moment to collect her wits. She hurriedly threw on a robe and answered the door. Homer stood in the doorway, looking apologetic for waking her, and told her it was six o'clock. She thanked him, dressed, and, after packing everything, went down to breakfast in the hotel dining room. At six forty-five she met Jake at the stage station.

The concern on Jake's face was plain as he looked at her. "You doing okay this morning, Rita? Looks like you might of had a rough night."

"Do I look that bad, Jake?" She smiled gently as he took her arm.

"Gosh, no, you look great. But your eyes are tired, and I thought maybe the noise at the hotel might keep you awake."

"Actually, the hotel was very quiet. I just dreamed a lot about the things that might happen once I start to operate the Golden Palace."

"You don't need to worry none about that. Between the two of us we'll let those who give us their business know that we ain't to be monkeyed with." Jake tried to ease her fears.

They loaded everything onto the stage and rumbled out of town on the eighty-mile trip to Pine Wood. They would be stopping for lunch at a small stage stop about halfway. The rough road caused the stage to sway from side to side, throwing the six passengers against each other and the sides of the coach. The spicy language of the wiry, impatient driver could be heard above the rattle of harness and rumble of wheels on the rutted road. Dust drifted in through the open windows. It would be suffocating if they were closed. Rita began to wish she'd taken Jake's suggestion that they ride the horses. Too late now, she just hoped she would be in one piece when they arrived in Pine Wood.

Stopping for lunch, the passengers straggled out of the coach, rearranging clothes and brushing off dust. The one other woman, a gentle lady in her late thirties, gravitated towards Rita and sat by her at the rough wooden table.

"Hello," she said pleasantly. "My name is Mrs. Juliette Johnson." She added with a twinkle: "Friends call me Julie."

"Rita Jackson," Rita said, extending a hand in her most ladylike manner. "Pleased to meet you."

"Jackson," mused Julie thoughtfully. "Are you related to the fellow who owned the Golden Palace saloon?"

"My father," Rita managed to choke out. It hurt all over again to think she was coming into Pine Wood but would not be able to see him.

"Oh my dear, I'm so sorry." The pain in Rita's eyes had touched Julie's heart. This young girl was about the same age Julie's daughter would have been had she lived beyond birth. "Are you coming to Pine Wood to sell the saloon?"

"No." Rita's chin came up defiantly. "I'm going to run the saloon."

Julie was astonished. "How do you expect-" she started to

ask, then took another good look at Rita. Seeing the strength and determination on her young face, Julie swallowed her words and said instead, "Good luck to you, Rita. If I can help in any way, please let me know. My husband owns the bank in town, so I'm easy to find."

Grateful, Rita said, "I'm hoping I won't need a bank too much, but I really appreciate having a friend."

As the conversation continued, they became better acquainted, and by the time they finished eating, a friendship had blossomed. After lunch, the stage left in a run again with fresh horses. If possible, the road became even rougher. All the passengers looked forward to another stop at the fort in Pipe Springs to change horses. The short stop also allowed the two ladies to continue their chat.

While the horses were being changed, the passengers strolled around shimmering ponds shaded by huge cottonwood trees and watched the ducks swimming in the water. It was cool there, and they were thankful for the short rest.

An old man leading an ornery-looking mule with a pack on its back approached Rita and Julie while they waited. Nodding briefly to Julie, he stared steadily at Rita as he came up.

"Seems I oughta know you, youngun," he said, squinting in the bright sunlight as his eyes took her in.

Studying the man, Rita was sure she'd never met him before. He looked like a prospector: grizzled beard, wrinkled, leathery skin, stooped and bow-legged as if time were gradually pushing him closer to the earth. His clothes were clean but worn, and there were sweat stains on his hatband and under his arms.

Smiling, she said, "I don't think I know you, mister. Maybe you say this to all the young girls you meet."

The prospector studied her some more, then grunted: "I'll bet yer old Bert's kid. He tol' me all about you. You shore carry his mark on you, young'un. I'm headin' in to see him now; he always grubstakes me. If I ever hit the big one, he gits half." He paused to spit, barely missing the mule, who gave an angry snort, laying its ears back. "Shore hope it don't take too much longer to find 'er. I'm gittin' too old to traipse around this here Strip anymore."

Doleful, Rita gave him the bad news. "I'm afraid you'll be disappointed, sir. My father was killed more than a week ago. I'm on my way there now to take over the saloon."

The prospector wrenched off his hat and slammed it to the ground. "Dad blast it, if that don't beat all. Cain't never tell in this country what'll happen next." Glaring at all of them, as if somehow they were responsible for the injustices of the world, his anger soon gave way to sorrow, and he bent over slowly, picked up his hat and murmured: "People call me Fuzzy Morton. Them that want just call me Fuzzy. Mighty sorry to hear such terrible news, young'un, but I guess the good Lord giveth and the good Lord taketh."

Rita could see the sadness and disappointment on the old man's face. Her heart went out to him: forlorn and bereft, he seemed lost, wondering what to do next. Impulsively, she put her hand on his arm.

"I don't know how much it takes to grubstake a prospector, but I have a hundred dollars if that will help."

The old man's eyes brightened. "By gum, you're a chip off the ol' block, lassie. That's what old Bert always give me, then I goes out to start lookin' agin. Someday I'll have so much gold, I'll be spittin' nuggets." He began to cackle. "Yesiree, young lady, I'll jist take you up on that. I'll git what I need here at the fort. Save me a long trip to Pine Wood."

Rita opened her handbag and gave him the hundred dollars. Well, that was that. She sure hoped there was money available at the saloon or she'd be in real trouble.

"Thankee, young'un'." Fuzzy took the money eagerly, then he pulled the stubborn mule toward the store inside the fort. "C'mon, Petunia, we got us some gold to find. Then you kin get shut of me and live on some fancy ranch with a bunch a good-lookin' stallions. We ain't too old too dream, by gum!"

He was still assuring the obdurate mule of her oat-filled future when Jake stomped out from behind one of the trees.

"Old Fuzzy's lived off your dad for the last two years. You made a mistake bankrolling him. He's never found anything other than a few small nuggets and never will. Giving him money is like pouring sand down a rat hole."

"I couldn't let him down, Jake. My father would have helped him if he were still alive, so there was nothing else I could do," Rita explained as they walked back to the stagecoach, Jake shaking his head in exasperation.

The horses were changed and the coach ready to roll. Looking up at the driver, Rita asked, "Would it be possible for me to ride up on the seat with you? It's been a long time since I felt the wind from running horses in my face."

The driver chuckled. "Sure thing, Miss Jackson. Just climb up and we'll be on our way. Pay no mind if my language gets raw; horses run a mite faster with some cussin' pushin' 'em along."

As soon as Rita settled on the seat, the driver snapped his whip and the coach rolled on for Pine Wood. The ride on top proved to be much cooler, and the dust didn't reach up to the two on the seat. The country was beautiful, with the varied colors of the cliffs providing a spectacular view. A cerulean blue sky contrasted with white clouds to make the colors more vivid.

Three hours later they rolled into Pine Wood and Rita got her first look at the saloon as they swirled past. The lights were on inside and over the swinging doors she could see diverse men mingling together, with fancy-dressed ladies sprinkled among them, adding little flecks of brightness to the mundane maleness.

Suddenly Rita became frightened of the responsibility that would soon be hers. What had possessed her to think this would be easy, a lark, so to speak? Reality had a way of bringing a person down to size, throwing in a small measure of humbleness along the way. The driver must have sensed her tension. He spoke reassuringly: "Don't worry, Miss Jackson, there's any number of people in town that'll help you if need be. All you have to do is ask."

She placed her hand on his arm. "Thanks for your thoughtfulness. And I'll bet you'd be the first one to come to my aid."

"You jist holler and I'll come running."

But she still remained frightened of the future. Up to now it had been something remote, something to tease her mind with; now she was almost face-to-face with it. The stage pulled to a stop, and Jake stepped out to help her down.

As her feet touched the ground, sudden gunshots roared from inside the saloon. A young cowboy staggered through the batwing doors, clutching his chest with crimson-stained hands, and crumpled slowly to the dust of the street. A tall, angry man dressed in black followed with a smoking six-shooter in his hand. A few of the more predatory customers pressed eagerly behind him. After gazing voraciously at the body and giving false praise to the tall gunslinger, they eventually turned and went back inside. No one cared that a man lay dead. Rita shivered and again wondered if she could handle this task— or if she even wanted to. Let Singer handle the killings and outlaws. She could marry some nice man and get away from all this. Then Jake took her gently by the arm, blocking her view of the dead cowboy, and led her away from the saloon towards the edge of town.

"Your house is the one standing off by itself. You go on in; I'll bring the baggage up shortly." He deliberately chose to ignore the shooting, not knowing how to soften such a jarring situation to a naive young girl.

Trying to forget the dead man, Rita continued on to the house. It was a single story, painted a muted beige color that would blend into the countryside. Inside she found a nice-sized front room, with a door leading into the kitchen and one leading into the bedroom. Walking into the kitchen, she saw a pump on the sink so water would be available inside. A good wood-burning cookstove dominated the room, with well-stocked cupboards lining the walls. She certainly would not starve for a while. Her father had equipped it with everything possible.

In the bedroom she found a small dresser and canopy bedstead, both made from knotty pine. Against the far wall, filling the air with its lovely aroma, rested a handsome cedar chest. Sitting on the bed, she sank into a mattress filled with feathers. It was so soft that she felt like she was floating on clouds. The pillows were also feather. The colors of the bedspread were deep maroon and blue, her favorite. Curtains on the bedroom window were of the same material. A lot of work and thought had gone into decorating this home. Tears came to Rita's eyes as she realized what her father had done for her and how much he loved her. This house was full of his dreams. Lightly stroking the smooth wooden post, she murmured, "Thank you, thank you, Dad. I love you too." Rising and wiping away the tears, she knew her choices were gone. She had to make a go of the saloon now.

Jake came in with her valise and trunk and placed them on the floor of the bedroom. She had noticed two chairs on the front porch when she entered, so she and Jake went out to sit and rest while observing the Saturday-night playfulness of Pine Wood.

"Tomorrow will be soon enough to get acquainted with your

new job," Jake mentioned after a bit. "I'll stay in a room at the saloon tonight and pick you up about eight for breakfast. There's a nice hash house about a block away."

Rita remained silent for a few moments, then said: "Thank you, Jake, I think I do need the rest after the long coach ride today. Things will be much quieter at the saloon in the morning, and that'll make it easier to get acquainted with everyone and learn what needs to be done."

Shortly thereafter, Jake excused himself. Rita remained on the porch, thinking of all that would take place tomorrow. Pine Wood seemed much larger than when she had left, and judging from the rowdy sounds coming from the saloon and various places in town, it appeared even more lawless. Realizing this was Saturday night, she could understand all the ruckus. Horses carrying eager cowboys galloped by slow-moving wagons filled with families, each looking forward to a different destination. Bright lamplight shone from all the store windows, beckoning those outside to step in and see the merchandise. A rough bunch of riders swarmed past her place, yelling and shooting into the air. People scurried in all directions to get out of their way. They whirled to a stop in front of the saloon, creating a choking cloud of dust. Swinging from their saddles, they tied, then burst through the batwings, laughing and shouting.

Rita noticed the dead body was gone. It certainly wouldn't be good for business to leave it lying around. Jake didn't mention it, so perhaps he worried about her sensibilities. Well, she was thicker skinned than everyone thought; she could handle it and anything else thrown her way.

Leaving the porch, Rita went inside. She opened a can of peaches from the cupboard in the kitchen, pumped some water into a glass, and sat down to eat. She was tired and the peaches would be plenty for tonight. The ice-cold water tasted even better than the what she drank on the train, probably because it was in her glass in her house, coming from her rain barrel.

After eating, she went into the bedroom, shut the door, and turned out the kerosene lamp she carried with her. Opening the window, she undressed, and fell exhausted into bed. Sinking into the softness of the feather mattress, she fell instantly asleep. Even the noise of the departing cowboys in the middle of the night did not wake her.

Five

hen Jake arrived at the saloon, he took note of the number of horses tied to the tie-rails in front. There were twenty-two, with more tied across the street. Saturday nights were apparently busy in Pine Wood. Going through the swinging doors, he found the place packed: cowboys, miners, ranchers, drifters, and bar girls were mixing together, creating a frolicsome atmosphere. At the bar he obtained a room and refused a drink, much to everyone's surprise. Was this their hard-drinking, carousing, fighting Jake? Grinning and giving no explanation, he headed up the stairs, followed by one of the bar girls. She caught him before he opened the door to his room.

"Would you like some company tonight, big fellow?" she asked suggestively as she pushed against him.

Jake smiled at her. "Not tonight, sweetheart, and would you spread the word that the new owner of the Golden Palace will be in tomorrow to get acquainted?" As a shocked expression spread over her face, he opened the door and stepped into the room.

Eight o'clock the next morning found Rita waiting eagerly on the front porch of her new home for Jake to arrive. She saw him coming down the street wearing the same suit as yesterday, it had been brushed clean, and he looked bright and happy. His buoyant attitude revealed that he'd left the drinking to others and looked forward to a new experience. As far as she knew, he'd not touched a drop since their arrival in St. George three days ago. If he could continue to hold out, he'd be especially valuable to her.

Tipping his hat as he came up, he said jauntily: "A good morning to you, Miss Rita. It was a lively place last night, but today all's quiet and peaceful. The good people are feeling righteous and the not-so-good are sleeping it off. Would you care to attend church today?"

Rita was more than surprised at this suggestion, coming from a rough character like Jake. "And how long has it been since you attended church, Jake?" she asked jokingly.

He bowed his head, and sweeping off his hat, said: "Since I was a wee lad about this high." He stood holding his hand about four feet from the ground. "Still and all, it would do you good to be seen there. The so-called respectable people would then be more considerate of you running a saloon. Paying the piper his due, and all that hogwash."

Rita knew a truth when she heard it. "You're right. It's important for me to get to know everyone in Pine Wood, no matter what their status. When we finish eating, I'd like a quick look at the saloon, then we'll attend church services."

Her hand on Jake's arm, they strolled to the cafe. A comely woman in her mid-thirties bustled around, busy waiting tables. A total of seven people were eating, all businessmen. Conversation around the tables stopped when Rita and Jake entered. Everyone in the room watched and listened closely to what was being said. The waitress hurried over, smiling coyly at Jake.

"You big ox, where've you been keeping yourself? Don't you know a lady gets tired of the same old company all the time?"

Jake folded her in his arms and gave her a sloppy kiss on the cheek. "Rita, this pretty young lady is Marie Purvis. she thinks I should spend all my time with her rather than at the saloon."

Marie reluctantly pulled away from Jake and turned to Rita. "So you're Bert Jackson's daughter. He was mighty proud of you, you know. Plumb wore us out with all his bragging. Bert was one of the best, and we all miss him."

Getting back to business, she shook the sadness from her eyes and led Rita and Jake to a table in the corner of the room. "This big ape can put away more food than six regular men, but I kind of like it when he visits Pine Wood."

Rita began to see why Jake was so anxious to help her at the saloon—that way he could look after his interests at the cafe. "Jake's consented to help me run the saloon my father left;" she said while they were being seated.

"Glory be," Marie gasped. A joyous smile spread across her face, and her eyes lit with love, settled on Jake. "Is it true, Jake?"

Embarrassed, Jake squirmed on his seat, then deciding everyone there already knew how they felt about each other, smiled back at Marie. "Yep, it's true, honey. You're gonna be seeing a lot of this old man."

Marie, overcome with happiness, clutched the menus to her bosom. The room, which had been silent, seemed to shuffle a bit and conversation resumed. This brought Marie out of her reverie. Smoothing out her emotions, she took their orders and hurried into the kitchen.

As soon as she left, a large man, dressed in his Sunday suit, rose from his table and came over to them. He looked to be one of the better-dressed patrons, an affluent air wafted about him.

Stopping in front of Rita, he bowed gallantly. "My name is Rex Johnson, Miss Rita. My wife Julie rode in with you from St. George yesterday and mentioned you very favorably. I'm the banker and Wells Fargo agent here in Pine Wood. It's a pleasure to welcome you to our fair town. Please accept my deepest sympathy on the passing of your father."

Rita held out her hand, which the banker took. "Thank you, Mr. Johnson. I'm looking forward to doing business with you. I intend to make the Golden Palace the largest and best saloon on the Arizona Strip. I'll need to go over any accounts my father kept with your bank."

Mr. Johnson smiled, pulled out a chair, and sat down at their table. Leaning towards Rita, he spoke in a quiet voice. "Your father kept all his money in my bank; there's a substantial amount there. Whatever you need, just let me know. I, for one, am glad to hear you're going to keep the saloon and that you have big plans for it. More people are moving into the Strip every month; they need a place like yours to unwind."

Happy to hear that she wasn't completely broke, Rita thanked him for his kindness and after a few more pleasantries, he excused himself to return to his table, where three other businessmen sat. She sensed these men held the same opinion as Mr. Johnson, for they all smiled and tipped their heads to her. She acknowledged their courtesies with graciousness, then turned to Jake, saying lightly, "It looks like some of the leading citizens are here this morning."

Jake glanced at the men. "They're the movers and shakers of Pine Wood, all right. If there's money involved, you'll find them very cooperative. It's probably common knowledge among them as to the amount of your father's account. He gave them a few gray hairs with his thriftiness but always remained ready to help folks who were bad-off. Bert's opinion counted for a lot here, and he was well-liked by both the businesspeople and the ranchers. Most of the rowdy bunch respected him as well."

This brought to Rita's mind the way the Arizona Kid seemed to feel about her father. She realized that filling her father's shoes wouldn't be easy and felt a little pang of fear. Could she do it? Then her youth and optimism asserted themselves, and she relaxed, confident in her abilities.

Marie brought their breakfast and sat down to flirt with Jake. The waitress seemed tickled pink to have him staying in town from now on. She gave him her undivided attention. Rita dove into her food, then remembered her training as to how a lady should eat. A smile spread across her lips, and she slowed down a bit. Picking at her meal, she thought- and not for the first time- about what a chore being a lady presented. Would her father have been happy trying to be an eastern gentleman? This brought a snort of derision, which caused Jake and Marie to pause in their preoccupation with each other and look at her curiously.

"I was just thinking of what my friends back at school would think if they were to see me eating breakfast with a big man like you, Jake."

Marie laughed. "I'll bet you're glad to be back, Rita. I went back East once and that was the first and last time."

"You never told me you hobnobbed with the Eastern establishment, Marie," Jake mentioned.

"How do you think I got so smart, Jake." She squeezed his hand as he looked sheepishly into her eyes.

Smiling benignly at them, Rita concentrated on eating until her plate was empty, then leaned back in her chair contented. Several new diners had come in, replacing those of the original group. She laughed to herself, thinking the news of her arrival would be all over town before the church bells tolled.

When Jake finished eating, Marie mentioned that church services were at ten o'clock, so they'd have time to see a little of the Golden Palace while waiting. Jake promised to stop by and get her when they went to church.

Leaving the cafe, they started across to the saloon. Several women strolled along the boardwalk in front of the Golden Palace and nodded to them cheerfully as they approached. "Good morning, Miss Jackson. Welcome back to Pine Wood." The news sure did spread fast in this neck of the woods. Rita knew this morning's walk in front of the saloon by the local ladies had been planned so they could meet her. Her eastern manners came to the fore: she smiled at each of them individually, making nice comments about particular parts of their clothing that was pretty. This made the women happy. They simpered and chattered a little about Pine Wood, how it had grown and what functions would be happening soon.

Finally excusing herself, Rita and Jake stepped into the saloon. A swamper busily cleaned the floors. He appeared to be in his late fifties, with white hair and a white beard, dressed in bib overalls and no shirt. His boots ran over at the heels, causing a slight hitch to his gait. Concentrating on the floor, he didn't notice them right away. When he finally glanced up and saw Rita he beamed, showing dark, stained teeth.

"It's good to see you back, Miss Rita. You sure are a sight for sore eyes. Too bad old Bert ain't here to see what a beautiful lady you are." Tears came to his eyes as he continued. "He'd be so proud of you."

Rita looked closely at the old man, then it came to her: he'd been the cook at the Lazy B-J for quite a few years. At first she'd not recognized him because he'd aged so much- his hair was brown when she left, and he'd been much slimmer.

"Pete, it's good to see you. Are you still cooking up those good steaks you used to fix at the ranch?"

Pete chortled. "You come back for lunch and I'll have the biggest steak you've seen in four years, girlie. I cook up the free meal they serve at the bar, so I ain't lost my touch."

Rita laughed and hugged him. "We'll be back after church to take you up on that, Pete. Right now I'd like to look around and see just what I'm getting into."

Pete put down his mop. "I'll show you the place, Miss Rita. Old Bert brought me with him when he sold the ranch, so the two of us kinda run it. There's a bartender who starts at noon, but I handle things till then."

He took them behind the bar and proudly showed them the stock of supplies. Everything looked orderly and clean. Next came the storeroom in the back, which had a rear door leading outside. Then they went into the office on the west side. The room was small, with a big roll-top desk sitting against the back wall. A wooden office chair, with carved claw feet for armrests, sat in front of the desk. Rita was startled to see the large picture of her mother that used to hang above the fireplace at the Lazy B-J. Now it rested directly over the roll-top, and there on a peg beside it hung Rita's thirty-eight caliber six-shooter, nestled in a brown leather holster attached to a full shell belt. She stepped forward, took it from the wall, and strapped it around her waist. For some reason it felt like it belonged there. Pulling the gun smoothly from the holster, she flipped the cylinder open and checked the rounds. Fully loaded, the gun appeared to have been cleaned recently and fit her hand like a glove. Slipping it back into its nest, she turned to Jake and started to speak, when a scream tore through the door leading to the barroom. Dashing out of the office with Jake in the lead, they heard the scream again. It came from the top of the stairs that led to the second floor.

The man was dressed in black and looked like the same one she had seen in the saloon doorway last night, after he'd killed the cowboy. He moved toward the stairs, dragging a partially clad girl from one of the rooms. The girl kicked and screamed at him, trying to pry his hand from her arm. Jake clenched his fists and was heading for the stairs when Rita stopped him by catching his arm. Cold with anger, she looked up at the man and shouted in a strong, commanding voice, "Let go of that lady!"

The man in black swivelled his head to see who dared to speak to him in such a tone. Seeing Rita, he pulled the distraught young woman towards him and said grimly: "Don't try to stop me, lady. I'm taking this whore with me- she's my girl and I don't want her here anymore."

The young girl squirmed in his grasp and pleaded, "Please, Miss Rita, I don't want to go with Nebraska. He thinks he owns me."

Rita stared steadily at Nebraska. "I said let the girl go, mister. She's one of my ladies. I'm Rita Jackson, the owner of the Golden Palace."

Nebraska watched Rita closely, his eyes narrowing. He pulled the girl nearer and growled: "I don't give a damn who you are. I say she goes, and who's going to stop me?"

The words were barely out of his mouth when a gun blasted and a small hole appeared in the lobe of his left ear. His hand went up to feel that side of his face and the wounded ear. Blood began to trickle through his fingers and drop onto his black neckerchief. His eyes widened when he saw smoke drifting upward from the gun in Rita's hand.

"Good Lord, woman, you could have killed me."

"If you don't let go of the lady, the next one will go up your right nostril." Rita spoke in a hard voice.

The man dropped the girl's wrist as though it had burned him. She scuttled back against the wall and watched him warily. The gun in Rita's hand slipped back into its holster faster than the eye could follow.

"That's better, Nebraska. I want you to know that the ladies who work here are not property to be hauled around without their permission. Now come on down to the bar and have a drink on me."

Nebraska stared at her: powder smoke still wafted around her, and with the sunlight glinting off the particles of smoke and dust, it looked to him like an angel stood there. He started down the stairs, shaking his head and holding his ear, completely bewildered by the sudden change of events. He prided himself on being the fastest gun in the Arizona Kid's gang- only the Kid himself was faster- yet he knew he would have been no match for this young girl waiting in the barroom for him.

While Rita prudently kept an eye on Nebraska as he descended the stairs, she became aware of several people looking over the saloon doors. She figured the story of her actions would spread through the whole town before church started. When she glanced back up to the second floor, she saw six girls in various stages of undress leaning against the railing, watching her. She smiled and nodded at them, then spoke to Pete.

"Pete, get behind the bar and pour Nebraska a drink."

When Nebraska reached the bottom of the stairs, Rita walked over to him and taking him by the arm, led him to the bar.

"I want you to know that you're always welcome here at the Golden Palace, but I won't stand for any rough stuff. My ladies are special, and they are not to be upset in any way." Rita spoke conversationally to Nebraska, who still appeared confused. He shook his head as if to clear it.

Pete poured a drink, and Nebraska picked it up and downed it in one gulp. He shuddered and sighed deeply.

"Pour him another, Pete." Smiling at Nebraska, she asked him, "Did you spend the night here?"

"Yes'm," he said with a groan.

Rita squeezed his arm in a friendly manner. "And did you pay the lady for her time, Nebraska?"

Nebraska was startled. "No, Ma'am, I aimed to take her with me."

Turning to Pete, Rita inquired, "Pete, what's the rate for one night's room with a lady?"

Pete was enjoying this by now. Old Bert's girl was tougher than rawhide. "Five dollars is the going price."

Rita turned to Nebraska, whose face was beginning to take

on a pink tinge. Then he laughed and reached into his pocket, pulling out a five-dollar gold piece and tossed it on the counter.

"Would you really have shot me in the nose, Miss Rita?"

"Pick up the gold piece, Nebraska," she said as she turned to face the room. Puzzled, Nebraska did as she asked. "Now toss it in the air."

Nebraska hesitated, then with a nod from Jake, he tossed it toward the ceiling. The gold glittered in the sunlight coming through the windows. As it reached the top of its arc, Rita's thirty-eight boomed, and the gold piece hit the ceiling then fell to the floor. When it stopped spinning and lay on its side, they saw the small round hole dead center. Nebraska took out his handkerchief and wiped his face.

"For a moment up there I was ready to call your bluff; now I see you weren't bluffing. Ma'am, I sure apologize for the trouble I've caused."

Rita spoke in a quiet but firm voice. "Spread the word around, Nebraska. Let everyone you meet know about the Golden Palace. Tell them that this is a good place to have fun and forget their worries, but we absolutely won't tolerate trouble. If they do cause any, either Jake there or I will take care of it. Now go up and apologize to the ladies, then fork your horse and come back next weekend."

Nebraska tramped upstairs to do as Rita suggested. The saloon began to fill with men, and the noise became too loud for Rita. She stepped out on the porch, and when Nebraska came through the doors, she took his arm and walked him down to the stable. Neither spoke until the saddle sat in place on his horse. Leading it outside, he stepped into the saddle and leaned down to take the hand Rita held up to him.

"No hard feelings, Nebraska."

"Shucks, Ma'am, if any man had done what you did, I'd not

rest till I nailed his hide to the barn door. But you have the same knack as my mother. She could whale the tar out of me and then make me feel like I was the greatest kid in the world. Nope, there's no hard feelings on my end, and you can be sure that the tale I tell back at camp tonight will bring all the boys into town in a hurry. You better stock up `cause they'll drink everything in sight." With that, he urged his horse into a run and disappeared in a cloud of dust.

Rita watched for a few seconds, then turned and retraced her steps. All along the street knots of men and women were whispering, sending admiring glances her way. She was glad when she went through the saloon doors, cutting off the sight.

"Pete, where do the ladies eat breakfast?" she asked as she walked through the barroom.

Pete indicated a door beside the office. "We have a kitchen back there where I cook the meals. They either eat here or at the cafe."

The young women were still standing at the top of the stairs. "You ladies get dressed and come down to breakfast. I'd like to meet each of you. We can get acquainted while you eat," Rita said. She followed Pete into the kitchen and helped him with the preparation of food. Jake took over the business at the bar. When the girls came in, Rita stepped over to them and took each of them separately by the hand, asking them their names and where they were originally from. Her soft warm voice and actions won them over quickly...before long they were all chatting with her just like old friends.

With the meal finished, she excused herself, saying, "I'm going riding after church so probably won't see you again today. I'd like you each to make a list of things you want for your room or for yourselves. As business improves, I'll see that you get whatever you want." With a chuckle, she added, "Within reason, of course."

Leaving them with happy looks on their faces, she stepped

into the main room. Pete who'd returned to help at the bar, and Jake were swamped with all the men asking for drinks. She stepped up to Jake and said, "It's almost time for church, Jake. Is there anyone else who can take your place while you go with me?"

A voice spoke from behind her. "I can tend bar, Miss Rita. I'll be glad to help in any way I can."

Rita turned to see the bar girl named Amy smiling at her. "Thank you, Amy, I really appreciate that."

Jake came from behind the bar, took Rita's arm, and hurried outside. They stopped briefly at the cafe to pick up a joyful Marie, who was dressed quite nicely with a perky hat perched on top of her head. Then all three walked quickly to the small church at the edge of town.

When they reached the doors of the church, the singing was just starting. A greeter stood just inside the door. He welcomed them, then glanced at the gun strapped to Rita's waist. "Would you like to leave that in the vestibule, Miss Jackson?"

Rita shook her head. "Do the men leave their guns at the door when they come to church?"

The man looked startled. "Why no, Ma'am."

"Then I'll keep mine on too."

There were still several empty benches throughout the room, but Rita, walking proudly with Jake and Marie in tow, went to the front row and sat on the empty bench. Rivulets of sweat formed at Jake's hairline. He kept running his finger around the inside of his collar, which had suddenly grown too tight. When he left home as a boy, he left everything behind, including church. Now here he sat beside this unconventional girl who insisted on wearing a gun in a holy place. He glanced gratefully at Marie...a nice, normal woman. She reached over and gave his hand a slight squeeze without taking her eyes off the pulpit. Jake settled back to endure the next hour. Keep this up and he'd become a regular "Amen" feller.

When the singing ended, the preacher stepped up to the podium and gave a long prayer that was almost a sermon in itself. Finished, he turned to Rita and in a kind voice said, "It's good to have you here, Miss Jackson. I hope you'll be a regular member." Rita acknowledged his welcome by nodding her head.

Then he proceeded with his sermon, which lasted for an hour. As the service ended, the organ played an old tune while everyone filed slowly out, greeting friends and neighbors. This was as close to a social club as most of the women ever got, since they were isolated out on ranches. The men had the saloon, their businesses, and their hired help to relieve the monotony of daily life. So while the men stood around chomping at the bit, anxious to leave, the women dallied in elfin clusters, hats bobbing like flowers in a gentle breeze as they chatted hurriedly, the words being absorbed much like water into parched earth.

Julie grabbed Rita's arm steering her toward a group of women. "I'll introduce you to several of the leading ladies. Their all anxious to meet you."

They stopped and talked with as many women as they could, and Rita complimented each one on something nice she noticed about them. She was charming and gracious, and the women soon forgot that she wore a gun...it became merely an added accessory. The men doffed their hats, kept their opinions to themselves, and waited for the womenfolk to finish their gossip.

When things began to break up, Rita, Jake, and Marie said goodbye and walked down the block to Rita's home.

"I think I'll ride out to the Lazy B-J and visit the new owners, Jake. You and Marie should take advantage of the beautiful weather and go on a picnic."

"That's okay, Rita. Marie won't mind if I ride with you." He sent an inquisitive look to Marie, who smiled her consent. "I don't think you should do this alone."

"No, really, I'll be fine. This is something I want to do by myself...just say goodbye to...everything. Okay?" She put her hand on Jake's arm, wanting him to understand.

Keeping his eyes lowered, Jake replied gruffly, "Okay, if that's the way you really want it." He hated to see her go through this ordeal without a friend to lean on.

"Thanks, Jake, and don't worry. I'll see you tomorrow." Rita removed her hand from Jake's arm, smiled at Marie, and turned towards her house.

Going inside, Rita changed into the riding pants and shirt she bought in St. George. Fixing a quick lunch, she made note of the things she needed to purchase tomorrow. Strapping on her six-gun and picking up her new, white, flat-crowned Stetson hat, she stepped out and hurried to the stable behind the house. Thunder, her father's horse, rolled his eyes at her. She located her saddle hanging on the wall. Patting the big bay on the neck, she spoke softly to him and bridled and saddled. Leading him outside, she mounted the eager horse and turned him towards his old home place.

The miles slipped away as Rita began to get into the old rhythm of riding again. It felt so good she almost shouted. Four years without the feel of a saddle under her was much too long. Sharing a horse with the Kid and riding from Joe's ranch to the train didn't really count- she wanted just herself, Thunder, and the familiar countryside. The air smelled clean, and the colors of earth and sky dazzled her mind and healed her heart as she rode. The top of the ridge overlooking their old ranch house came before she realized it.

She sat a moment, remembering her life in this place. Nothing ever stayed the same, but how she would've loved coming back to this ranch and seeing her father. Giving herself a shake, she gigged Thunder into motion. Nothing moved in the yard and only three horses stood in the corral. Riding down the hill, she drank in the smells and the sounds of animals, trees, and earth.

As she entered the yard, she hallooed the house. A kind-faced man with a white-haired woman beside him stepped out the front door.

"Howdy, Ma'am," the man said, looking her over from hat to boots. "Are you lost, or just riding for the joy of it?" His mellow voice and friendly manner eased her hesitancy. He was a tall man, whip lean, with broad shoulders and strong arms from working on a ranch all his life. He wore a gray short beard with matching grey hair, neatly combed. His legs, stuffed in boots, were bowed from long hours in the saddle.

His jolly, pretty wife came from behind him, saying, "Land-a-Goshen, girl, light, and come on inside out of the heat. We can chatter in there. My husband sometimes forgets that others don't like the warm weather as much as he does."

Rita slipped from the saddle and wrapping the reins around the hitching pole, stepped up to the porch. She smiled warmly at the couple.

"I'm Rita Jackson. Bert was my father. I wanted to see the ranch again after being away from it for so long."

"Well bless your heart, honey," the wife said as she took Rita's arm and ushered her into the house. "We're Glen and Susan Jacobs." She hugged Rita. "It's a real treat to have you come visit us."

Susan Jacobs was the epitome of motherly: a sweet, loving face with crinkly dark eyes surrounded by a wealth of white hair, set on a compact frame. Rita instinctively knew this woman was a good cook and ruled her house with a kind, firm hand. Susan motioned Rita into the kitchen, where she pulled down a rich-looking chocolate cake and sliced three big pieces for them. Glen went to the cellar and came up with some cool homemade apple cider that he poured into glasses.

They sat around a large oaken table, worn smooth as silk from years of use, and talked about the ranch and about Bert, how they'd wanted him buried beside his wife on the knoll behind the house. They mentioned that today all the hands were in town for the weekend and would probably be tired and broke when they returned. Rita wanted to know if any of their children still worked the ranch with them.

Glen scowled. "We only had one son. He's off in Colorado somewhere. We get a letter occasionally but haven't seen him since we bought the ranch. He wanders from place to place. Sometimes his letters arrive from as far south as Tucson." He sent his wife a furtive glance. "We think he's on cattle drives, but don't know what he does for sure."

Placing her hand comfortingly on her husband's arm, Susan interrupted. "He was always a rather wild boy, carrying a gun and shooting at everything when he was growing up. It wouldn't surprise me at all if he was a gunslinger by now. I just hope he's okay."

The conversation continued as they talked about their son. This must be the way her father felt with her gone for four years, Rita thought, except he knew where she was and what she was doing. She learned that their son would've just celebrated his twenty-third birthday and they wished they could be with him.

After a while Rita bid them goodbye, promising to come visit occasionally. Before leaving the ranch, she rode to the hillside where her parents were buried. The graves lay close together under the branches of a large pinon pine tree, overlooking the ranch where they had been so happy. Kneeling on the soft green grass she said a final good-by to her beloved father. Eyes blinded by tears, She rose and quickly stepped into the saddle, letting the horse take her away.

Dusk had turned to darkness by the time she reached home. She unsaddled, turned the horse into the corral, and fed him hay and oats. Entering her home, she fixed herself a sandwich, then crawled gratefully into bed. Her dreams were all mixed up, with her father, the Arizona Kid, and Nebraska changing places until she couldn't tell who was who. They all were outlaws, then businessmen, then cowboys.

Her restless night left her still tired when she woke the next morning. Rita wondered about the day. With all the men back at work, Monday shouldn't be too busy. She sighed and snuggled under the covers, intending to sleep only a few more moments, but that was not to be.

Six

omeone pounding on her door roused Rita, who struggled awake to see who was up at this hour. Seeing the sunlight streaming through the window, she glanced quickly at the clock: eight-thirty. Darn it she'd overslept again. Would she ever get used to waking up early? The days seemed to be so long and the nights so short. Throwing on a robe, she hurried towards the door, glancing through the front window as she passed it. She could see Jake fidgeting outside, dressed in work pants and a plaid shirt. He had a six-shooter strapped to his right hip. This must mean trouble, she thought uneasily as she opened the door.

Jake removed his hat and entered the house. "We got problems at the saloon, Rita. Three hung over cowboys are there and starting to give Pete a hard time. I don't want to shoot any of them, and since we haven't hired a bouncer, I'm not sure I can handle them alone."

Rita stared at him for a few seconds. She had feared something like this would happen. How did Jake think she could handle three tough cowboys? Somehow it must be done without bloodshed—that would be bad for business.

"I'll get dressed and come right on down, Jake. Stall things as long as possible."

Hurrying into her bedroom while Jake left for the saloon, she started to put on pants and a shirt, then stopped, thinking: Maybe if I wore a real fancy outfit, I could distract the punchers enough to get them to leave. Throwing the pants and shirt on the bed, she went to the closet and picked out the ornate gown she bought in St. George. Dressing rapidly and strapping her thirty-eight to her hip, Rita left at a fast walk towards the saloon.

The news had spread already. People all up and down the street watched her progress. They showed surprise at her appearance, but she nodded to them politely and hurried on. It wasn't every day they saw a young girl dressed in fancy clothes with a gun on her hip. Everyone smiled at her, but it was obvious she created quite a stir. When she reached the saloon, she went around to the rear door to make her entrance.

Rita heard rough talk and derisive laughter as she entered the back room. She stepped silently through the door leading into the barroom. Jake stood helplessly just inside the batwings. Three slaphappy cowboys surrounded Pete with their guns out, ready to fire at his feet. Obviously they were still a little drunk from the night before and had decided that making the bartender dance to their gunshots would show how tough they were. Her heart pulsed in her throat as she moved toward them, but she made sure no one could detect this from outward appearances.

Walking defiantly up to the group, shoulders back and fire in her eyes, Rita elbowed one puncher aside and stepped up to Pete, who heaved a mighty sigh of relief upon seeing her. Taking him by the arm, she glared at the stunned punchers and led him over to the bar. All three were so amazed at the sudden appearance of such a beautiful girl, they forgot all about Pete.

Over her shoulder, Rita called, "You boys are up mighty early this morning. Won't your boss be looking for you back on the ranch?"

Stopping at the bar, she whispered to Pete to get behind it and set out four shots of whisky. Turning to the punchers with an easy smile, she said, "Are you going to let a lady drink alone, gentlemen?"

The cowboys stood rooted to the floor with bewilderment, admiration, and surprise on their faces. Their apparent leader, a young reedy fellow, finally found his voice as Pete began to pour the drinks. Sweeping off his Stetson, he mumbled: "Sorry,

Ma'am, we didn't mean no harm, just wanted to have a little fun." He kept staring at her and rolling the brim of his hat up more and more.

"Fellows, let me introduce myself. I'm Rita Jackson, Bert Jackson's daughter. I own the Golden Palace now and Pete works for me. Surely you wouldn't want anything to happen to him, would you?" She spoke the words softly, but they carried to each man plainly. She was the most beautiful girl any of them had ever seen, and their faces began to turn red. They could not hold her steady look; each began to mumble something unintelligible and stare at the floor.

Their leader apologized meekly: "We're plumb sorry, Miss Jackson. We heard how you shot Nebraska's ear off yesterday; we sure don't aim to give you any more trouble. We spent the night upstairs with some of your ladies, and I guess we ain't exactly sober yet."

Rita motioned to the drinks sitting on the bar. "They're on the house this time, boys, but when you stay over next weekend, take your lady out to breakfast, then you won't be so apt to cause trouble."

All three stepped quickly to the bar, avoiding her eyes, and downed their drinks. When they finished, Rita told them, "Jake will walk with you to the stable to get your horses. Remember, I want to see you in town every weekend. Our ladies will be singing and dancing in a special musical show, so tell all your friends to come join us."

"We sure will, Miss Jackson," they said in unison, then doffed their hats and hastily stumbled after Jake. The cowboys would remember this morning for a long time since they were more or less herded to the stable in front of the whole town. As they slouched along with heads held low, they realized this was just what Rita wanted. They swore under their breaths that they would never cause her any trouble again. She was all woman, and each one of them felt protective of her. They'd done wrong, and she had politely put them in their places.

When they were gone, Pete let out a shout and danced a little jig behind the bar. "By golly, boss, I ain't been so skeered and then so happy all at once in my whole life. My feet had plumb growed to the floor. If you hadn'ta come along, I'd be pushin' up daisies right about now."

Rita's glance picked up the house girls leaning on the upstairs railing, and she knew they had witnessed the whole episode. She read real respect in their eyes. Heaving a sigh of relief, she pushed the remaining drink toward Pete.

"I don't drink, Pete, so you can have this, and if you could see my knees knocking now, you'd know how scared I was too."

Pete laughed and slapped the bar. "You sure din't look it when you come charging through that circle—looked like you was the lion tamer smack dab in the middle of the lions. Yes Ma'am! You really know how to handle men. I betcha you could take on any outlaw in the Strip and whittle him down to nothin'."

Rita winced at this thought, then turned towards the office door. "I'll be in the office if you need me for anything else." Then she hesitated and turned to him. "Have the cafe send over some breakfast for me—I don't feel like facing the townsfolk right now."

One of the girls hanging over the balcony spoke up. "I'll go get you some breakfast, Miss Rita."

Looking up, Rita saw the same girl who had the trouble with Nebraska. Dressed in a riding outfit, she'd apparently been on her way to the livery stable when the trouble started. Rita traversed the intervening space to meet her as she came down the stairs.

"I should get to know all you young girls much better than I did on our first visit, since we're going to be working together." Then speaking directly to the one girl, Rita remarked, "When you get back, come into the office and we'll talk some more."

Rita took the hand the girl offered and pulled her close for a friendly hug. The girl hugged Rita back, saying: "Sure thing, Rita, I'll be right back." She hurried out the door.

Rita turned to the office and went inside. Closing the door behind her and dropping into the chair behind the desk, she considered what had just happened. She was surprised at the way she'd reacted to the situation. To her way of thinking, it was quite brazen; she could still see the men looking at her. Then she realized that the looks were all respectful, and she began to laugh to herself. Apparently men could be handled easily if you played your cards right.

Rita got up and went to the office window facing the street. Standing there, she saw Jake leave the stable and head back towards the saloon. Several people intercepted him, and she understood by the gestures made that they wanted to know what had gone on in the barroom. Jake was having a great time spinning out his story, acting both parts with a lot of hand movements and facial changes, and before long they were all laughing and slapping him on the back. The story would be embellished and told all over the Strip before tomorrow. Well, that should bring more business into the saloon: everyone on the Strip would want to come into town and see the lion tamer. She turned from the window and sat back down in the office chair.

Jake knocked on the door shortly thereafter. She bid him enter, and as he came in, he swept off his hat and bowed.

"If you ain't the wildest young woman I ever met! I truly believe you'd walk up to a bear and spit in his eye. Too bad old Bert isn't here to see you in action." He chuckled and sat down in the chair facing the desk. "With you handling things, we don't need a bouncer. In less than twenty-four hours, you've shot the ear off one of the Arizona Kid's gunhands and sent three wild cowboys packing like misbehaved schoolboys." He leaned back in his chair, admiring her.

Laughing at herself, Rita said jokingly: "And if my help give me any trouble, I'll do the same to them."

"You don't have to worry about me. I've seen you in action, and I don't want no part of your brand of punishment."

Just then the young girl came in with Rita's breakfast and set it on the desk.

"I want you to know, Miss Rita, that I'm proud to be working for you. I know you inherited all us girls, and if you had your druthers, you'd probably want to be rid of that responsibility. But we like the way you handle things, and all of us would like to stay on." She said the last in a faltering voice.

Rita picked up her fork and started eating as Jake and the young girl watched. She chewed the food contentedly, swallowed, then addressed the young lady.

"I'll admit I was rather scared to take on the running of a saloon. I wasn't sure how to take you young girls, but I told myself if my father let you work here, you must be the cream of the crop, and that's what I think also. You all have a place to stay and work as long as you'd like."

The young girl sighed with relief and gratitude. "I hoped you'd feel that way. By the way, my name is Rosy, and if you like, I'll bring the other girls in so they can talk to you and express their feelings."

Rita smiled up at Rosy. "That won't be necessary at the moment. I want you to stay and talk so we can get to be friends. Then later I'll visit with each of the girls separately."

She would have to let everyone who worked for her know they were special, but it would really be Jake's responsibility to manage them.

"Jake will be the one directly in charge of your activities. If any man treats you badly or doesn't pay his bill, let Jake know. He'll take the necessary action."

To Jake she said, "While I'm talking with Rosy, would you go to the house and bring me back my handbag? If Pete needs anything, please help him."

Jake realized Rita wanted privacy while she talked with Rosy. That was fine with him...there were a few more people who hadn't yet heard about this morning's exploits, and he wanted to be the one doing the storytelling. That way, he could tell them that if Rita's way hadn't worked, he'd have shot them all where they stood. Standing up, he beamed at both of them and left the room.

Rita got right down to business, wanting to know where Rosy grew up and all about her family. The talk between them became easy and before long she felt she knew the young girl very well. Broaching a subject resting heavily on her mind, she inquired: "What do you know about Nebraska? Is he really one of the Arizona Kid's men?"

Startled, Rosy stammered, "Wh-where...where did you hear that?"

Rita's eyes bored into Rosy. "I met the Kid on the train when he held it up. Since arriving here, I've heard rumors that Nebraska is his number-one man."

Rosy was having trouble speaking. Rita felt bad for putting her on the spot, but she wanted to know about the Kid and the only way to do that was through Nebraska. She sat calmly and waited until Rosy, decidedly uncomfortable, finally mumbled: "Yeah, he's one of the Arizona Kid's men, but no one except me knows for sure. He confided in me a long time ago. But he respects the Kid a lot and says he never killed anyone," she added defensively.

Restless, Rita got up and went to the window. In her mind she saw the tall, slim figure of the Kid; his devil-be-damned attitude was fresh in her memory. She could see why most women looked on him as a romantic figure: they liked that edge of excitement he carried. Where was he now? The thought had just crossed her mind when she heard herself say, "Do you know where his hangout is?" She was startled that she had been so bold as to ask such a thing.

Thinking Rita was talking about Nebraska, Rosy answered: "He never told me that, but I think they may be somewhere around the Hole-in-the-Rock country. Nebraska says they never stay in one place long enough to really call it home."

Rita came back to the desk and sat down. Watching Rosy closely, she inquired, "Does Nebraska come to see you often?"

When Rosy nodded, she proceeded. "Next time he comes, I'd like to talk to him. There's no law on the Strip, and I want to make sure the Kid's gang will leave us alone here. I expect the Golden Palace to become very well known in the West, and trouble with the Kid's bunch would spoil my plans."

"You won't have to worry about that. Nebraska won't let any of the gang cause trouble here in Pine Wood. He knows this is the only place where they can come and not worry about the law." Rosy spoke as though she were proud of the gang.

Rita tried to place her own feelings and wondered how she would react if the Kid came to see her.

"Rosy, they're still outlaws with a price on their heads and wanted for robbery all over the West. I know we can't do anything about that, but as long as we have to put up with them, they need to understand our position as far as the saloon goes. They're welcome, but if they start trouble, I will exert all the influence I have to getting them caught. Until then we'll have a truce."

Rita felt strongly about this point, and from what Rosy had seen so far, she knew Rita would stand by her convictions.

"All right. I'll have Nebraska talk to you when he comes in Saturday. I know you can count on him to keep his men in line."

"Does the Arizona Kid ever come here?" Rita asked with hesitation. She wanted to appear nonchalant about this but was afraid Rosy would tumble to her real feelings.

"Not that I know of. Nebraska says he stays away from Pine Wood. When he goes to a town it's usually down south in Phoenix or Tucson. Nebraska thinks the Kid knows someone here and doesn't want to be recognized."

They continued chatting for a time, then Rita went upstairs to talk with the other ladies. They were all about her age, and most of them were fairly pretty. Some were content with their lot, feeling that sooner or later they would get married and get out of the trade. But a few hard-edged, plainer girls knew this was their only road, and going down it would not be a smooth ride. Rita didn't know how to help these girls but was wise enough not to show pity. Seeing them, she realized again how lucky she was and sent a silent prayer of thanks to her father.

By the time Rita spoke with all of the girls, the day was drawing to a close. Pete fixed her a late lunch, then she went home to change into riding clothes. She needed to get out in the fresh air. She saddled Thunder and started to step up in the stirrup when a man approached her. Delight mingled with awe was plain to see as he gazed at her. Full of curiosity, he wanted to talk about how she'd handled the three cowboys and wanted to see for himself if it was true. It was his opinion that she handled the whole affair exactly right.

Stepping into the saddle, Rita assured him dryly that such affairs would not be a daily routine. Taking her leave of the stranger, she rode out of town and wandered aimlessly over the range, enjoying the smell of sage and the rustling breeze. She thought for a moment of all the people in New York and the other big cities who couldn't even conceive of riding on a range, nor would they want to. In a way, they reminded her of young pine-cones with their petty, sharp points, always ready to prick anyone who came too close. What they needed was time with the beauty of nature—it never failed to enlarge the heart. Well, it worked with her anyway.

Out on the open range her mind was like a sieve: a thought would drop into it, only to be pushed on through to the morass of her subconscious. She'd only truly been at the saloon one day, but it had been one thing after another, with so much to learn, so many people to meet, and no time to relax. Now she just wanted to drift, to be free for a while from making decisions and taking responsibility.

Passing a large stand of cottonwood trees, she heard banjo music through the branches. Amazed, she stopped to listen and heard a mellow voice singing "Awfully Gone at the Knees," a song she knew well. As a little girl, her father often sang it to her.

> *"Come listen a while and a story I'll tell*
> *Brim full of misfortune and woe.*
> *I must have been born 'neath an unlucky star*
> *For it to equal the story I'll tell.*
> *Like a lot of young men I fell deeply in love*
> *With a girl I thought loved me as well.*
> *I met her one evening intending of course*
> *My tale of affection to tell.*
> *I said my sweet Phoebe allow me to tell*
> *My greatest misfortunes are these,*
> *I've nothing to offer except what's in these*
> *And I'm awfully gone at the knees.*
> *Gone at the knees, gone at the knees,*
> *Yes, I'm awfully gone at the knees.*

It came by degrees, do not laugh at me so
But pity me please, for I'm awfully gone at the knees.
Yes, I'm awfully gone at the knees."

After the song ended, she rode into the stand of trees, calling out to alert the singer that she was approaching.

A middle-aged man with a derby hat rested on a log, holding a decrepit banjo. His clothes were ragged and dirty, and more than a week's growth of beard covered his cheeks. Holes were worn in the knees of his pants, and his threadbare shirt was torn in several places. His eyes were sad and tired; it looked like he was on his last legs. How could that beautiful bass voice come from such a debilitated man? Rita wondered as she gazed at him.

Open-mouthed, he returned her stare. Then his eyes lighted and he cried out: "The good Lord sent an angel to be with me at last." Tears spilling down his cheeks, he bent his head in thankful prayer.

Rita was astonished to see how emaciated he was: this man had not eaten for days. Where on earth did he come from? Hurriedly, she dismounted and, disregarding the dirt and stink, leaned over to take his arm.

"Let me help you onto my horse, mister. We can ride double to my place."

Tugging him to his feet, she half carried and half pulled him to her horse and, with a mighty effort, pushed him onto the saddle. Climbing up behind him, she gigged the horse into motion towards town. The man clung to the saddle horn, mumbling his thanks.

When they reached her home, Rita slid from the saddle and stumbled through the door, half dragging the man with her. Placing him in a kitchen chair, she fetched water for him, then started the fire in the cookstove, heated coffee, and sliced meat into a skillet. Taking down a can of corn, she dumped it into a pan to heat. While the food cooked, she took time to wet a rag and wipe the man's face and hands. He seemed to revive as she washed him.

"Thank you, Ma'am," he said in an eastern accent. "I've been walking for a long time. I knew there was a town around here somewhere but couldn't find it. Sure glad you came along when you did. Don't know if I could've lasted till morning without help."

Rita poured some coffee for him, which he drank sparingly, then, as the minutes went by, he drank more. When the meat and corn were done, Rita put some on a plate for him and took some herself. His hands shook at first, and he couldn't get the food to his mouth fast enough, but by the second plateful, he'd settled down and remembered his table manners. They ate in silence, while she studied the man.

After they were finished, she asked, "What were you doing out there without a horse?"

Leaning back in his chair with a contented look on his face, he replied: "I left the fort over at Lee's Ferry ten days ago. Was headed to St. George to see about a job in the saloon there. My horse stepped in a hole and broke his leg five days out. All I had was my derringer, but I put the bullets where it counted. Hated to do it—he'd been a good horse." His mind drifted. "This is the most barren land I've ever seen. Not a soul anywhere till you showed up. Thought you were an angel at first—come to think of it, you are."

Excitement began to build in Rita. "What kind of job were you going to in St. George?" She hoped that her wish would be granted.

He studied her for a moment, then, standing up, bowed and proclaimed: "Meet Sam the Piano Man. I wanted to get a job playing the piano and dealing cards at a saloon owned by Mr. Singer. I played for a musical show in Santa Fe, New Mexico, but it went broke." He stopped, watching her cautiously. "I, ah, borrowed a horse to get out of town and headed this way. Ma'am, I surely hope you don't get into any trouble because you helped me."

"Sam, you don't have to worry...there's no law here, and when you get on your feet, we'll send back money to the sheriff in Santa Fe to pay for the horse," Rita replied happily.

Sam was the welcome answer to one of her problems. She had wanted to start a song-and-dance routine in the evenings, something that could be presented to the whole town at times.

Sam stared at her as though he hadn't really heard what she said. "You said, 'we,' Ma'am." He figured his head must still be a little foggy from the close call with death. This girl couldn't be very old. She looked mature in the eyes, but her body spoke of bold, exciting youth. How was it possible for her to be in a position to help him out?

"That's right, Sam. I'm Rita Jackson, owner of the Golden Palace here in Pine Wood. It just so happens I'm in need of a piano player. I want to start a weekly musical show on Friday and Saturday nights. Occasionally, it will be necessary to bring in other performers from all parts of the West, or even some from back East, and you may have ideas that would facilitate doing that. You can live in one of the upper rooms at the saloon, deal cards most of the week, and on Friday and Saturday do our shows."

Rita became more animated as ideas began to fill her mind. She wiggled in her chair, fiddled with her hair, and her eyes were sparkling. What luck to find such a talented man when she needed one. This would help immensely in making the Golden Palace a first-rate saloon.

Sam stared at her as though she were some sort of angelic being. "Miss Rita, I would be most happy to assist you." He bowed again and his face lit with a smile. "As a matter of fact, I've produced many shows back East. I only came out West for health reasons. I still have quite a few connections back there that we can use to provide special shows when we want." Sam too began to see all sorts of possibilities in working with someone as progressive as Rita. She had saved his life, and anything he could do to help her would not come close to paying off that debt.

The two of them discussed ideas as Sam continued to drink slowly and fill his parched body with liquid. He'd done a lot of praying since losing the stolen horse, and at the last moment the Lord answered his prayers in the form of this beautiful girl. Not only did she save him from certain death, but she was providing him with a job, which he really needed, plus a place to live. He would not let her down. With his conceptions and talents, he knew her plans would be successful.

Realizing Sam was exhausted, Rita pointed the way to the Golden Palace and told him to go there and tell Jake she said to give him a room. She would be up shortly after changing into a dress and freshening up some. Sam left with as jaunty a stride as he could muster. Rita heated water for a bath and climbed in the tub to wash the dirt and grime off, hoping Sam would have time to bathe and clean up also before she arrived at the saloon. She put on one of her new dresses, fixed her hair, and then hurried down the street.

There were quite a few people for a Monday night. Jake met her and said that Sam had bathed, dressed in some clothes Pete lent him, and was in his room sleeping.

"Where did you find that broken-down sponger?" Jake grumbled when they were in Rita's office. He had visions of Rita bringing in every tramp who crossed her path, giving them a room and providing them with money. She'd spent her last dollar on an old prospector, and now she was giving a handout to an impoverished stranger who smelled like a pig sty. Thinking along this line, Jake knew he would have to council her on being as firm with panhandlers as she was with business dealings. It was beyond him how she could act so tough when trouble started, but was such a soft touch where bums were concerned.

Rita told him about finding Sam singing what to her seemed to be his last song, and by the time she finished talking, Jake changed his mind about the man. He still cautioned her about picking up any strays that might be wandering around, but knew in his heart it wouldn't do any good. His boss was one for the books as far as he was concerned. Then he smiled to himself. In a way, she had picked him up: She gave him a job working for her after knowing him for less that twenty-four hours.

Rita stayed at the saloon talking to the patrons and the bar girls till it closed at midnight. Then she spent some time in the office just musing about how to use Sam and planning for the future of the Golden Palace. Her father certainly left her with an interesting responsibility, and she anticipated the challenges more all the time. Her fears of being inadequate were rapidly disappearing.

Leaving the office, she found Jake and Pete straightening things up in the barroom. Bidding them a warm goodnight, she departed and strolled home, not noticing the balmy evening, her eyes turned inward, her mind a jumble of future possibilities that were all exciting and fun. Little did she know that much more responsibility waited just around the corner.

Seven

The following week seemed to fly by, with Rita settling into a routine of getting up in the morning, going for a ride for two to three hours, then coming back and spending the late afternoon doing the necessary book work, settling disputes among the girls, and checking supplies with Jake and Pete. When all this was done, she mingled with the patrons of the Golden Palace, to everyone's delight, until it closed at midnight.

The amount of business increased rapidly, with cowboys she suspected were part of the Kid's gang coming in all the time. Sam fit right in, and finding that Rita had an excellent soprano voice, he worked out a duet with her. Each night the two of them entertained the cowboys, ranchers, and businessmen with an hour of singing. Then the bar girls pranced around on the stage Jake constructed at one side of the barroom. Sometimes they danced through the crowd, causing ribald comments and a clamor so loud that no one could hear the music. By the weekend, the saloon girls had worked up a lively song-and-dance routine that was sure to pack the barroom every night. If this kept up, Rita would have to enlarge the place to accommodate everyone. It was amazing what had been accomplished in just one week.

By Friday evening, Pine Wood bustled with people. Punchers from all over the area were in town, and nesters and ranchers rubbed shoulders with miners and businesspeople. Most of them eventually made it into the Golden Palace, much to Rita's delight.

She finished a song and was starting to circulate among the patrons when a large hand settled gently on her arm. Looking up, she recognized Rex Johnson, the banker.

"Good evening, Miss Rita," he said genially. "I've never seen so many people in this town before, and I think it's largely due to those shows you're putting on. You've done a mighty fine job here."

"Why, thank you, Rex." Rita beamed. "And how's your lovely wife?" She felt a small prick of guilt—she hadn't seen much of Julie since the stagecoach ride but hoped that would change when things settled down.

"Julie's doing just splendid, thanks. But she did ask me to inquire if there was any way the more respectable part of town could see the nice parts of your show." He flushed slightly, realizing Rita might take this the wrong way, then rushed on: "There's not much to do in a place this size, and I'm sure a lot of the womenfolk would appreciate some diversity."

This notion appealed to Rita. "You may have something there, Rex." She began working it out in her mind. "If we could build a small stage in back of the saloon and put benches out in front of it, we could bring all sorts of quality entertainment into Pine Wood."

Mr. Johnson's face lightened upon hearing Rita's suggestion. "That would be terrific, Rita, and maybe Julie could help with costumes. If I can get the carpenters to do the work, can you pay for the materials?"

Rita answered fervently, "You get the men and order the lumber, and we'll bring in the talent and pay for the materials. If any of the wives want to help, we'll be glad to have them."

The women weren't really needed, but a happy wife meant a happy husband, and then there'd be less bickering when the man wanted to visit the saloon.

Mr. Johnson left, eager to discuss the idea with other business friends. By morning the plan seemed to be in motion, and his wife Julie organized the ladies of the town so the men working on the stage would be fed and housed. In less than two weeks the stage would be ready for Rita and her show; that would be a boon to the whole town. If Friday night was any indication, there would be good business all over Pine Wood from now on. Thinking of all Rita had managed to do, it was hard to believe she lacked a couple of months of being twenty years old. She stood the town on its ear in a short time and all the men were eating out of her hand, so to speak.

Saturday night, Rita finished her song with Sam just as Nebraska came in. Rosy met him and ushered him right into the office. While they were waiting, Rosy filled him in on what Rita had discussed with her.

"Honey, I really like Rita." Rosy's arms were around Nebraska's waist, and she gazed up at him lovingly. "I'm sure your secret will be safe with her."

Melting under her look like warm butter in the sun, Nebraska found it hard to keep his mind on what she was saying. Restraining himself to a fairly gentle squeeze, he agreed.

"Rita's strong-willed but fair-minded. If she gives her word, you can bet she'll keep it. After all the things I've heard about her, I'd sure rather have her on my side than against me." Having reassured Rosy, he was leaning forward to sneak a kiss when Rita entered the office.

After greeting most of the men in the barroom and hearing their compliments, Rita arrived in a good mood. She knew her duet with Sam went over very well. Smiling at Nebraska, she said, "I see the ear is healing fine. Good thing I don't carry a forty-five, or there wouldn't be any ear left."

Nebraska turned pink and gave a weak smile. "You sure won't get a chance to ruin the other one, Miss Rita. I'm on my best behavior from now on."

"Just call me Rita, Nebraska, there's no need to be so formal since I'd like to be your friend."

Sitting in the office chair, she studied Nebraska, while Rosy tried to sit still. Rosy was nervous because she wondered what Rita would say. "Did Rosy explain what I wanted from you, Nebraska?"

Admiring her for the forthright way she approached a subject, he decide to cooperate. "You won't have any worry about the Kid's men causing trouble in Pine Wood, Rita. We all know this is one of the few safe places for us. None of us want to ruin that." His voice was serious, and Rita knew he meant what he said. Her next question would have to be phrased carefully or he would divine her real motive. "What do you know about the Arizona Kid, Nebraska?" She held her voice steady, with as little inflection as possible.

Nebraska thought for a few moments, then shrugged. "Not much really. He never talks about himself or mentions anything about his family. I've been in his bunch for over three years. I don't think any of us know where he came from or what his prior life consisted of."

He tried hard to remember anything that had been mentioned about the Kid. "I can say he treats all of us fairly. When he says he'll do something, you can stake your life on it. I'd sooner have the Kid by my side than anyone I know or have ever met."

This was exactly the impression Rita had goten of the Kid. During the short time she'd been around him, she had formed a similar judgement.

"Is there any way I can get in touch with him?" The words were out of her mouth before she realized what she asked.

Nebraska concealed his surprise. What could this young girl want with the Arizona Kid? Did she know him? The Kid certainly never mentioned anything about her. Maybe she or her family was the reason the Kid wouldn't come to Pine Wood. Well, whatever the connection, it was none of his business.

"That's impossible, Rita. If you'd asked me that ten days ago, I'd have gladly taken you to him. But I don't know where he is now. You see, after we held up the train you were on, we went to the appointed rendezvous and waited for the Kid. For a long time he didn't show up. When he finally got there, he told us to divide the money between us, packed all his gear, and said goodbye."

"You mean he just left the bunch without any explanation?" Rita was astonished at this disquieting news. Why would he do something like that? Was it possible she had affected him the way he had her? Now she would never know anything more about him.

"That's right. No one knows where he went. He told me to take charge and disappeared, didn't even take his share of the split. The way I figure it, something happened after the train robbery that caused him to rethink his life. Maybe the posse almost caught him, I don't know. Whatever happened in that time, he came back a changed man from when he left the bunch. He was thinking serious, not like his usual light-minded self." Nebraska was sorely puzzled at the Kid's behavior.

The more Rita thought about it, the more she liked what she heard; because of her, the Kid gave up his lawless ways. She just knew that was the answer. Her heart told her he'd changed—he had been so concerned for her safety. She hoped she'd made an impression on him; he certainly had on her. Anytime she faced a problem, she found herself wishing the Kid were there to help. Thinking of him as an outlaw had been very hard; now he had given up his wild ways, and maybe someday they would meet again.

Bringing her mind back to the present, it dawned on her that with the Kid gone, Nebraska must be the leader of the gang since he'd been the Kid's right-hand man. "So you're running the gang now, Nebraska?" She knew the answer before he replied.

"Yes, Rita, but it ain't the same without the Kid. He did all the planning before; no one was ever hurt seriously while he rodded the bunch. Now some of them are getting big ideas, and I'm not the one to ride herd on them." Nebraska knew he didn't have leadership qualities and sorely missed the Kid.

Rosy broke into the conversation. "You could work here in town, Nebraska. You have some schooling and could do anything you wanted." She wanted to quit working at the Golden Palace; with Nebraska in town, they could get married and settle down. After a few years, his outlaw days would be forgotten, and because no one knew for sure he belonged to the Kid's gang, they could live a peaceful life.

Nebraska considered this for Rosy's sake. "I'm not sure I could take town life, honey. I'll stick with the bunch for awhile, but if they get too wild, I'll leave."

"You could help Jake around the saloon, Nebraska." For some unknown reason, even to herself, Rita wanted to keep him around almost as much as Rosy did. Maybe subconsciously she thought if he stayed in town, the Kid may look him up sometime.

Nebraska studied her. "No thanks, Rita, that sounds like too much of a handout for me. I know cattle and ranching. When I quit the bunch, I'll hire on with a cattle outfit either up in Utah or somewhere on the Strip."

Seeing that Rosy and Nebraska needed to talk, Rita excused them. They left the office, and Rita turned to the books—they should be brought up to date. It was past eleven when she heard a commotion in the barroom. Stepping to the office door, she opened it and peered out. Jake was ushering a sorry-looking cowboy out the batwings. When he came back, he saw Rita in the office door and came over to tell her about the problem.

"Another freeloader. Wanted a drink but didn't have any money. Tried to get Pete to let him have one on the house." At the look on Rita's face he sighed, turned on his heel, and went after the cowboy. Rita smiled since she knew what Jake thought. She had given two down-and-out cowboys a free drink and a meal before they went on their way already this week. If she kept grub staking all the prospectors and giving free meals to any stray cowboy, they'd all be beating a path to her door.

Jake came back with the cowhand in tow. Rita asked him where he worked last. Sheepishly, he stated that he'd worked for the Bar-K up in Skutumpah, Utah. The foreman disagreed with him on some work, and he'd been forced to quit. He wanted to hire on with a spread on the Strip.

With her eyes assessing his needs, Rita asked, "What was the trouble with the foreman?"

He hesitated, then mumbled, "I don't wanta say, Miss Rita."

"You know who I am?"

"Shucks, Miss Rita, the whole country knows who you are. The stories comin' outta the Strip are colored with things you've done. Why, you're more talked about than the guv'nor."

Shocked by his answer, Rita wondered if she was a thing of gossip everywhere. Reading her thoughts, the man continued, "All that's said is good. When someone yarns about you, there's always the greatest respect. You treat everybody the same, no matter what their way of life."

Contemplating the man for a moment, she turned to Jake. "Give him one drink and a good meal. He can sleep in the stable tonight— maybe some rancher will give him a job tomorrow. They'll all be in town for the dance at the church." Turning, she went back to her book work in the office.

Finishing just at closing time, she said goodnight to those still in the bar and strolled down the street to her house. She was tired, she found herself looking forward to Sunday. Riding out to the Jacobs to spend some time with them, relaxed her.

The Jacobs were almost like family to her. They enjoyed hearing about her experiences at the saloon and could always be counted on to give good advice. Try as she might, Rita couldn't understand why their son stayed away and why he didn't write more often. The Jacobs rarely mentioned it, but Rita knew it had to hurt. If she'd known how to get hold of him, she had a few choice words—and some not so choice—to tell him. It purely did get her dander up just thinking about it. It also made her appreciate the relationship she'd had with her parents even more, and she never left the ranch without visiting their graves.

The next week seemed to whiz by, and Friday night came again before she knew it. There were even more people in town than last weekend. The outdoor stage was coming along nicely, and Sam scheduled a noted magician to come as entertainment for the opening. When the bar girls sang and danced on the outdoor stage, the routine would be changed to fit the thin skins of the more conservative people in town. The two performances would be a great show for everyone who attended, and at a dollar, apiece there'd be money left over to apply to the next spectacular. Sam was chock-full of plans for well-known performers to come to Pine Wood.

One week blurred into the next for Rita, and before she realized it, fall was in the air. The leaves were changing, the air turned crisp, and the residents bustled around like squirrels storing up for the winter. Pine Wood had grown so much she didn't recognize it. It didn't seem possible that one successful saloon could generate so much growth, but obviously it had. She danced with all the businessmen at the church socials, every one of whom remarked on the good the Golden Palace did for the town. The women welcomed her to their social clubs, and she tried to attend as many as possible. With all that plus her saloon work, she was so busy she felt like she needed a twin.

The morning rides were the only thing that kept her sane; she could relax out in the wild country of the Strip. Everything there had to struggle to live, but that only made the survivors stronger. Rita knew she was strong, but, oh, there were times when she wanted to escape from all the hubbub and responsibility and be at peace in a home with a man she loved, and who loved her...to have strong arms around her and a manly chest on which to rest her weary head. Rita didn't wallow in this trough for long, though—she knew too many people were dependant on the business the saloon generated. So with a sigh, she'd pull up the invisible bootstraps and carry on. Less and less was seen of Nebraska, and Rosy worried about him. In late September he came into the saloon one evening to see Rosy. After he left she came to Rita's office. "I'm worried about what's happening to Nebraska. From his last few visits, I'm certain things are getting bad with the Kid's old gang, and he doesn't know what to do about it."

Rita tried to figure the best approach to take with Rosy. "What seems to be going wrong, and how can I help?"

"The men won't listen to him anymore, and the last raid they went on, two people were killed. The Kid never let something like that happen when he bossed them."

"Maybe it's time Nebraska left the gang. Tell him he's welcome here anytime. I'm sure we can find a place for his talents." Rosy left with hope shining in her eyes after hearing this.

Leaves were falling when Nebraska came into the saloon again to see Rosy. After he left, Rosy came crying to Rita: "Nebraska has signed on for a job in Tucson and will be gone till next summer. He wants me to go with him." The tears streamed down her checks.

"Then why don't you go with him Rosy. I know you would like to quit your work here."

"I'm afraid that if he left the safety of the Strip, he'd be recognized as one of the Arizona Kid's men and thrown in jail." She wrung her hands.

Rita could see that the Arizona Kid still got all the credit for any holdup or killing in the West. His old gang had turned vicious, and the Kid's reputation had changed for the worse, even though he wasn't with them anymore. Because of this if Nebraska was recognized he would be hung without a trial.

Rita tried to comfort Rosy, but the girl was so distraught that she wouldn't listen. Finally Rita suggested they go for a ride. In the past they'd ridden together often, and this seemed like a good time to do it again. Probably nothing would be solved, but just getting away would help.

By early afternoon Rosy had settled down, so they returned to Pine Wood. Saying goodbye to Rosy, Rita stopped at her place. A carriage sat in front of her house...it was the Jacobs, come to visit.

Seeing them on the front porch, Rita rode over, waving a hello. She told them she'd put up her horse and be right back. After rubbing down and feeding Thunder, she hurried to the house.

"To what do I owe this visit, folks?" she asked, smiling as she approached.

Glen was worrying his hat with his hands and glanced at Susan before replying: "Hope you don't mind getting right down to business, Rita, but we'd like to sell the Lazy B-J to you." Noting the surprised look on Rita's face, he continued. "We're both getting older, and without our son to help, we feel we'd like to live in Tucson where it's warm in the winter. We hoped when we bought the ranch that our son would come home to help us and eventually take over the place." He sighed. "That hasn't happened—we haven't heard from him for months now, and who knows, maybe he's dead or has left the country. Anyway, we don't want to stay another winter here. Since you once lived on the ranch, we thought you might want to buy it."

This news was hard for Rita to get a hold on. She didn't want to lose two very good friends, yet she'd give almost anything to own the Lazy B-J again. She had some money saved, but not nearly enough to buy the ranch. Most of what she made went into expanding the saloon.

"I'd like to buy the ranch very much, but I don't have enough money right now to pay for it." Then the answer popped into her head, and she leaned forward eagerly. "If you could wait for a week or so, I may be able to sell the saloon to Mr. Singer. He's visited every month, wanting to buy me out; his offering price has gone up every time. It might just be that I could get enough from the sale of the saloon to pay for the ranch."

"You could borrow the money from Mr. Johnson's bank—I'm sure he'd loan it to you," Susan said, trying to be helpful.

Rita laughed. "I'm sure he would, but I've always been taught to pay for what I get. You can't tell what the future may bring, and if times get bad, and I can't pay the mortgage, I'd lose everything. No, Susan, I'll pay cash or not buy."

Glen was disappointed, but Susan could see her point. "We don't mind waiting, Rita. If you say you'll buy it, we'll plan on that and make preparations to leave as soon as the deal is finalized."

Rita was becoming excited at the possibilities. "I'll have the money inside of three weeks, so plan accordingly."

They continued to discuss the ranch and the future sale. Rita chatted with them and was assured that they would send her their address in Tucson, where she could write to them occasionally. She fixed lunch for them, and they left after eating to go back to the ranch.

Rita had been considering what to do while she conversed with them. Hurrying to clean up after the lunch and her ride, she donned one of her finer dresses and walked to the saloon. There were quite a few men in the barroom, and the three new girls she took on several weeks ago were mixing in with the bar patrons. Each girl had come through town looking for a place to live and had stayed to work in the saloon. Rita had hired another bartender, which made Pete, in his own words, "happier'n a dog with a new bone."

Now, catching Pete's attention, she asked, "Has Rosy come in yet?"

"She's up in her room wailin' over Nebraska agin." Pete, having never been married or seriously in love, felt little sympathy for these addle-brained females and their dubious relationships.

With an inward smile, Rita climbed the stairs and knocked on Rosy's door. When Rosy answered, looking like purest misery, Rita took her gently by the hand and led her to the bed. Sitting by her side, Rita asked, "How soon can you get hold of Nebraska?"

At the puzzled look on Rosy's face, Rita went on. "The Jacobs are selling their ranch, and I'm going to buy it. I need Nebraska to help me run it."

Rosy could hardly believe Rita. It took a few moments for the facts to sink in, and then joy suffused her face. She'd been so despondent about Nebraska's leaving that the sudden possibility of his staying was unimaginable.

"I-I'm meeting him tonight to say goodbye," she answered, stumbling over the words as her voice rose in excitement. "I'll bring him to the office so you can talk to him." Then, looking down at her hands, which twisted in her lap, she asked hopefully, "Do you really think it might be possible for me to quit my job here and live on the ranch with him?"

Rita knew how much this meant to Rosy, and with the three new girls, it would be easy to let her go. She put her arms around her friend and said: "Why, I wouldn't have it any other way. You belong with Nebraska. And that way I'll have a woman to talk to when I'm at the ranch."

Rosy literally vibrated with anticipation by the time Nebraska showed up. She met him on the porch of the saloon, and practically dragged him into Rita's office. As he looked at Rosy, he figured something had come up, and he supposed Rita would try to talk him out of going to Tucson. He prepared a counter-speech and started to open his mouth when, without any preliminaries, she said: "Nebraska, I need you to run the Lazy B-J for me."

Nebraska thought he'd heard wrong. The Lazy B-J belonged to the Jacobs. He stood with a frown on his face, trying to get a handle on this new development and staring intently at Rita.

"Did I hear you right? You want me to run the ranch?"

Rita enjoyed the surprise, and Rosy fidgeted so much she could hardly contain herself. She blurted out, "Rita's bought the ranch from the Jacobs. They're moving to Tucson to live."

Her words spilled out so rapidly that he was having trouble keeping them straight. "Rita says I can live on the ranch with you...I won't have to work here anymore." She was crying as the words tumbled from her lips.

Nebraska took her in his arms and kissed her cheeks. Looking over her shoulder, he spoke to Rita.

"Is this the gospel truth?"

"It's the gospel truth, Nebraska," Rita answered. "The only problem is, I haven't closed the deal yet. I thought you and Rosy could catch the stage to St. George tomorrow, talk to Mr. Singer, and tell him I want to sell the saloon. You could get married while you're there and after a honeymoon, come back here. By then the Jacobs will be gone and you can go right to the ranch. How does that sound to the two of you?"

Rosy didn't give Nebraska a chance to answer. She threw her arms around Rita, exclaiming, "That sounds wonderful." Then remembering that she had someone else to consider before giving that answer, she turned back to Nebraska, who laughed at her impulsiveness.

"Rita, Rosy spoke for both of us. There's only one thing— we'd like for you and Jake to be with us at our wedding, wouldn't we, darling?" he said and Rosy nodded, too happy to disagree with anything.

"We sure would like to be there, Nebraska, but it'll be hard for both of us to leave the saloon. We'll just have to be satisfied with giving you a reception here when you come back."

The two happy lovers left the office and went out to discuss their plans. Jake came in, shaking his head. "What's gotten into Nebraska and Rosy? They left the saloon laughing and talking like they just discovered Christmas."

"Well, not quite, but to them it's probably just as good." Then Rita told Jake of the new events. As she talked, she saw Jake's face take on a worried look and stopped to let him speak.

"That doesn't sound so good to me. With you not running the saloon, it won't go near as well, and Singer sure won't like me running it. I never did cotton to that man, and my job's gone soon as he takes over."

Rita was brought up short by the thought. Before, she'd only considered herself—now she could see that scores of people would be affected by her decision. The whole town would be up in arms if she sold the saloon.

"What can I do, Jake?" she asked with a sinking heart. "I've already told the Jacobs I'd buy, and Rosy and Nebraska are going to catch the morning stage for St. George, where they'll get married and tell Singer I want to sell."

Jake worried it over, not coming up with any solution. "Let's sleep on it...keep the word from going anywhere else for now. Maybe something will turn up. I'll catch up with Nebraska and Rosy—tell them to not say anything to anyone else." Deciding in his own mind that a way would be found, he added, "Let them go on to St. George. By the time Singer gets here, we may have something worked out."

Jake left the office, and Rita went out to mingle with the men in the saloon and to get ready for the show with Sam the Piano Man and her girls. She didn't know what to do about the ranch, and staying busy kept her mind free of the disappointment she felt. When closing time came, she was glad to leave for home. There seemed to be no answer to her dilemma that would keep everyone happy. If only the Arizona Kid had carried her off, she wouldn't be faced with all the work and problems. Then she chided herself: what would her father think if she took the easy way out of all her troubles? Besides, she was well thought of all over the Strip. There just had to be a way to make the ranch hers without letting any of her friends down.

Reaching her house, she climbed into bed without even lighting a lamp. Since leaving school back East, it had been one crisis after another. She'd survived by using her wits so far, but what would she do this time? It would take a lot more than wits now—what she needed was a savior. The image of the Arizona Kid dressed in shining armor and carrying a lance, charging to her rescue on a big white stallion, made her giggle. Her mind relaxed a smidgen, and she became less tense. Maybe Singer would come up with a solution where she could sell the saloon, work for him, and still get the ranch. That wouldn't be the same as owning the saloon but it could work if Singer was agreeable...and it might just be the best solution.

But things don't always work out the way they're planned.

Eight

The stage left Pine Wood on time with Nebraska and Rosy aboard, happiness enveloping them like a cloud. Rita desperately hoped she wouldn't have to disillusion them. It would be a few days now before she would know, maybe as long as a week if Singer couldn't come to Pine Wood right away.

The first day dragged for her and Jake both. They talked extensively and decided that Rita's idea of still working the saloon after Singer bought it was the logical solution. That weekend was extremely busy. There were people everywhere: ranchers and their wives in town for Saturday night festivities and to stock up on supplies; cowboys and businessmen just wanting to relax; husbands and wives and children waiting for the stage show.

Rita and her girls had just finished a song-and-dance routine when the saloon was rocked by a sudden blast. The batwings burst open, and two masked men stood with their guns covering the room.

"Just stay put, folks. No one'll get hurt if y'all will be good. All we want—" The harsh Texas drawl ended abruptly.

Rita acted before thinking: her gun slipped from the holster at her side with lightening speed, belching flame and lead. One of the masked men crumpled to the floor with a groan, dead before he hit. The other one was so startled that a lady on the stage had shot his partner that he hesitated for a split second before bringing his gun up to fire at Rita. He was too late—her smoking gun spoke again, and he staggered back with hot lead lodged in his shoulder. While his pistol fell from nerveless fingers, he stumbled through the batwings, clutching his bloody arm, scrambling to get to his horse and out of there as fast as possible. He almost made it before Jake came flying through the swinging doors and landed on top of him, slamming him solidly against the hard-packed dirt of the street. The outlaw tried to squirm free, throwing a futile punch with his good arm, but Jake's fist came flying through the dust to land on the man's jaw with a solid thud. Going limp, the outlaw lay unconscious, bleeding slowly into the uncaring earth.

Pandemonium came from the direction of the bank: six masked men carrying bags of money sprinted out of the building, their guns blazing. Townsfolk were ducking into doorways, hiding behind barrels, scattering everywhere to get out of the line of fire. A few guns were fired sporadically by some brave cowboys, but those shots were answered by the six men and soon silenced. The bandits jumped onto horses that were running before their riders were even in the saddle, vanishing in a whirlwind of dust and powder smoke. By the time Rita rushed from the saloon, they were gone.

Jake grabbed the wounded outlaw by the collar and dragged him roughly into the light. Tearing off the mask, he studied the face of the hapless bandit while others crowded around. Jake was sure he'd seen the man in the saloon earlier in the week. Someone else mentioned seeing him buy supplies from the general store, and another person recalled him cashing a bill at the bank. Apparently this man had cased the town and reported back to his gang.

The other outlaw lay face down on the floor of the saloon, a blood stain spreading from under his chest. When Rita started back inside, Jake quickly grabbed her arm, propelling her away from the door. Leaving the unconscious outlaw to some of the townspeople, he gently led Rita towards her house. It was bad enough for her to have killed a man, but to see the results of her quick action might be too much for her. Holding her close, he guided her home, opened the front door, and took her inside. Her face was white and her hands and lips were trembling when he got a lamp going. She dropped into a chair and leaned over, hanging her head in her hands. Jake patted her clumsily on the back, trying to talk with a soothing voice to calm her jittery nerves. It was several minutes before Rita raised her head, showing tear stained cheeks.

"Is he dead, Jake?" She knew the answer, but the hope that she was wrong would not be quieted.

Jake sat in a chair beside her, and taking both her cold hands in his, he rubbed them gently. "Rita, honey, you saved the saloon from being robbed, and possibly friends from being killed. You let the gang know the Golden Palace is a very dangerous place for them to cause trouble. Because of your quick action, other outlaws will consider going elsewhere to rob and steal. The whole town will be proud of you and call you a hero...you saved their future."

Rita watched him while he spoke. She certainly didn't feel like a hero. She felt small and uncertain and a little frightened. All she could think of was that she had drawn and fired without a thought as to the consequences, and a man lay dead because of it.

Knuckles rapped briskly on the door. Jake answered it and talked quietly with a man on the porch for a few moments. The man left and Jake stood there, shoulders slumped, face haggard, as if waiting for time to release him from these unwanted problems. Then he straightened and walked firmly back into the house.

"Rita, you're needed at the Johnson home." He paused when he saw the disbelieving look on Rita's face, which said: I can't go anywhere like this. He spoke gently. "Rex was killed in the robbery; Julie needs your care and support."

Shock washed over her. Rita bounded to her feet, forgetting her problems in an instant. She rushed out the door with Jake close behind. Running the two blocks to the Johnson house, she burst through the door to find Julie crying uncontrollably, her head in her arms on the table. Rita went over and sat in the chair next to her, pulling Julie's head onto her shoulder. The sobs got louder as Rita murmured softly, doing her best to comfort the distraught woman. There were other friends standing around the room looking sad and upset. While Rita held Julie, she overheard Craig, the grocer, muttering to Jake. "There's three more that was hit by flyin' lead—one's a little six-year-old girl belongin' to a nester family."

"How bad are they? Any killed?"

"Don't know yet. They was takin' 'em to the doc's place last I heard."

Jake left to go see what could be done for the others. He found they had all been taken to the doctor's house and placed on tables and a bed there. Formerly the only medical person on the Strip, the doctor had hired a nurse, who bent over the whimpering little girl, to bandage her wound. Jake went up to them and saw where the girl had been hit in the shoulder. The nurse gave him a smile and a nod, indicating that the girl would be okay. Going to the two men stretched out on tables, he discovered they were both dead. Thinking this was one hell of a way to end a weekend, he walked over to the saloon to check on the wounded outlaw.

The dead outlaw had been removed and the floor scrubbed clean- there would be no telltale evidence for Rita to see when she came back to work. The other renegade had been sloppily bandaged —why waste time on an impending corpse?—and was just regaining consciousness when Jake came in. The man was being loosely guarded by several gun-hung cowboys, their trigger fingers itching, hoping the outlaw would try to make a break. When Jake approached, one of them spoke to him.

"This piece of trash ain't goin' nowhere." He shot a venomous look at the sullen man. "What we need's more people like Miss Rita —she's the only one had sense enough to act quick. Because of her, there'll be two less gang members to rob decent folk." Jake knew this would be the sentiment all over town. "Has anyone gone after the others?" he asked.

There was a general shaking of heads. Someone mentioned that they found a few drops of blood on the trail out of town, but no one risked chasing after the gang. Jake decided it would be useless to try in the dark anyway, but at least one or more of the outlaws were wounded. It would be a long time before they tackled Pine Wood again: the cost in gang members turned out to be too high.

Jake spoke harshly to the outlaw: "Are you part of the Arizona Kid's gang?"

The outlaw scowled at him through pain-filled eyes. "Go to hell," he muttered weakly.

Jake glared at the man and his voice was ice cold when he said: "That's just where you're going, mister. Your crowd killed the banker and two other good men tonight. Now you're gonna pay."

Turning to one of the cowboys, he snapped, "Slim, go fetch a rope from your saddle. We're taking this pile of puke down to the stable and stringing him up."

Two men jerked the cringing outlaw up by the arms and shoved him savagely out the batwings to the stable. The rest of the angry cowboys followed. They would've liked to stomp him to death, but being civilized, hanging would have to do. Reaching their destination, the rope was thrown over a rafter and the noose placed roughly around the outlaw's neck.

Jake stepped up to him and asked one more time, "Are you part of the Arizona Kid's gang?"

The man glared back at him with undisguised hatred.

"Why did the Kid decide to rob the bank here? Doesn't he

realize the Strip could be the only safe place for him?" Jake was truly puzzled.

The outlaw lashed out: "There ain't no more Kid. He left eight, nine months ago. If he'd still been runnin' things, this wouldn'ta happened." Then he clammed up and refused to talk, waiting sullenly for the inevitable.

Jake gave the signal, and the rope went taut as several men hoisted the outlaw off the floor. He kicked and struggled for a few moments, then went still. They held him up till they were sure of their work, then slackened the rope and let the body fall to the earth. Several men carried him out to the back of the stable and left him till morning to be buried with the others.

Justice delivered, a dispirited Jake trudged to the saloon, followed by the men who helped hang the outlaw. Entering the Golden Palace, he stepped behind the bar, where Pete was pouring drinks as fast as he could.

Jake made an announcement: "The drinks are on the house for the next ten minutes, then the bar is closing till Monday. It will be a sad day tomorrow when we bury Rex Johnson and those brave men who died with him."

Everyone there felt sorrow for the dead men and their families and friends. A general nodding of heads and a chorus of amens echoed Jake's speech. Talk was subdued while the men took their drinks, tossed them down, and silently left. Jake and Pete closed the doors and mingled on the street a short time, sympathizing with a few cowboys who were still riled up. Then they walked slowly to the Johnson house to wait for Rita.

A group of worried businessmen standing outside discussed what should be done about the outlaws and getting the money back. Comments ranged from calling in the U.S. Calvary to sending for an Arizona Ranger. Someone suggested getting up a posse and going after the bandits. This was met with a wry laugh.

"You know how many posses have gone after the Kid and returned empty-handed?" the blacksmith snorted.

A man answered: "All of them." This brought more laughter, although it was toned down.

Jake told them, "According to the outlaw we hanged, the Kid isn't rodding the gang anymore."

"How can you believe scum like that?" a rancher asked bitterly.

"Well, Ed, think about it for a minute. What did he have to gain by lying? Could be it's the only truth he ever told in his whole rotten life."

Several more opinions were tossed around, but in the end they all agreed that was probably the case. The Kid would never attempt to cause trouble on the Strip.

Then Nebraska's name came up. Jake told them Nebraska had taken the stage to St. George that morning and didn't run with the gang anymore. He added the fact that no proof Nebraska ever did run with the gang existed, and if he had, he certainly wasn't mixed up with them now. Taken aback, they wanted to know why he felt this way. He looked them over and asked, "Do you trust Miss Rita's judgement?"

They all agreed in the affirmative, and Slim added, "I'd take Miss Rita's word on anything. If she thinks Nebraska is okay, then I'll back her all the way."

Others voiced the same opinion, and the conversation turned to how Rita had acted so quickly. The general consensus was that no one on the Strip could shade her draw. A respectful silence followed, until one scalawag said, "But I sure don't want my wife wearin' a gun!" This brought an easy chuckle, choked off immediately when Rita stepped out on the porch, calling to Pete and Jake.

As they approached, she said: "I'm going to sleep here on the sofa tonight, where I'll be close to Julie in case she needs anything. She wants the funeral to be held in the church at ten o'clock in the morning."

The two men went along with this and left to spread the word. The two cowboys killed in the gun battle were single, with no family to consult, so they would be buried at the same time.

Pine Wood still hosted a slew of people the next morning. Jake dispatched a cowboy to ride to St. George and telegraph the news of the holdup to the Arizona Rangers, requesting a Ranger be sent to Pine Wood. It hadn't done any good before, and he didn't think it would do any good now, but it was worth a try. Besides, it seemed to be the only plan he could think of.

Marie Purvis went with Jake to accompany Rita and Julie to the funeral. It seemed like the whole population of the Strip came to show their respect. The nester girl sat with her parents and the town nurse; she was recovering well from her bullet wound. The preacher made the services mercifully short out of consideration for the widow, and the burials took place at the cemetery east of town. After everyone left, the two outlaws were hastily buried in barren ground at the edge of the graveyard...no one grieved for them.

When the funerals were over, everyone went back to the general store, where the Jacobs provided a barbequed beef. Side dishes, cakes, and pies filled the table, an abundance of food for people with dulled appetites. Only the children were immune to the sorrow-laden air.

By early afternoon Pine Wood began to empty out as those from the range and other parts of the country left for their homes. Without the saloon open, the men were at a loss with nothing to do. Jake and Pete walked Marie home, then went in the Golden Palace to prepare for Monday. The bar girls were changing into more comfortable clothing after returning from the services and luncheon.

Pete worried aloud as they stood around the empty barroom. "With the bank money gone, it's really gonna put a damper on business—it's gonna slide right down the old chute."

Jake agreed. "I doubt the bank will ever open back up. Wells Fargo's gonna pull out and do all their business from St. George. I understand they had forty thousand dollars in the bank last night, brought in from the four corners area on its way to San Francisco. I guess the robbers got wind of it and decided this was the most remote place to hit it."

Sally, one of the bar girls, asked: "Do you think Wells Fargo will send men after the gang?"

Pete laughed dryly. "Oh, they'll try all right, but nothin' will ever come of it. That's one thing the Kid taught them boys well, how to hide a trail and lay low after a big job. They're probably scattered all over the West by now, about as easy to find as a sober cowboy on a Saturday night."

The conversation limped to a halt, and Jake decided to go spend the rest of the day with Marie. Pete finished his chores, which had been interrupted the previous night, then made an early night of it.

Rita stayed with Julie again Sunday night; she awoke Monday morning to the sound of Julie moving around in the kitchen. Smoothing out her rumpled clothes, she brushed her hair back and went into the kitchen. Julie had breakfast almost cooked. Her eyes were swollen, but she tried to put on a brave front.

"I couldn't sleep, and I couldn't take being in the bedroom alone any longer, so I came out to start breakfast," she said defensively.

"That's what I would've done, Julie," Rita said as she stepped to the washbasin to clean up. She wasn't feeling any too happy about facing the world herself. Going to the stove, she helped Julie finish their breakfast. Without saying any more, the women sat down to eat. Rita took several bites, then pushed her plate away. Casting a glance at Julie, she saw her food hadn't been touched.

Julie returned her look and sighed. "I'm just not hungry this morning. After twenty years of cooking for Rex, it seems so strange not to have him here and to know he never will be again."

Rita got up to answer a knock on the door. When she came back, an older lady followed behind her. The lady went over to Julie and hugged her. "I'm going for a drive in the buggy this morning—I thought you'd like to go along," she said, concern and sympathy in her voice.

"That sounds like a wonderful idea, Ida. Just give me a minute to get ready." Julie rose from her chair and went into the bedroom to change clothes.

"I'm Ida Smith, an old friend of Julie's. We used to play together when we were growing up in Pine Wood. I just heard about the shooting this morning. I knew you'd need to get on with your business, so I'll take over now. Sorry I didn't make it to the funeral, but I live way out in the wild canyons of the Strip. Usually, news carries to me pretty fast, but this time I guess my son stayed in town too long, and no one else came by to tell me. He woke me up when he got home, about three o'clock this morning, told me about the trouble, and I hopped in the buggy. Been driving ever since."

Obviously, Ida wanted someone to talk to, and Rita decided that would be good for Julie...she could just ride along and listen to Ida chatter.

Ida was still chatting quietly about the shooting when Julie came out of the bedroom. Rita put her finger to her lips to shush Ida. Ida stopped in mid-sentence and looked around at Julie.

"I guess I'm ready to go, Ida. Let's pack a lunch so we won't have to come back so soon." The two ladies got busy putting a lunch together, so Rita excused herself and went home to bathe and clean up before going to the Golden Palace.

At the saloon, a meeting of businessmen took most of the chairs in the barroom. She nodded to them and went into her office. Shortly after, Jake knocked, and when she said, "Come in," he stepped into the office.

Taking a chair, he watched Rita for any sign of nervousness. Seeing none, he said: "The men out front are concerned as to what'll happen to the town now that the bank will be closed."

"I hadn't even thought about that, Jake. Won't the bank continue to operate without Rex?" Here was another problem, and she would bet her bottom dollar that she was expected to be one of the main decision-makers for the town. After all, she owned the biggest business.

"I don't know how it can—this loss places all of us in a tight spot. Most of the people kept their money in the bank, and now it's all gone. You're probably one of the few who kept enough in your safe to run on for several months. But we can expect business to be bad all over town, and that will impact us."

While Jake talked, Rita realized the truth of what he said. "What about Mr. Singer? When he arrives he may be able to take over the bank and keep it going."

"I hope that'll be the case, but he might not want the saloon after he understands the problems facing it and the town."

Rita would have to rethink everything now—the robbery Saturday night could affect all her plans. Was this to be the end of all her hard work? She sat there in a dilemma, pondering this new situation. It would take a long time to get back to the same level of prosperity she'd known before the robbery. Trying not to worry about it, she decided she would go about her daily business, hoping for the best. The stage would arrive late that evening; she could only pray Singer would be on it.

Around ten o'clock that night, Rita paced restlessly outside the saloon, breathing in the fresh air while waiting for the stage. Then she heard it rolling into town. She left the porch and hurried down to the stage depot.

Arriving in a cloud of dust and dirt, the stage came to a stop. The door opened and Nebraska stepped out. Turning, he helped Rosy down the steps. Rita was so surprised at seeing them, she stopped dead in her tracks, staring from one to the other. They should be on their honeymoon by this time. What were they doing back in Pine Wood? Something definitely went wrong or they would not be here. Rosy spotted Rita and rushed over to her, with Nebraska following.

"Rita, we heard about the shootout from the man who came to send a wire to the Arizona Rangers."

Rita almost laughed as she realized that Nebraska and Rosy had come back to comfort her. What a relief! All her immediate fears vanished with this knowledge. She hugged Rosy, who started crying almost uncontrollably. The tears ran down her cheeks and onto Rita's dress. Rita thought they were tears of happiness.

"Now now, don't worry about that—we're doing fine. Congratulations on your marriage, and I want to hear all the details. Let's go sit down so you can tell me all about it. Okay?"

Over Rosy's shoulder, her glance fell on Nebraska, who stood looking at her with a pained expression on his face. She suddenly realized the reason for their return had nothing to do with comforting her.

"What happened in St. George, Nebraska?" she asked, stepping back from Rosy, her joy turning to anxiety.

Nebraska came right to the point. "We're not married yet. Your plans for buying the Lazy B-J may be changed." He stopped, swallowing hard, not wanting to be the bearer of bad news.

"You're not married? Why in the world would you not get married while you were in St. George? That's why...." Then she stopped talking as his last statement sank in. She switched her gaze from one to the other.

"What do you mean my plans will have to be changed...didn't Mr. Singer want the saloon?" This could not be. Singer tried constantly to buy the Golden Palace. "Did the robbery change his mind?"

Rosy wiped her eyes and, in a strangled voice, said, "Mr. Singer is traveling in Europe till the middle of summer; there's no way to get hold of him till he gets back. Nobody knows where he'll be, so a letter can't be sent. That means Nebraska will have to take the job in Tu-Tucson, and we ca-can't get m-m-married." Rosy began to stutter and wail as the last words came tumbling out.

Rita put her arms around Rosy once more, wondering what else could go wrong. Friday night she had been so happy, thinking she would own the Lazy B-J again, and now everything had fallen apart. She killed a man without thinking, and now she might lose the Golden Palace. She felt like crying with Rosy but knew she must appear strong in order to comfort Rosy and the other girls at the saloon. She would have to set an example, hoping the whole town would follow. The solution to their problems lay in banding together and helping each other, which could be done. But they needed a strong leader, and Rita knew she might be pushed into this position, much against her will. Joseph, the general store owner, would be her sidekick, so to speak, since he owned the next most prosperous business.

She felt so young to be responsible for a whole town. Why did they expect her to solve everything? Did they think someone who'd lived in the East was smarter than someone who lived in the West? That could be part of it, but the main reason, she knew, was because she'd made such a success out of the saloon.

Savvy business knowledge was the criterion by which they judged everyone. Well, so be it.

Nebraska still stood there waiting for her to tell him what to do. The other passengers had left the stage and gone their, separate ways, with the exception of one middle-aged man-dressed in a cowboy shirt and pants, his vest sporting a badge—who was standing there listening to their conversation. When he saw Rita looking at him, he stepped forward, introducing himself.

"I'm Bert Logan, Miss Jackson, the Wells Fargo investigator. I'm here to see if the stolen money can be recovered." He put out his hand, which Rita took while wondering how she could possibly be involved with this problem. He let her know: "It seems from all I hear that you'd be the most likely person here in Pine Wood to help me in this task. Everyone I talked to on the stage told me to look you up and enlist your help."

What made them think she could help? Rita wondered as she listened to Mr. Logan. Did owning a saloon automatically make you the mayor, a law enforcement officer, or perhaps some wise oracle that knew everything? Or did he think she had previous knowledge of the robbery, the saloon being the only business that might stay afloat during this hard hit? Well, she'd do what she could and hoped to be of some assistance.

"Mr. Logan, I'll be glad to assist you in any way I can, but I don't know anything about the gang that did the robbery."

"I realize that, but the man who brought word to St. George said the wounded robber claimed the Arizona Kid's gang pulled the job. We've heard that some of his men hang out at your saloon."

For some reason Rita felt defensive about Logan implying the Kid was one of the robbers, so she replied with some asperity, "He also told the men before they hanged him that the Kid left the gang a long time ago, and that if the Kid still rodded the gang, they would never have robbed this bank."

Logan watched Rita closely as she spoke. She was protective about the Kid, and he wondered what had happened to make her that way. Before he could pursue this line of thought, Nebraska put in a comment.

"Mr. Logan, can't this wait till morning? Rita has enough to consider at this point. I'm sure if you dropped by the Golden Palace around nine o'clock, she'd talk with you then."

Logan got the hint and, tipping his hat, excused himself, saying he would come by the saloon at nine in the morning.

When Logan left, Rita thanked Nebraska for coming to her rescue. The three of them walked to her house, where Rita fixed them some steak and potatoes to eat. They both appeared famished, and the food disappeared rapidly. When they finished eating, Rita brought up the subject of the ranch and the saloon.

"Nebraska, would it be possible for you to stick around as long as Mr. Logan is here? I may need your help, and we might come up with a solution for both problems. I know there's no possible way Logan will recover the money, but he may be talked into keeping Wells Fargo's business here, since the chances of the gang trying to rob us again are slim—at least that's what most of the businessmen and Jake think."

Nebraska mulled it over for several moments, then, seeing Rosy's hopeful face, agreed. "Okay, Rita, I'll stay for a month. Knowing what I do about the gang, I think the town folks are right, and if Mr. Logan can be convinced of that, the bank may be saved, and Pine Wood will pull out of this a lot faster."

"Then I really need you to help persuade him," Rita said. "Perhaps he'll listen if a man tells him."

They discussed related matters for a while before Rita sighed and told them she would see them at the Golden Palace in the morning. It had been a discouraging day for all of them, and they were glad to see it end.

Nine

Two weeks passed with no arrests made or money recovered. Adamant that the forty thousand dollars would eventually be found, Bert Logan would not give up. The people of Pine Wood, who felt they knew more than some uppity Wells Fargo agent, didn't agree.

Another two weeks slipped by with no results. The Wells Fargo investigator enlisted Nebraska to manage the bank on Rita's recommendation. She put money into it and let others borrow in order to keep them solvent as much as possible. At first Nebraska resisted vehemently.

"I'm not some namby-pamby sittin' in an office. I know how to rob banks, not manage them. Besides, if anything goes wrong and some money is missin', they'll think I took it!"

Rosy, afraid her man would go to Tucson and find some other woman, pleaded with him.

"Sweetheart, please try it. It won't be forever, and at least we can be together." She gave him a look like warm honey, which seeped into his very bones and discouraged further resistance.

With encouragement from Rosy and Jake, he grudgingly gave in, and as the weeks passed, he began to like his job more. It kept him in town close to Rosy, who had moved into a vacant home and started a dress-making shop, which Rita backed. They were waiting for Rita to decide what to do about the ranch.

The Jacobs decided to stay on a while longer, also hoping Rita could complete the purchase of the Lazy B-J. The town limped along, shop owners barely holding even. The saloon managed fairly well since Wells Fargo continued to operate out of the bank. The company brought money in to mix with Rita's and keep things going. This helped the saloon, which was really the only business in town showing a small profit.

It was the week before Christmas. About a mile out of town, in the early evening, an old man began changing clothes. Sitting on a rock by his mule, he pulled on rather fancy boots, stood, and admired as much of himself as he could see. Then he reached into his pack and pulled out some ribbons, which he tried to tie on the mule. She fought him all the way, kicking and biting. Grabbing her by the ears, the old man put his face eyeball to eyeball with her and yelled: "Stop it, you ol' flea-bitten nag! If'n we don't git there in style, you don't git there at all! So quit yer belly-achin'."

Understanding the intent, if not the words, the mule reluctantly settled down and let the old man festoon her with the ribbons. Thus they approached Pine Wood in great style.

Rita was working in the Golden Palace that night, worried about the poor Christmas the town would be having, when she heard a commotion outside the Saloon. Expecting trouble, she hurried to the swinging doors and looked out. There, tying an unhappy mule in gaily colored ribbons to the hitching post, stood an old man dressed in an expensive business suit. He wore a derby hat on top of graying hair. When he stepped onto the porch, she saw that his boots were custom-made and costly. A crowd that had apparently followed him down the street gathered behind him. He strutted into the light from the saloon, and Rita saw a brown leathery face with a big smile on it.

"Well, lassie, I told ya I'd be back," he chortled as he walked towards her.

Rita stepped back from the doorway so he could enter the barroom. For the life of her, she did not recognize the man, though he apparently knew her. When he came inside where the light shone full on him, she still felt sure she'd never met him before.

Then Jake hurried past her with his hand outstretched, saying, "Well, bust my britches, if it isn't Fuzzy Morton, and all dressed up like some slick dude from back East."

Shocked, Rita realized this was the old prospector she had given her last hundred dollars to on the way to Pine Wood. She'd only seen him for a few moments that day, so he wasn't familiar to her. And he sure did look different now. If Jake hadn't recognized him, she didn't think she ever would have.

Fuzzy shook Jake's hand and then turned to confront Rita. "Howdy, pardner," he said as he put out his hand. "I told ya I'd strike the mother lode sometime, and by gum, I did. It's producin' more gold than a body can keep track of, and half of it's yours."

Rita's head felt funny, and for a moment she thought she was going to fall right into his arms. To cover her unsteadiness, she wrapped her arms around him and gave him a big hug.

"Fuzzy, come on over to the bar and tell us about it. And you don't owe me a thing; I'm just glad I was able to help you," she whispered in his ear.

He reared back away from her and snorted, "Why, girl, if it hadn'ta been for you and your pa, I'da been buzzard bait a long time ago."

She took him by the arm and led him to the bar. "Pete, the drinks are on the house in celebration of Fuzzy's good fortune."

A mad stampede descended on the bar, forcing Jake to come to Pete's rescue and help pour the drinks. Pete poured Fuzzy's glass full. Fuzzy stared at it for a moment, then turned to Rita by his side.

"Missy, I ain't drinkin' one drop till you admit we're pardners."

"Fuzzy, I can't accept half your mine. I didn't do anything to earn it. You knew my father; he wouldn't accept it if he were here either."

Fuzzy inspected her, thinking hard. Here was a strong-willed young filly; she looked a lot more growed up than he remembered. As pretty as a desert cactus in bloom, to his way of thinking. Yet with that gun on her hip, he got the impression she could be hard as nails if the need arose.

The men in the saloon became quiet as they listened to the exchange between Rita and Fuzzy. All of a sudden Fuzzy's face lit up and he laughed out loud.

"If'n I go pardners with someone, I go all the way." Turning to Pete he said, "Top those glasses agin, Pete. This here saloon is half mine now that Rita and I are pards. She owns half of everything I got, and I own half of everything she's got."

The men started shouting and slapping each other on the back at Fuzzy's statement. Rita took Fuzzy firmly by the arm and led him into the office, motioning for Jake to follow them. Amy and Sally went behind the bar to take his place. Fuzzy carried his drink with him, still untouched.

"I told ya, missy, I ain't touchin' this till ya admit we're pards." Obstinate, he plunked himself down in one of the office chairs. Rita sat in one facing him and Jake took a third.

Rita looked at Fuzzy for what seemed a long time. What should she do? Fuzzy's luck was the answer to her problems, yet she felt he would be getting the raw end of the deal. The Golden Palace certainly didn't equal Fuzzy's mine.

"Fuzzy, I just can't accept half your mine. You're the one who spent all those years looking for it."

Fuzzy leaned forward, speaking earnestly. "Ain't no one got more right to half than you, missy. Old Bert staked me many a time, and you give me your last dollar to keep me going after the mother lode. If'n I'd gone into Pine Wood for supplies, I'da done went the other way when I left. You givin' me that money aimed me and Petunia in the right direction. I found that thar gold jist layin' there, shinin' like a young girl's hair. Kin't no one say you ain't responsible for me bein' where I was at the right time."

Jake threw his two cents into the conversation: "He's right, Rita, that's the way things work out here in the West. A prospector strikes it, his backer gets half the strike. If it wasn't for you, he'd never have found it. Fuzzy knows that after he left you at Pipe Springs, he went directly to the place and found the gold. Half the mine is yours."

"You're darn tootin' it is!" Fuzzy snorted. "We're pards, missy, ain't no way you kin get outta it."

Rita stared from Jake to Fuzzy, trying to determine the right thing to do in this situation. She was young when she left the West, so she'd encountered nothing like this before. She wondered what the Arizona Kid would do in a case like this. But why in the world was she thinking of him again? He left the country and would never be back. Clearing her mind, she had an idea.

"All right, Fuzzy, on one condition. I'm buying the Lazy B-J ranch that Dad used to own. You're a partner in that also, since you said all I have is half yours and all you have is half mine. That's the only way I'll consent."

Both Fuzzy and Jake leaned back in their chairs with a sigh. "You got a deal, girlie," Fuzzy said and then let out a shout that could be heard all over town. He hoisted his drink and downed it in one gulp, not even blinking an eye as the fiery liquor ran down his gullet. He jumped up and headed for the barroom. Jake followed him while Rita sat behind the desk, a glazed look on her face, trying to figure out what had just transpired.

With Fuzzy and her as a team, they could buy the bank from Julie. Get it up and running even better than before. Pine Wood could be prosperous again, settlers would come in and ranchers would have a source to borrow from. All sorts of possibilities raced through her mind: Nebraska could run the ranch, Jake would run the Golden Palace, and maybe Fuzzy could be coached to run the bank—although she'd have to watch that part closely... she didn't know much about his abilities as a manager. It might be better if she kept Nebraska on as banker and let Fuzzy run the ranch; he seemed to like the outdoors. After all, she would be at the ranch a lot to help him. She decided that if all the others agreed, that's how it would be done.

A lot of noise flowed from the crowd in the barroom; everyone on the Strip would be in town tomorrow to celebrate Fuzzy's luck and spend his money. The news would travel fast.

While she sat thinking, a knock came at the door. When she bid them enter, Rosy walked into the office. Her face flushed and vibrating with excitement, she started talking immediately.

"Rita, this means Nebraska and I can get married now. I'd like to have the wedding tomorrow. Could we use the saloon?"

Rita laughed at Rosy's eagerness. "We'll put on the biggest wedding this place has ever seen, Rosy. Does Nebraska know he's getting married tomorrow?"

Rosy squealed from sheer happiness. "No, but he will in a few minutes I'm going to find him and tell him right now." And she dashed back to the barroom.

Almost time for the girls' performance. Rita left the office and went to the stage to meet the other ladies. Sam banged out a wild western ballad at the piano, adding to the general hubbub. The saloon girls formed their chorus line and Sam changed his tune to the one for the song and dance. A wild show followed. Everyone was in a jolly mood and the girls danced and sang better than Rita thought possible. After the performance the men shouted for more and it seemed the roof might come off the place.

Rita left the stage and grabbed Fuzzy from a table with five other card players. Taking him with her back to the stage, she signaled Sam, who played a waltz. She stepped into Fuzzy's arms and the two of them danced, with Fuzzy kicking up his heels and really showing off. Rita hadn't expected such a wild dance, but Sam played faster and Fuzzy twirled her around again and again. The crowd shouted, cheered, and clapped their hands. When the dance ended, Rita was exhausted. Fuzzy picked her up and carried her off the stage amid the whistles of all the men.

Rita decided this was one night she would not stay to close up; Jake could handle it. She only hoped the Golden Palace would still be in one piece tomorrow. Telling Fuzzy goodnight and excusing herself to all those who wanted to congratulate her, she left the saloon.

Halfway home, Jake overtook her. Falling into step, he seemed hesitant to say what he wanted. Finally he blurted out, "Marie and me want to get married at the same time as Nebraska and Rosy tomorrow."

Stopping in her tracks, Rita turned to him. "That's wonderful. We can have a double wedding. Most everyone on the Strip will be in town...it will be a great celebration." Then she went quiet, a worried frown on her face. "How on earth are we going to handle the crowd at the saloon with you gone on your wedding night?" she asked.

Jake gave her a big smile. "I already got three friends to help out at the bar. They get all they can drink free after the bar closes, plus five dollars apiece. There sure will be a bunch of hungover men in church Sunday." He laughed as he spun around and hurried back to the Golden Palace.

Rita continued on home. What an exciting evening she thought, She owed a lot to Fuzzy; he showed up at exactly the right time, just like Santa Claus. She fixed a light snack and went to bed. Lying there thinking of tomorrow, she grew happy again.

Because of the mine, her dreams of owning the Lazy B-J would be fulfilled. With her three friends running all the businesses, she could ride as much as she wanted.

Before the weddings, Rita and Fuzzy visited Julie to see about buying the bank. Happy to sell, Julie wanted to be out of the banking business. The arrangements were made for the changeover to take place next Monday. Fuzzy had brought several thousand dollars with him—no one suspected he carried so much money. The rest remained in a Nevada bank and could be transferred anytime. All monies from the Nevada mine would also be sent to Pine Wood if necessary.

The weddings went off without a hitch. Fuzzy contacted the Jacobs, who happily barbequed a steer for the wedding dinner. Sam the Piano Man dressed the bar girls up as bridesmaids. Fuzzy acted as Rosy's father to give her away and Pete acted as Marie's father. The saloon had been spit-shined and filled with evergreen boughs—there weren't any flowers available in December. But the bar girls adorned every available spot with colorful ribbons, giving the whole place a festive air. A raw and windy day, the weather deterred no one from coming, for they were celebrating not only the marriages, but what promised to be a better future for them all. Both couples left town in separate buggies and headed into the high country for a few days' honeymoon. The party continued at the Golden Palace. Rita and Fuzzy met with the Jacobs to finish the sale of the Lazy B-J. Fuzzy was particularly happy about this, since his loyal Petunia would at last be retired to live out her days in comfort.

"Maybe now we'll get to see our son more often. We heard he was in Tucson, and that will be nice," Susan mentioned as the papers were signed.

Glen shook Fuzzy's hand, then turned to Rita. "We sure are glad you bought the place. It was beginning to wear us down.

Not sure I can take city life, but since Susan is looking forward to it so much, we'll probably both enjoy it."

"Remember, you're always welcome back at the Lazy B-J." Rita gave Susan a hug.

After closing the deal, Fuzzy stayed in the saloon, playing cards and having a good time. During the afternoon, Rita and the bar girls prepared a special show for all the people in town, to be held in the outdoor theater. Even some of the Paiute Indians from the reservation around Pipe Springs were in town. Every now and then some cowboy would get a little too rambunctious and want to shoot things up. Rita kept a sharp eye on them in the saloon, but when they got outside there was no one to ride herd on them.

She finally convinced Glen Jacobs to enlist two of his former ranch hands to help keep order. Patrolling the streets, they let the cowboys have fun, but if they got too rowdy, Glen or one of his men would throw them in the horse troughs. This always cooled them off, and no one was hurt.

After the show, Rita went inside the saloon to relax in her office for a while. It seemed lonesome without Jake and with Rosy gone. Fuzzy weaved through the door and plopped in a chair, watching Rita.

"Missy, we sure have a rip-roaring place. I ain't had this much to drink since my wife's funeral, and that were a long time ago." He belched loudly, obviously soused.

"Why don't you go upstairs and sleep it off, Fuzzy. Then we can ride out to the ranch in the morning and see what shape the place is in," she ventured, hoping to forestall a bad hangover.

"That's a right smart idea." He reached for his vest pocket, missed once, then pulled out a roll of bills. "Keep this wad in the safe for me; I won a little tonight." He chuckled.

Rita took the money and placed it in the safe. When Fuzzy left, she walked into the barroom and over to Pete.

"We won't close tonight until most of the men have either left or passed out. I'll mosey through the barroom occasionally to watch things."

"It's sure been a great night for business. Maybe we oughta have a weddin' every Sunday," Pete told her.

After a short time she drifted towards the office door again and went in, closing the door behind her. Instantly, she knew she wasn't alone, but scanning the room, she saw no one. Glancing at the office safe, she was dismayed to see its door open. Rushing over, she checked all the contents—everything was still there. Maybe she had forgotten to lock it. Pushing the door shut and making sure it was locked this time, she went around the desk to sit down. She let out a yelp as an Indian came up from under the desk. But her reactions were still without thought, and her gun appeared in her hand. The Indian fell back, mumbling, "No hurt, no hurt."

Getting control of herself, she motioned for him to sit in one of the chairs.

"So you speak English. How did you get my safe open?" she asked, holstering her gun.

The Indian simply sat, obdurate and stubborn. He looked rather thin and she began to wonder if he was hungry. Stepping to the office door, she got Pete's attention and signaled him to bring some food into the office. Going back to her chair, she sat down and watched the Indian, keeping silent.

When Pete entered, he almost dropped the tray of food.

"What in hell is he doing here?" he asked, startled.

Rita took the tray from him, saying, "He's hungry and came into the office to ask for food." She didn't mention the safe.

Pete glanced at the Indian, then leaned in for a closer look.

Surprise again came over his face. "Well, heck's fire, if it ain't old Spit-So-Far. He use'ta do odd jobs round the ranch. When Bert sold it, he worked here at the saloon. Stayed for about a year then disappeared." Pete paused and his look became grim. "That was about the time old Bert missed some money from the safe. He thought this Injun took it but never could prove it. Besides, the Injun ain't been seen round here for a long time, till now. You better watch him—somehow he knows the combination to that safe."

"I'll watch him close, Pete. You go on back to the bar, and if I need you I'll call."

Pete gave her an inquisitive look, glared at the Indian a moment longer, then left.

Rita handed the tray of food to the Indian and he dug into it. She watched as he ate, keeping quiet, waiting for him to finish. He ate it all, using his fingers, then looked up at her. She said nothing, just stared back at him.

"Why you no tell Pete about safe?" He finally asked.

With a shrug, she stood up and walked to the window, her back to the Indian. After a few minutes of letting him wait and wonder, she turned.

"I remember an Indian bronc-buster who worked on the Lazy B-J when I grew up there. He braided me a horsehair rope once."

The Indian stared at her, then his face began to break into a grin. "You Rita;" he stated, then came to his feet. "I not know you boss here."

Rita laughed at his expression. "You think you could make me another rope, Spit?"

Spit was tickled to death. "You pretty. Me make rope, bring you two days," he said, and going to the office window, slipped through it and disappeared.

Rita thought back to the days when Spit did so many things

for her on the ranch. Puzzled at not recognizing him, she decided it must be because he was so skinny now and his hair was short. For whatever reason, he seemed a lot older—perhaps the guilt of stealing money from a friend ate at him. And the dim lamplight had made him less visible. Besides, she'd been shook up by the safe being open. She would have to get the combination changed since there may be others around who knew it.

A short time later she returned to the barroom and could tell it would be closing before long. Most of the men were gone and those left were a little unsteady. She floated around the room, letting them know that closing time was near and she'd been glad to have their business. They drank a few more shots, played a couple more hands of cards, then began to drift out the batwings. When all the revelers were gone, she helped Pete clean up and then left for home. It was two in the morning when she got there, and she fell into bed, exhausted.

Ten

The next six months in Pine Wood passed rapidly. Jake hired carpenters to build a home on the lot next to Rita's for him and Marie. With the help of the townspeople and some of the ranchers, the house went up fast. When they completed it two weeks later, Fuzzy consulted with Rita. "Why don't we move the carpenters to the Golden Palace and enlarge it. Business will be even better if we add more space and hire more girls."

"That's an excellent idea. We can build an imposing stage and add another bar." Rita became excited about the prospects.

Upon deciding to increase the size of the saloon to cover a full city block, they made plans to put in a large gaming room with roulette wheels and card tables where games could be played twenty-four hours a day. They included a few secluded card rooms for gentleman who wanted their privacy.

The Golden Palace employed more men than a lot of the ranches, including a boy who cleaned the horse manure off the street in front. A great many people felt this was pretentious, but it not only kept the floor cleaner, it also made the saloon smell better.

The size of the outside amphitheater was increased and covered to keep out bad weather. Sam the Piano Man scheduled weekly attractions on its stage; Rita and her girls performed each weekend in the early evening with a milder version of their routine. Later in the evening they performed inside with a more robust and wild show. Sam capitalized on Rita's pleasant singing voice and her popularity by making her the lead entertainer. She held all the men's hearts in her hand when she sang, whether standing on the stage or moving through the crowded barroom, always wearing a fancy dress and a gun belt.

Every single man, and many of the married ones, wished they could marry her. Over time she received proposals from most of them; she always let them down easy, and each left feeling she belonged to all, not just one. Much covert discussion went on about whether she would ever marry, and sometimes she wondered about this herself. When she looked in a mirror, she no longer saw the naive young girl who arrived a year and a half ago, wondering if she could run a saloon. A certain maturity in the eyes, a firmer mouth, and definitely a sense of self-confidence defined her. Marriage was not out of the question, but none of the men in Pine Wood interested her that way, and right now she was too busy.

With the outdoor stage complete, she put the carpenters to work building a first-rate hotel, with a plush dining room and foyer. The bedrooms were decorated and furnished with velvet drapes and fine linens. She hired waitresses to serve the patrons and outfitted them in nice dresses. The popularity of Pine Wood spread through all the adjoining states, as well as further east and west. She became known as the lady who ran the town, and as a gun-toting female who could best any man in a shootout, but who could win the hearts and respect of any man or woman she met.

The week of the Fourth of July was planned by Jake, Pete, and Fuzzy with Rita's approval. A big parade began the holiday, led by Rita on Thunder and Fuzzy on a big white stallion that Spit-So-Far had caught and tamed. Each of the businesses decorated a wagon for the parade, and Sam the Piano Man's wagon sparkled, with his saloon girls singing and dancing on it.

A rodeo scheduled in the afternoon brought many of the Indians and cowboys in to participate. The big celebration was held in the amphitheater that evening: Sam had persuaded a special orchestra and a well-known lady soloist to perform. People mingled everywhere, and the new hotel was completely sold out for the whole week. There were newspaper men, miners, bankers, cowboys, saloon owners, and fancy-dressed ladies from all over the west. Even a few people from back East, who had read about Rita, the gun-toting lady that ran a town on the Arizona Strip, were there. Rita was especially surprised to see Mr. Singer. Every time he visited her and saw the new changes in town, he kicked himself all over again for being gone that fateful day. But he was happy for her and spent a few days enjoying the revelries. All in all, it was a wild week in Pine Wood.

After the special performance in the saloon that Saturday night, Fuzzy bounded to the stage and grabbed Rita by the hand, bowed with her, and, raising his bull voice, shouted: "Ladies and gentleman. Three cheers for the Queen of the Strip." The roof almost came off as men and women shouted their approval. Hats were tossed into the air, and the word quickly spread outside the saloon, where guns began to go off, with men riding up and down the street shouting, "Hail to the Queen of the Strip." This embarrassed Rita, but the crowd would not be quieted. It took Jake, Nebraska, Fuzzy, and Pete together to get her through the crowd and into her office.

Rita was white-faced and surprised at all the rowdy activity over her. All she had done in Pine Wood benefitted her as well as the town, and she couldn't understand the fuss over it. "Do you think the Golden Palace will still be standing by morning?" she asked Jake.

Jake let out a hearty laugh. "Can't be helped, Rita. This town knows that if it weren't for you, it would hardly exist. I think Fuzzy was great doing what he did. We should have done it a long time ago." A chorus of amens came from the others.

Nebraska added: "He's right. From now on you're going to be known as Queen Rita. Won't anyone be calling you Miss Rita anymore."

"That sounds a little pretentious for a gun-toting saloon girl.

Besides, I still prefer that you call me Rita." She laughed at them. "You four men, along with Sam, deserve the credit. Especially Fuzzy, who persisted till he found the mother lode."

Fuzzy stood up and proclaimed: "Since we're airin' the sheets, there's some changes we wanta make in this here organization." He glanced around, making sure he had everyone's attention. "We all been talkin' since you up and bought that other ranch last week. Nebraska wants to be quit a the bankin' business—he's hankerin' to be out in the open and livin' on your new ranch with Rosy. I don't cotton to ranch life— give me the saloon where I kin drink all I want and spin big windies to any sucker who'll listen." Having said this much, he paused, watching Rita sit with her eyes wide, and a puzzled look on her face.

The import of what Fuzzy said finally registered on her. "But who will I get to run the bank if Nebraska leaves it?" she asked.

Jake spoke up. "That's where I come in. Being married puts a different light on the way I think. Marie told you last week she was going to have a baby, and I want the young'un to grow up somewhere other than in a saloon. I ain't saying anything against a saloon, Lord knows I've spent enough time in one, but, well, Marie and I think it's better if I run the bank. I've always been good with people and figures, and you know you can trust me." With that speech, Jake closed his mouth and waited for Rita to decide.

Glancing from one to the other, she said: "It looks like my advisors have come up with a great plan. I like it." A general sigh issued from the men as she continued: "So Fuzzy will be in charge of the saloon; he'll be responsible for all the saloon girls, which I'm sure he'll be happy about. And I know that with his keen mind, he can keep track of all that needs to be done. Jake will take control of the bank, and Nebraska will be general manager of all our cattle ranches." She sat gazing up at the ceiling. "Sounds good to me."

They discussed the changes and decided they would have everything in place by Monday morning. The men went back into the saloon after Rita bid them goodnight and left for home. It had been a wonderful week in Pine Wood. The businessmen were all happy with the crowds that turned out, the weather cooperated with sunny days, and no one had been killed or hurt when the rambunctious cowboys let off steam by shooting their guns. Who could ask for more?

Well, come to think of it, she could. Sometimes it was downright lonesome coming home to an empty house. This was not her goal in life—she wanted a man she could love. Jake had Marie, Nebraska had Rosy, Sam had one of the bar girls he was sweet on, and Fuzzy had his bottle. When would it be her turn? Self-pity rose like bile in her throat till she shook herself, said, "Enough of that," and strode through her front door into her lonely house.

The next morning she rode to the Lazy B-J since the town was still crowded with people. When she topped the rise above the ranch house, she could see Spit-So-Far and his Indian friends working horses in the corral. She rode up to the fence and watched them. It was a quiet and peaceful scene. Spit-So-Far's special way with horses brought buyers even from other states. A rancher in New Mexico had tried to hire him, but he remained loyal to Rita. After all, she gave him the second chance he needed. Rita thought back to the night she had caught Spit trying to rob her safe. What a lucky break for both of them— she had put him on her payroll the very next day.

Spit would take a wild mustang, start from the head with gentle rubbing of the muzzle, then proceed up the face and down the neck, constantly talking in a soft soothing voice as his hands worked over every inch of the horse. He would watch the horse's ears and eyes as he worked. With the slightest twitch of the ears or rolling of the eyes, he'd go back to the front and start all over again. As time went on, he would lean against the horse, then pick up its feet, rub its legs, work to the back, and with his body pressed close to the horse, he'd slowly ooze around behind the horse and then up the other side. Soon he was able to touch and stroke the horse anywhere. A pile of fresh-cut green grass or oats always lay in front of the horse, and Spit left the most difficult procedures till the horse was occupied with eating.

When it came time to get on the horse's back, he would lead it out to a nice patch of grass, where he started from the neck, rubbing and stroking, before sliding up onto the horse's side, then quickly slipping off. He would repeat this time and again while the horse grazed, till he could soon slip all the way onto its back and off the other side. The horse got so used to Spit being everywhere, it wouldn't move even when he spent more and more time lying along its back. Eventually he would sit up, and as the horse wandered around, grazing on the grass, he'd sit on it and talk to it. There was never a moment when the horse didn't hear Spit's voice speaking softly, or feel his hand touching it somewhere.

One to two months of this gentle training and the horse was broken to ride and trained to double rein and run on slight knee pressure. Spit turned the horse by leaning into the turn or shifting his body in the direction he wanted it to go. It was a real lesson in patience to watch him work, and Rita could watch for hours as he and his men gentled the horses, all using the same method. But it was left to Spit to really fine-tune a horse for the rider he sold it to.

Spit took a break and came over to the corral fence, with the horse following, to talk to Rita.

"Have good time in town?" he asked.

Rita laughed because she'd seen him at the rodeo. "A very good time, Spit. I really like the way you work with horses; I wish men could be trained that way," she joked.

Spit-So-Far squinted up at her. "Some men no good. No try train. Get killed. Horse never too mean to train."

Again Rita laughed and leaned over to take Spit's hand. "By the way, Spit, Nebraska will be running the ranches from here on; Fuzzy will be in town at the saloon."

Spit's face broke into a full grin, which was rare. "Nebraska heep good cowman; Fuzzy talk too much, better he in saloon."

This Indian didn't miss anything, Rita thought. She might have to consult with him more often. Waving to the other Indians, she turned her horse and rode to the house.

Tying up in front, she went inside. The ranch house always smelled the same this time of year; the aroma of leather and wood mixed with sage brush and wild desert roses permeated the room. She truly loved this ranch. It was a part of her, and she enjoyed the time she spent here. She decided to stay overnight and go back to town in the morning.

Fixing lunch, she called Spit-So-Far and his crew into the kitchen and fed them all they could eat. The other ranch hands and Nebraska would be back at the ranch tonight. She made an apple pie and baked it while they ate, its sweet aroma infusing the air. When she placed it in front of the Indians, it disappeared so fast she couldn't believe it. "You come next week, make more pie?" Spit asked as he swallowed the last mouthful.

"I'll have to have my own apple tree if I keep this up, Spit," Rita said as she rose from the table to wash the dishes.

"Me plant," Spit announced as he left the house with his men.

When Rita left the ranch early the next morning, the ranch hands were just riding out for the day's work, and the Indians were working the horses in the corral again. Nebraska rode a short distance with her.

"It sure feels good to get in a saddle again and off that banker's chair. Hope I never see a chair like that again," he said with a chuckle.

Rita rode a few paces, then said: "You may be wishing you had that chair back, Nebraska, after riding between two ranches all the time to keep the cowhands on the job."

Nebraska gave a short bark of laughter. "I don't think so. When I rode with the Kid, we would ride for three, four days without stopping except to catch a little sleep. There wasn't a posse in the West that could keep up with us." His voice faded, and Rita believed he was reliving the old days with the Arizona Kid.

"Yes, he was quite a man, Nebraska." The words slipped out before she realized she had spoken them aloud.

Pulling his horse to a stop and looking Rita in the eyes, he asked, "How do you know what kind of man the Kid was?"

Rita's horse stopped of its own accord when Nebraska's did. "I met him on the train, remember?"

Nebraska stared hard at her, and she knew that her statement did not fully satisfy him. "I always wondered what happened to change the Kid after that train robbery. Now I wonder if you didn't have a hand in that."

He sat still on his horse, staring at her, waiting for her to confirm or deny his suspicions. How could she tell him that the short time she spent with the Kid had made such an impression on her, he was never far from her thoughts, even though she hadn't heard from or seen him again? She didn't even know what he looked like—a bandana covered his face each time she saw him. Would Nebraska understand her fantasies involving the Arizona Kid? Of course not. She knew no one could understand how she wanted to meet him again, talk to him, and listen to his soft, gentle voice.

Suddenly she realized that Nebraska still stared at her with a grin on his face, and that she hadn't answered him. Flustered, her face turning pink, she stammered, "I talked with him during the train robbery."

Chuckling, Nebraska said, "That's okay. Ain't none of my business anyway. But I was on that train, in the express car, and the Kid didn't have much time to talk before we got the money and rode out. It took him an awful long time to meet the rest of us at the rendezvous point, though," he added suggestively.

Getting control of herself, Rita said: "You're right—it isn't any of your business, Nebraska, but you are one of my best friends. In fact, the only one with a hole in his ear." He laughed with her as they both started their horses to moving again.

After an interval, Rita said in a wistful voice: "He took me on his horse that day to my friend's ranch. He met me again after I heard the news of my father's death and went to the stream behind their house to commiserate with myself." Her crystal-clear memory reconstructed the sight of the tall, lean, broad shouldered Kid.

Holding his tongue, Nebraska waited. When she said no more, he told her: "Your secret is safe with me, and if you like, I'll try to get a message to the Kid."

"Thanks, Nebraska," Rita said. "But it's just a young girl's fantasy about an outlaw. With time, I'll get over it, and besides, the Kid has probably forgotten he ever saw me."

Nebraska didn't think so...he knew the Kid too well. And judging by his sudden change of character, he figured the Kid still remembered Rita very well. Nope, he would just have to try to get in touch with the Arizona Kid.

They parted company, and Rita rode on into town. Between

the two ranches, the bank, the saloon, and the hotel, she was back to sleeping little and working till midnight or later every night. Her associates did their work well, but there always seemed to be questions to answer and decisions to make.

Fuzzy took to the saloon like an old hand. He worked with the young girls and took a lot of the load off Rita as their counselor. All of them enjoyed crying on his shoulder occasionally, and Fuzzy always had a story to tell to ease their worries. He spent a lot of time either in the barroom playing cards and drinking or out on the front porch sitting in a chair, telling stories to anyone who would listen. To Rita's surprise, there were always several people and a few young kids hanging on his every word; even the ladies of the town would stop to engage Fuzzy in conversation. He wore a flower in the lapel of his suit, and his memory kept track of each person he met and their birthday. When a lady came by the saloon on her birthday, he presented her with the flower from his lapel. It got so that some ladies would walk their husbands by the saloon while Fuzzy sat out front so he could remind the husband of his wife's birthday by giving her a flower. In this way, Fuzzy became a favorite of all the ladies in Pine Wood.

He was sharp at cards as well. He played while telling a story and drew comments out of his opponents that let him see the real person behind the face. Rita learned to trust his judgement, and when he said a man was a cheat, Rita politely told that man to leave Pine Wood and never return. It didn't happen often, but when it did, the man left, no questions asked. None of them wanted to face Rita's gun.

Fuzzy became so popular and adept at running the saloon that Rita spent less and less time there. But she still showed up most every day and mingled with the customers, joking and talking with each as much as possible, because that's what they expected, and she wouldn't let them down. She had her reputation to keep up, and she did that very well. She also still participated in the song and dance during the evening show on weekends.... This was also what all the men wanted.

Fuzzy hired two more dealers and several more girls, since the size of the saloon made it imperative. There were so many people traveling into and through Pine Wood now that the saloon was busy all the time. They heard some talk of the railroad coming, but Rita figured it wouldn't happen: the large canyon at the south end of the Strip was a natural barrier, and no railroad would ever be built across it. Besides, where else would a railroad go? One already ran through southern Utah, taking travelers east and west.

The weeks slid into months, and before long the time for a Christmas celebration came again. Sam outdid himself this year with the most spectacular show presented so far. Despite the cold, people from all over the country came to Pine Wood.

Rita was lingering at the bar one night just before Christmas Eve when a young man came in after arriving on the stage. He was slim, of moderate height, with red hair and a pale face. His clothes spoke of a New York life style. Stopping in front of Rita, he removed his hat, saying, "Miss Rita, do you remember me?"

Rita turned her gaze from the card game she was watching to rest on the young man's face. About her age, she figured. Then it hit her: this was Jim Stout, a friend from her school in New York. She had dated him several times, and liked him, but that was all. He was just one of the many friends she left back there.

"Sure I remember you, Jim. I don't forget my school friends. Come on into the office so we can talk over old times." Turning to Pete, she said, "Pete, bring a bottle and glass to the office for Jim when you get a chance."

Taking Jim by the arm, she led him into her office and motioned him to a chair, going behind the desk to sit in hers. The way Jim watched her, she figured he wanted to become more than friends, so she started talking about school chums they knew, asking how they were and what they were doing. Jim soon got caught up with old memories, and when Pete brought the bottle and glass, they were laughing about some funny instances that had happened on campus.

"Pete, this young man wants to stay in Pine Wood so he can become a leading citizen," Rita said as Pete set the bottle and glass down.

"Actually, I'm interested in starting a newspaper so Pine Wood will get more notoriety," Jim stated.

"Humph. That's all we need, more folks traveling through this here place and a lot more outlaws. You start a paper and things will get even worse." Pete ground out as he left the room.

When closing time approached, Rita took Jim out to meet Fuzzy, where she asked one of the card dealers if he would take Jim with him to the hotel and make sure he got a room. Then she left the saloon for home. What with the increased attention Bert Logan, the Wells Fargo investigator, paid her, and the arrival of Jim, who always expected a lot more than he got, she may decide to stay at the ranch all the time.

Turning out the lamp, she settled into bed. If only the Arizona Kid would come back, then she could see if she still liked him as much as she thought she did. If not, then maybe Logan would not be such a bad catch; and with that thought she fell asleep.

Eleven

anuary brought the new year in with a rush of cold weather, but no let up of the outlaws activity. It also brought changes to the country around the Arizona Strip: an increase in train, coach, and bank robberies emerged, with the Arizona Kid getting all the blame. Each time a robbery took place, the gang doing the holdup was led by a tall, slim, broad-shouldered young man with a mask covering his lower face. Mr. Logan constantly chased after the gang, and countless posses were sent out without so much as sighting one of the outlaws. Conjecture abounded that the Arizona Kid had been severely wounded and laid up for at least a year but was now back in business—only now his gang did more than just robbing. There were killings at every holdup, and cattle were being rustled from everywhere but the Strip. In fact, the outlaws stayed completely away from the Strip. This led some of the lawmen in other states to suspect the Kid may be using the Strip as his headquarters.

Both Jim Stout and Bert Logan were courting Rita, each trying to get her to commit to marrying them. When Logan went on one of his numerous trips to hunt outlaws, Jim took over. She liked both men, but she knew in her heart that neither would have her as long as the Kid was alive.

Reports kept coming in of the Kid's outlaw shenanigans, and she became more worried than ever. She feared the reputation being plastered on him would cause someone to end his life with a bullet before the real truth came out, not realizing he was innocent of the charges being levied against him. She felt she knew the Kid and he would never do what people said he was doing, and, besides Nebraska had said the Kid had retired from his outlaw ways. But she still listened closely to each account of outlaw activity brought to town, just in case one of the outlaws, drinking at the Golden Palace, might know where he disappeared to, in hopes that somehow she would be able to locate him.

Jim opened a newspaper printing office in town, so news from other states came in daily over the telegraph machine put in by the government. Rita let Jim court her mainly for this reason, since she was usually the first to learn, through him, of the robberies. She held her breath every time he reported on a coach, bank, or train holdup.

Most people she talked with couldn't believe how the Kid's luck seemed to keep him from being captured. Several of his gang were killed in shootouts, but the Kid himself always escaped with the money and left no trace. How the Kid knew where the money would be each time was a mystery to everyone.

By the time the Fourth of July rolled around again, money was almost impossible to transfer anywhere. Fuzzy couldn't get money in from his mine, and money from Pine Wood couldn't be safely transported out. The Strip became an island where no outlaws operated, but where business transactions could only be handled locally. A large amount of money collected in the Pine Wood bank and in Rita's safe, to the point where it was feared the outlaws would surely hit one of these days.

Mr. Logan turned one end of the bank into a small office and operated from there. This, coupled with Rita's gun skill and popularity, was the only thing keeping the gang away. People from other areas began to transport small amounts of cash at a time into the bank of Pine Wood, it being the only safe place. Jake was kept busy with all the bank transactions. He consulted with Rita frequently, and they tried to keep about equal amounts in both the bank and Rita's safe...then if one place was hit, there would still be money left in town. When goods were brought in, they used a bank draft with special codes on it for payment. This way the Strip stayed alive and people were able to obtain supplies.

Logan called a meeting of all the important men on the Strip to see what could be done about the outlaws and to find out if anyone knew where their hideout was. The meeting was held in one of the large gambling rooms of the Golden Palace. Rita was the only woman present, since she was the real power on the Strip. Ugly rumors started by people in other states, who didn't know Rita, said she was obviously the real leader of the outlaws. When Logan brought this up at the meeting, the men got very indignant— no way would Rita harbor outlaws.

Logan announced: "I have petitioned the governor of Arizona many times for a company of Rangers to be sent here, but he always ignores the request. It seems to me he'll have to do something before long because he's getting pressure from other states."

"Dad gum it, we gotta take the bull by the horns," Fuzzy stated. "Cain't depend on nobody else. Ya want somethin' done, do it yerself, I always say."

Rita objected. "Fuzzy, if we send men out from here, that leaves us wide open for the gang to hit. Other businesses are depending on us to guard the money they've entrusted to us."

"That's right," Logan said. "If we lose the money we have here in Pine Wood, the other businesses in the states surrounding us will never trust us again. We have an opportunity to become the banking capital of the territories; we can't afford to lose that advantage. Surely the rangers will eventually catch the Kid and his gang; we just need to put more pressure on the governor."

Jake weighed all the options and thought he might have a feasible plan. "Let's send Rita on the next stagecoach south—she can meet with the governor personally and maybe he'll listen to her."

The men in the room brightened at this suggestion.—if anyone had influence, it was Rita. Logan was the only one who objected to this—he didn't want to risk Rita's life on one of the stagecoaches. They all knew how he felt about Rita and understood his reluctance to consent to the plan.

Rita listened to their comments and made her decision. "Gentlemen, I accept the responsibility. I'll leave on the stage tomorrow and do my best to pressure the governor into sending in the Arizona Rangers." She waited as they nodded their agreement. "Remember, I always wear my gun. If the stage is stopped, the outlaws will wish they were somewhere else."

This brought a laugh, and when the quiet was restored, Fuzzy joked: "You got that right. I sure wouldn't wanna be one of those boys tryin' to stop a stage with you on it."

Again there was laughter and the consensus that none of the others would want to be in the outlaws' shoes either. The meeting broke up and Logan wanted to walk Rita home. She refused his offer pleasantly, saying she needed to go over the saloon business with Fuzzy, so wouldn't have time tonight. He was disappointed but could see her reasoning since the stage left early.

Rita left the meeting holding onto Fuzzy's arm. Pressing close to him, she murmured, "Fuzzy, come to the office with me. I have a plan I need to discuss with you."

They walked out of the room, going directly to the office. There were several people with greetings along the way, which they acknowledged, but they didn't stop to palaver.

Entering the office, Rita drew a chair close to hers and motioned for Fuzzy to sit in it. Puzzled, he obeyed. When they were both seated, she leaned towards him and spoke in a whisper.

"I'm going to transfer the contents of my safe to a bank in Phoenix when I travel in the morning."

Fuzzy reared back and started to object, but Rita stopped him with a finger to her lips.

"I'll stop here at the office in the morning with my suitcases—they'll be packed with clothes. As I come into the saloon, one of the cases will come open, spilling my clothes for everyone to see. You'll rush in from outside to help me stuff the clothes back in. We'll then bring the suitcases into my office, take out all the clothes, and load them with money. No one will know the clothes were left here in the office. If the stage is stopped, the outlaws won't bother with my luggage since my spilling it will let anyone watching know it contains only clothes."

Fuzzy listened closely to her whispered plan. "By golly, missy, you're slicker'n snot on a doorknob." Then he chuckled. "Them town folk will be flabbergasted when you git back and half their money's in Phoenix." Fuzzy got up and danced a little jig around the room. "Sure wisht I wuz twenty years younger— I'd give that Logan fellow some competition."

He stopped dancing as what Rita said sunk in. "Ya think some weasel in town tips off them outlaws about gold shipments?"

Rita, still speaking softly, said: "I don't know, Fuzzy, but we must be careful." Then she smiled. "You already give Logan competition, you old phoney. You know I'd rather be on your arm than anyone else's."

Giving her a cynical look, Fuzzy snorted, "You ain't hoodwinkin' me. Every feller on the Strip wants ya, but ya don't give any of 'em so much as a flirty eye. Ya got some feller on the string out in the boonies?"

Taking Fuzzy by the arm and ushering him towards the door,

Rita said, "You know that's a very personal question to ask a young, innocent girl like me."

"Innocent my eye. Ya got more guts than any man I ever knowed. But all the same, ya be careful. I don't wanta lose my best girl."

"I've seen some of these ladies giving you the eye," she teased.

"An they ain't gittin' no closer. It was some sweet-talkin' thing what turned me to drink, and I plumb forgot to thank 'er." He patted her hand as he went out the door with her.

Rita left the saloon to go home and pack. It would be at least a week before she returned to Pine Wood. She hoped her plan to transfer money would be a safe one; with that accomplished, they could continue to pay bills without any worry of the money being stolen. The Phoenix bank had never been robbed and with all the Rangers around, probably never would be.

She left on the stage the next morning, and no trouble occurred along the way. Her plan worked perfectly, and the stage arrived safely in Phoenix after a four-day trip. She went straight to the bank, opened an account, and deposited the money into it. It was such a relief to her to have that job over. Then she went right to the largest hotel in town, and after bathing and freshening up, she went down to the hotel dining room to eat, her gun still on her hip.

Dressed that way, she caused quite a stir in the dining room when she entered. Then someone mentioned "The Queen of the Strip," and puzzled faces turned to smiles. The hostess led her to a table in the center of the room, much to Rita's chagrin...she would have preferred one less obvious.

When Rita took a seat, a large man, dressed impeccably, approached her table and introduced himself as Charles Albright.

It took a moment for the import of his name to sink into

Rita's mind, then she quickly rose from her chair, saying, "Why Governor, it's a pleasure to meet you."

As she put out her hand, he bowed over it and gave it a kiss. Straightening up, he said. "Queen Rita, it's a pleasure to welcome you to our fair city. To what do we owe this honor?"

Pink began to steal over Rita's face as she answered, "Please call me Rita, Governor. The Queen part was none of my doing, and I'd rather not be called that. As to my reasons for being here, I came to see you."

"In that case, Rita, why don't you join my wife and me at our table. We can get better acquainted and set up a time for you to visit with me about your business."

Understanding that her purpose for coming would have to wait, Rita put her hand on the governor's proffered arm and walked with him to his table. His wife was a lovely lady with brown hair and lively brown eyes. The governor introduced her as Lila.

She welcomed Rita with a hug, saying, "We've heard so much about you. It's nice to finally meet you and see you're only human after all."

The two women laughed at that statement while they sat down at the table. The governor's wife made Rita feel at ease, and while they all talked about the Strip and the people they knew there, Rita decided the wife was the real power behind the governor. She had certainly helped him get elected to office.

The governor asked Rita, "Do you know the Jacobs that have a ranch on the Strip?"

"They were two of my best friends."

Lila's face went white as she said: "You said were. Has something terrible happened to them?"

Rita said quickly, "No, nothing terrible has happened. They sold their ranch to me and moved to Tucson about two years ago."

Relaxing, Lila said gratefully: "Thank heaven they're all right. I wish we'd known when they came through here."

Charles pointed out that about that time they were in Washington for a conference and regrettably missed them. The waitress served their food, and they talked less while eating. Lila still carried on quite a conversation though, making the meal more pleasurable. After an excellent dessert, she told her husband that she would walk a little with Rita and then meet him at the hotel afterwards.

While they walked, Rita learned that Charles liked to play a hand or two of cards at the hotel before going home, so the walk with Rita was much better for Lila than sitting in a chair gossiping with all the old ladies.

Lila told Rita about her four children, who were grown and living in different areas throughout the West. The conversation shifted to the gang operating in Utah, Nevada, and Colorado. In Lila's opinion, whoever ran the operation bossed many different gangs, with someone in a good position to tip them off when a large shipment was sent out.

Rita agreed with her, saying: "That's why I'm here, I want to enlist the governor's help in getting a company of Rangers up to the Strip to put a stop to the outlaws doing all this robbing and killing."

Lila turned to Rita in surprise. "My land, Rita, a company of Rangers would be out of the question. Charles never lets Captain White send more than one or two men on a job. Why, there aren't enough Rangers in the force to send a whole company."

What a disappointment, Rita thought. She'd hoped that through Lila, she could convince the governor to send help.

"The Wells Fargo investigator's been on the job for over a year and hasn't accomplished anything so far. One or two Rangers aren't enough to solve the problem."

"Well, I can assure you there is no way a company will be sent, but you can count on Charles to come up with a solution. That man can solve any problem if you just give him enough time." Lila was obviously proud of her husband.

While they walked back to the hotel, Lila continued chatting, but Rita's mind wasn't on what she said. Rita answered questions automatically and tried to concentrate on Lila's words, but when they reached the hotel, she was glad. Telling Lila she was really tired after such a long coach ride, she excused herself and went up to her room. Apparently her trip would be wasted. Staring at the window she considered the trouble facing her and those on the Strip. If the outlaws continued to make the transfer of money next to impossible the bank and her saloon would eventually be robbed, and more people killed.

Rita was right on time for her meeting with the governor the next morning. His secretary ushered her into his office, and he was very warm and polite with her. He passed a moment or two with talk about how his wife had been impressed with Rita, and then asked what he could do for her.

Taking a deep breath and keeping her fingers crossed, Rita said: "Governor, the situation is very bad on the Strip and in the territories surrounding it. We need help or commerce will come to a complete stop before long. Anytime money is shipped anywhere, it's stolen, and the worst is that innocent people are being killed."

The governor studied the wall behind her, then, bringing his eyes back to hers, asked: "What do you want me to do, Rita? There aren't enough Rangers in the whole outfit to cover the northern part of the state, plus southern Utah."

Sitting up straight, Rita plunged right in. "I know that, but something has to be done. It's the general feeling in Pine Wood that you don't care what happens up there. We sent several requests for help, and you didn't bother to answer. Do you think that's fair, Governor Albright?"

By the time she finished, he had realized this strong-willed woman would not be put off. He decided to change the subject.

"My intelligence sources at the bank tell me you brought over fifty thousand dollars with you on the stage from Pine Wood."

Surprised at his sudden comment, Rita said, "Yes, I did that. It was the only way I knew to get it into a bank that wouldn't be robbed. With that money, we can keep businesses on the Strip alive."

"Who knew you were carrying that money?"

Rita looked down at her hands, then met his eyes steadily. "If you think I'm part of the Kid's gang, Governor, then there is no use talking anymore."

She rose with great dignity from her chair, and with a solemn and sad face, she strode towards the door. She was almost there when the governor chuckled.

"My wife told me you were a worthy opponent, but I had to know for sure where you stood. Stay a few moments so I can tell you what's being done."

He got up and walked to the window and looked out on the street. Rita went slowly back to her chair and sat down. After a time he went to the door of the office and said to his secretary, "I don't want to be disturbed by anyone, period, until I'm through talking with Miss Jackson." Then he closed the door and came back to the chair behind his desk.

Looking gravely at Rita, he said: "What I'm going to tell you is known by me only; you will be the one other person on earth to have this information. Please don't, under any circumstance, reveal it to anyone—take it to your death with you if necessary."

Rita met his eyes, thinking she really didn't want to be privileged to that kind of information, but it was too late now.

"Governor Albright, you have my word."

"And from what I hear, your word is your bond. Now, I've had an undercover man working in Mexico for two or three years. He's been very efficient and valuable to me by getting the Mexican government to cooperate with us on several problems. I work with him through a special code and use people who don't even know they're carrying a message. Furthermore, they don't know when that message is delivered to him. This man is known only to me. No one, and I mean no one, knows who he is or that he's been working for me. He's the slickest man I've ever met. I could tell you stories by the hour of things he's accomplished that seemed to be impossible."

He stopped talking and Rita held her breath. This must be more than a man, she thought. He must be a magician. The governor finally continued.

"There's no need for you to know more on that subject; just be assured that he can be depended on to deliver the goods when asked. His job in Mexico is finished, and one week ago today I sent him a message to go directly to the Strip and make sure the gang operating in that area is apprehended. I don't know when he'll arrive—he'll still be working undercover, and no one will know what he's there for or who he is. As far as I know, he may already be there."

Rita sat there, mesmerized, staring at the governor. It was hard for her to get this fact under control. A few moments ago she had accused him of not caring about her people, and now he said help was on the way.

"I'm truly sorry I misjudged you. My father taught me never to jump to conclusions, but I guess I'm a slow learner."

The governor smiled, saying: "I used to know your father when he was a young man. I'd say he instilled in you his characteristics. Of course, you have your mother's looks, and that's to your advantage also."

Rita hated to ask this next question, but she couldn't go back to Pine Wood without knowing the answer. Taking the bit in her teeth, she asked, "What will be done to the Arizona Kid if he's one of the gang?"

Again the governor chuckled. "The old Arizona Kid who started all this trouble is no longer a problem. Someone else is pretending to be the Arizona Kid and is now rodding the gang."

Rita caught her breath, saying: "You mean the Kid is dead?"

"No, he's not dead. You see, a couple of years or more ago, I was with several Arizona Rangers in Tucson when they caught sight of the Arizona Kid. We went after him, but he's a slippery devil, got clean away. We chased him clear over the border into Mexico. He settled on a ranch there and hasn't been back across the border since."

Rita heaved a quiet sigh of relief her faith in the Kid had not been misplaced. Nebraska had been right, the Kid was no longer an outlaw.

"How do you know he's stayed in Mexico, Governor?"

"The man I told you about has been keeping an eye on the Kid. In fact, he uses that ranch as his base of operation—the Kid doesn't know he's being watched. So you see, the real Kid went straight after his last train robbery in southern Utah. He owns the ranch now and has become one of the areas leading citizens." The governor paused, reflecting. "I sometimes wish he still rodded the gang...at least when he was boss there were no people killed."

Thankful to hear the Kid was all right and had settled down, Rita wanted to ask if he was married but knew it wasn't a wise thing to do. Maybe someday she would visit Mexico and see for herself what the Kid was doing.

The two talked for a while longer, then Rita thanked the governor for his time and started to leave. Just as she was opening the door, she remembered to ask: "What will I tell the people back in Pine Wood, Governor?"

"Tell them we'll consider their request, and as soon as possible, we'll send help."

Rita smiled at him, saying: "You're a true politician with an answer like that."

He laughed and turned back into his office, pleased with the way he'd handled a sticky situation. Rita left the mansion to do a little shopping and to find some gifts for her friends in Pine Wood.

Twelve

he stage trip back to Pine Wood was worse than the one to Phoenix. The wind kicked up, and traveling across the northern Arizona desert became just plain miserable. Every time the coach stopped, all the passengers got out and headed for the watering trough, where the men stuck their heads in the water to wash the dirt and sand away. All Rita and the other lady could do was wet a rag and try to wash as much dust off as possible. She wished she were a man, so she too could dunk her head. When the coach stopped for the night, she sponged off and fell into bed, exhausted. By the time she arrived back in Pine Wood, she felt that even the look of a stage would turn her stomach.

Jake waited with several friends to meet the stage. Taking her by the arm and signaling a couple of men to get her luggage, he led her into the saloon. Everyone there shouted a welcome to her, and it felt wonderful to be back. Sam played a special song for her as the girls danced on the stage. She truly felt like a real queen coming home—it was nice to be missed.

Entering the office after her impromptu reception, Jake, Nebraska, Fuzzy, and several businessmen followed her, anxious to hear what she learned. The questions started coming hot and heavy, so she raised her hand for quiet.

Not being able to tell them the whole truth was going to be hard, but she had given her word.

"Gentlemen, I'm afraid I didn't accomplish much. The governor is aware of our problems. He promised he would consider our request and see what he could do about it."

There was absolute silence for several moments, then the grumbling started.

"A politician always gives that answer," the grocer muttered. "I knew he didn't care about this end of the territory," Nebraska said, flushing with anger.

"He's probably holding out for money. I haven't seen anyone in politics yet that couldn't be bought," Jim observed bitterly.

Many other like statements were made. It was so hard for Rita to sit and watch their discouragement.

Fuzzy sputtered: "Dad gum it, missy, I told ya we'd have ta take keer of this ourself! Now ya know what I mean. Ain't no other way ta do it."

Rita knew she had to stop this thinking, so she said: "I had a long talk with the governor's wife—she seems to be the real power behind the governor. Why don't we wait and give her a chance to work on him. You men all know what a wife can do if given enough time."

Jake realized the situation was like a bomb that needed defusing, so scratching his head and looking a little embarrassed, he muttered: "It don't take my wife long to get her way."

A chorus of relieved laughter eased the tension in all of them. Rita joined in. For now at least she had averted a crisis; they would wait, and that's all she could expect.

After a little more grousing and complaining, Jake led them out to the bar for drinks and then most of them went home. Shortly afterwards, Rita also left to go home and clean up. It would be her first bath in four days, and she felt that not only was she made of dust and dirt and sweat, but she smelled pretty whiffy too. Dawdling in the soapy water, she thanked God that tomorrow was a Sunday.

She intended to relax and spend time at the ranch before

getting back to the grind on Monday. If she got away early enough, she might avoid having to talk with anyone. Jake and Fuzzy knew where to reach her if they needed her.

The next morning a false dawn eased over the blood-colored hills as she saddled Thunder and headed for the ranch. Such a beautiful day for riding: a gentle breeze ruffled her hair, the sky blazed a vivid blue, and a meadowlark sang it's unique melody. She felt like a new woman. The Kid was safe in Mexico, and she would positively quit thinking about him anymore. Besides, being a successful rancher, he probably had a string of pretty senoritas at his beck and call.

When she topped the rise above the ranch house, she saw the place looked deserted—the ranch hands were still in town and wouldn't be back till late tonight. Even the Indians were gone somewhere. The luxury of being alone after the turmoil of the last week, a chance for peace and quiet, delighted her. She began to hum a tune as she rode into the yard.

The tune abruptly broke off when she saw a strange horse tied to the hitching post. The color of burnt sand, he blended in so well with the surroundings that she hadn't noticed him from the ridge. Regret at losing her peaceful morning warred with an innate curiosity.

Stepping down from the saddle and tying up, Rita glanced around but saw no one. Maybe the visitor was in the barn, she thought, or asleep in the bunkhouse, but she knew no self-respecting cowboy would leave his horse tied and saddled while he slept.

Giving up the visual search, she stepped onto the porch and went in the house. Someone was singing softly in the kitchen. Puzzled, she pushed through the kitchen door and saw a tall, slim cowboy heating coffee on the stove.

"Howdy, miss. Sit and have a cup of coffee with me."

His soft and pleasant voice showed no surprise at her arrival. His Stetson was pushed back so she could see all of his face and a shock of sandy brown hair. The western-style shirt he wore was fancy and clean. His Levi's were dusted off, and also his well-worn boots. He stood looking her up and down, a pleased smile on his face, while she did the same to him. They stood poised that way for several seconds before he spoke again.

"Welcome to the Lazy B-J ranch, miss. I guess my folks are in town with the crew—no one was around when I came up a while ago."

The mystery was solved for Rita: this young man had to be the Jacobs' son, and he apparently didn't know they had sold the place and moved to Tucson.

"Don't mind if I do, Mister...?" She let the sentence hang in the air.

He poured two cups full of strong black coffee before answering. "Name's Dusty Jacobs, miss. I was always playing in the dirt, and Mom would say, 'Look at that dusty boy.' Guess it kinda stuck. I've been wandering the West for a few years...suppose my folks thought I'd disappeared from the face of the earth, I've been gone so long."

He paused, gulped down some coffee, and when Rita remained silent, started again. "Fact of the matter is, I ain't never been here before. Dad bought it several years back, and this is the first I've seen it. Looks like a real nice spread to me."

On a lark, Rita decided to play along for a while. He seemed like a really nice young man. And he was more handsome than any man she presently knew. She took a sip of her coffee and sat at the table. This might be fun.

"I've been friends with Glen and Susan since I moved back to Pine Wood. In the past I came out to the ranch to visit on

Sundays and to enjoy Susan's delicious apple pies." She paused to let him take the lead again.

Dusty thought for a moment, gazing into space. "By golly, I do recollect her apple pies...the best ever." His granite eyes shifted to pierce hers, causing her heart to skip a beat. "No wonder you walked in as though you owned the place—they probably adopted you like you were their own."

Rita burst out laughing at this. "Yes, that's exactly what happened, and I guess that makes me your adopted sister."

Dusty almost choked on a swallow of coffee at this statement. "Heaven forbid, miss. It wouldn't be any fun at all with you being my sister. But I suppose it won't make any difference, 'cause I won't be around very long. You can keep our mom and dad company while I'm gone."

This young man was quick on the think, Rita decided. Flustered for just a moment, he had recovered nicely. Then she reconsidered: possibly that choke on the coffee was faked, and he wanted to tease her. Watching him closely, she couldn't make up her mind as to which it really was.

"Do I pass inspection, miss?" he asked, grinning. "I didn't have time to clean up before you got here—saw you out on the flat headed this way when I topped the rise; just had time to tie up and get the coffeepot on." Dusty enjoyed her scrutiny; it wasn't often he got to sit with such a beautiful girl. "By the way, you haven't told me your name yet. If you're my sister, I'll need a handle so I can introduce you to all my good-looking friends."

Things were moving almost too fast for Rita; it had been quite a while since she participated in this type of easy banter— the last two years or so had left little time for it. She suddenly realized that even though she spent quite a bit of time with Logan and Jim, they never wisecracked like this. She sat there wondering why.

"Cat got your tongue, Sis?" The softly spoken but humorous words brought her back to the present.

"Nope. I just realized how nice it was to have a brother to look after me. I was an only child, and Dad wanted a boy, so that's what I became. I only look like a girl. I can ride and shoot with the best of the herd," she stated flippantly. "And my name is Rita Jackson...my friends call me Rita."

Dusty started to answer when a stove-up old cowpoke came into the room.

"Miss Rita, there's an hombre out by the corral, forking a Mexican saddle, and wearing a Mexican hat, with a horse carrying a Chihuahua brand on its left hip. Wants to know if you need those horses in the corral broke."

"Does he look hungry, Cookie?" Rita asked as she got up from the table to go look through the front window, Dusty and Cookie following her.

"Yep, seems like. Traveled a right smart way too."

Watching the cowboy sit his horse by the corral, Rita saw a man of light skin color, dark hair, and dressed in Mexican garb, carrying a brace of pistols on his hips, a rifle in the saddle scabbard. Immediately she thought this must be the man Governor Albright sent. She turned to Cookie.

"Tell him if he wants something to eat, to work on the woodpile behind the cook shack while you fix the food. Nebraska will be in by mid-afternoon to talk over the ranch operation. He does the hiring—he'll talk to the stranger then."

"Yes, Ma'am, I'll tell him. He sure do look hard as nails," he mumbled as he left the house. Rita watched him talk to the stranger, hoping this was the undercover agent from Mexico. Her thoughts were interrupted by Dusty.

"It seems I made a terrible mistake, Miss Jackson. I haven't been in touch with my folks for several years, and I guess I offered you a drink of your own coffee."

Turning, Rita laughed at the expression of repentance on his face. "Brother, I bought the Lazy B-J from our folks over a year ago," she joked.

"Please don't call me brother anymore, Miss Jackson. Boy, you don't know how happy I am to know we aren't brother and sister. Life here on the Strip will be much more exciting now that's settled," he teased.

Rita gazed at him a moment before commenting: "Okay, Dusty. I won't call you brother if you don't call me Miss Jackson." She paused, considering him. "You've been away from girls for a long time, haven't you, Dusty? Well, if you ride into Pine Wood, I've several young girls who might interest you. They work at the Golden Palace."

Dusty didn't blink an eye at this. "Nope, I think I'll just wait till you ride into town and go along to protect you from all those wild men on the Strip...after that you can introduce me to the prettiest girl of the bunch."

"You got a deal, Dusty. Now I have to go to the office and check the books before my foreman gets here. Feel free to wander around and look the place over. You may want to stay and make yourself useful," she bantered.

"Oh, I already decided on that. Figured I'd ask that Nebraska hombre for a job on the ranch. Then I can come into town every weekend and spark that pretty saloon girl you're offering me."

Rita smiled and went into the ranch office, getting out the tally books and other records, in order to be ready for Nebraska. She opened the tally book, which recorded how many cows were with calf, how many steers were ready to ship, and other figures that soon began to blur. The face of Dusty Jacobs kept getting in the way. She tried to shake it off, but after reading a few more lines, it sneaked in again. Disgustedly, she slammed the book shut and opened the ledger. The balance grew steadily, and with the acquisition of the second ranch, her net worth was more than she ever dreamed possible.

Her vision blurred again, and staring at the office window, she visualized a tall, broad-shouldered, sandy-haired man standing there in an easy, lackadaisical pose. Foregoing all pretense of working, she got up and went to the window, watching the stranger and Dusty in conversation. Shortly they went around back of the cook shack and were lost to sight. What ailed her? She wondered, shaking her head. She'd seen all shapes and sizes of men before this. The only one who ever affected her this way was the Arizona Kid. But he was fading into the past, perhaps because he remained inaccessible. Before, hope that he would show up somewhere on the Strip lingered in her heart—now she knew better.

Rita walked around the room. This didn't clear her mind any, so she left the house and stepped into the saddle. A good hard run with the wind blowing in her face might do it. The horse leapt into a fast gallop, and she left the yard in a swirl of dust.

After a mile, she pulled Thunder down to a walk and cut across country to a watering hole, two miles from the ranch. Several cows and one big bull stood in the water, drool dripping from their mouths. Cattle always did this, and she wondered if it was to keep cool or just to stay there till they drank all they could hold and then move out on the range.

She never ceased to be awed at the many colors of the Arizona Strip country. She'd traveled all across the United States by train, and nothing compared with it. She rode around the water hole and up the next ridge. She owned the land for as far as she could see. The picture made her thank Fuzzy for finding the mother lode and sharing it with her. She'd helped many prospectors since coming home from school, but Fuzzy was the only one who succeeded so far. After riding aimlessly for the next two hours, Rita suddenly remembered she hadn't eaten before she left the ranch. Her stomach was beginning to complain, so she headed Thunder back to the ranch house.

She noticed Nebraska's horse in front when she rode up. Dismounting, she tied up and walked briskly into the ranch office. Sitting there talking were Dusty and Nebraska. They broke off abruptly and stood when she entered the room. Tossing her hat on the desktop, she sat down in the chair behind the desk.

"I see you two have met. Did Nebraska give you that job, Dusty?"

"He said you were the final authority on that, but there's an opening available."

"What about the visit you were planning to make to your folks when you came here?"

Dusty gazed innocently at the ceiling, saying, "Nebraska's been telling me how you transported fifty thousand dollars to the bank in Phoenix. He says you're the heroine of the Strip and they call you Queen Rita. Sure glad you ended up not being my sister. I wouldn't know how to act, being brother to a queen. Anyhow, I figure when you get another fifty thousand, I'll ride with you to Phoenix to protect you, then go on to Tucson to visit my folks."

Rita slid a stern glance in Nebraska's direction. "Don't believe anything this stranger says, Nebraska, he's been full of baloney since he arrived here. Maybe you can work some of the smarts out of him... that is, if you can get him to work at all."

Nebraska swivelled his head from one to the other, not understanding any of this. "You two know each other?" he asked.

Dusty jumped in before Rita had a chance to speak. "I

thought my folks still owned the Lazy B-J when I got here today and that Rita was a visitor come to see them. She led me on, making me think she was an adopted daughter. Cookie finally came in and set me straight."

Nebraska smiled at this. "I find it hard to get the best of this young lady. After all, she's the one put this hole in my ear."

They all laughed at that, then Rita spoke to Dusty: "So you see, Dusty, I won't need any protection when I take the next bunch of money to Phoenix. Besides, how do I know you're not an outlaw? It would be easy for you to steal money away from a poor defenseless girl like me." She couldn't resist batting her eyelashes at him and twisting her hands in a helpless gesture.

Barely controlling his laughter, Dusty responded wryly, "If Nebraska's ear is your doin', I'll be sweet as a puppy around you. You can even rub my ears if you promise not to shoot."

Then he got up and excused himself. He walked out the door, stepped into his saddle, and rode out of the yard to look the place over.

Rita opened the ranch books again. "It looks like our calf crop has been good, and there must be at least three hundred head of steers to sell. Are you planning a drive to the railhead soon?"

"That's why I thought I'd sign Mr. Jacobs on—we'll need extra men on the trail drive. He seems to be easygoing and levelheaded; that will come in handy if we run into trouble, and a big herd's gonna be tempting to outlaws." Nebraska pulled his chair closer to the desk so he could look at the books also.

Rita leaned back, considering. "Why don't we contact the other ranchers? They would be wise to throw their cattle in with ours and make the drive with us."

"I took the liberty of talking with most of them while you

were gone. I think they'll do it. It'll make quite a large herd, so we should wire the railroad to have enough cars on the siding to handle it."

"That's my responsibility, Nebraska; I'll get on it when I'm in town tomorrow. When do you plan to start the drive and approximately when will you arrive at the railhead?"

"Hmmm. Well, it'll take about three weeks to gather our cattle and bunch them with the other ranchers. At least another three weeks for the drive. Give us a little extra time in case of trouble. That would be about seven, eight weeks at the most. If we have to wait a few days letting the cattle graze at the railhead, it'd be to our advantage—they'll put some of the tallow back on they will lose on the drive."

"Then I'll plan the cars to be there eight weeks from tomorrow. We'll be taking Cookie with us, and I can help with the cooking. You think there'll be enough trail drivers for that large a herd?"

Nebraska looked thoughtful. "We'll take Spit-So-Far and two, three of his Injuns,—should be plenty of men and still leave enough here on the ranch till we get back. Do you think you should go on this drive? If we run into trouble, it could be dangerous. You'll be gone over two months—can you leave your businesses that long?"

Thinking things over, Rita decided she had good managers running her various enterprises. They were all loyal, and actually, she didn't have that much to do in any of them anymore. The romance of a cattle drive was hard to resist; the fact that Dusty would be along was an added attraction.

"I want to be on this drive, Nebraska. It'll be my first one since going off to school. The businesses are in capable hands, so there'll be no worry. I'll arrange to stop in a town along the way and wire back to make sure everything's okay."

The two of them discussed all the details and then Rita went out to the cook shack to grab a bite to eat before going back to town. Nebraska tagged along...it had been a while since he ate breakfast. Cookie saw them leave the house and head for the cook shack, so he put three large steaks on the stove. There were fried potatoes and fresh-picked asparagus from the banks of the stream behind the house. He always fed Rita good when she came to the ranch.

They all three sat down to eat and Nebraska detailed Cookie on the cattle drive. It would be his responsibility to get the chuck wagon in shape and stocked.

Rita finished her meal and left the table to go back to town. She found Thunder in the barn eating oats from a nose bag. Dusty was tossing down hay for the other horses, and the stranger with the Mexican hat was nowhere in sight. Rita had almost forgotten about him with so many other things on her mind.

As Dusty climbed down from the hayloft, she asked: "Who was the man forking a Mexican saddle earlier in the day, Dusty?"

Slapping his hat against his legs to brush off the hay stems, he answered: "Some fellow who's been down in Mexico for a time. Seemed like a nice guy; you might consider hiring him if you need more help. He went on to Pine Wood to check out the town. I think he's just drifting through and could probably use a job for a few weeks. If you can't use him, maybe one of the other ranchers can." Checking the saddle cinches and tightening them, Rita told him, "We'll be starting to gather the cattle for a trail drive tomorrow—if you see him again and he wants a job, tell him to check with Nebraska. He'll be rodding the drive."

Stepping up to remove the nose bag from Thunder, Dusty patted the horse on the neck, speaking to Rita as he worked.

"Thought I'd ride in with you, then I can talk to him in town tonight. Besides, there's no use putting off meeting that pretty saloon girl you've picked out for me."

"You better plan to come back to the ranch early, Dusty. A handsome fellow like you'll tire out fast, fighting off all the females that'll be chasing you. Why, I won't even get a chance to introduce you: as soon as you step through those batwings, the girls will scream and go crazy," Rita said, a solemn expression plastered on her face.

Scratching his head and appearing to think seriously about Rita's statement, Dusty suddenly brightened. "Shucks, I won't have anything to worry about. I'll just latch onto your arm when we go through the door, and those other girls will fall back, knowing they haven't got a chance."

Rita laughed at this and picked up the reins, swinging into the saddle. Gigging Thunder to a trot as she left the barn, she called back to him: "You better hurry then, because I won't waste time waiting for you."

Two miles down the road Dusty finally caught up to her. Mopping the sweat from his brow, he mused: "When you decide to do something, you sure don't wait for the iron to heat. What if some outlaw had been waiting in the bushes back there and I wasn't around to protect you? My folks would never forgive me for letting that happen."

"You know, Dusty, it's absolutely amazing how I've survived this long without your protection. Maybe I've just been lucky," she observed with mock humbleness.

Dusty sighed in frustration. "One of these days I'm going to say something that you can't come back at so fast. Course, it may take me an awful long time to think of it, so I guess I'll just have to stay close to you till it comes to me, no matter how long it takes. May even be white haired by that time."

Looking demurely at him with her eyelashes fluttering, Rita asked, "Why, Dusty, is that a proposal?"

Mumbling something unintelligible, he kicked his horse into a run and left her in the dust. Looking back, he saw Thunder gaining on him and tried to outrun Rita. She easily overtook him and waved with a laugh as she went by, calling, "See you in town, slowpoke."

Thirteen

The next three weeks were spent getting things ready for the drive. Jake would be responsible for making sure all Rita's businesses ran well while she was gone. He took over the bank and it did very well under his capable hands. He bantered with the locals, but when bank policies needed to be enforced, he didn't falter. His marriage to Marie worked better than anyone expected— she not only settled him down but helped keep the books as well.

After Dusty arrived in town that first Sunday night, Rita saw him only twice. The next morning he couldn't be found. She thought he went back to start work at the ranch, but when she saw Nebraska and asked how Dusty was doing, he said he hadn't seen him. This worried Rita, then she decided he may have gone to visit his folks. To her surprise, he showed up at the ranch the next Sunday when she went out there to spend the day.

Noncommittal as to his whereabouts, he said only that there were some loose ends to tie up before the cattle drive. He spent most of Sunday afternoon riding with her and seemed to have a wonderful time. She certainly did anyway. Then after they got into town that night, he disappeared. She didn't see him again until two days before the cattle drive was to start, when he came into the saloon looking dirty, tired, and worn out. Clearly, he'd traveled a lot of miles since she saw him last.

Concerned, she invited him to dinner at her house, but he declined, saying he needed a bath and a good rest. Thinking perhaps this was too blunt, he apologized, explaining that he'd sure like to but wouldn't be a good dinner guest, as tired as he was. He slept around the clock at the hotel and left late the next day; she didn't even get to say goodbye before he was gone. Needless to say, she was extremely upset over his actions.

The day the drive was to start, Rita arrived at the gathering place just as dawn broke. Cattle were strung out as far as the eye could see. Dust drifted on the light wind, choking the air into a hazy web. Steers bellowed and tossed their horns, hooves churned the dry dirt. A trail ride was no picnic. Days would seem to drag by, the riders caked with dust, sweat stained, thirsty, and saddle sore. Nights, almost too tired to eat, they would drop their bone-weary bodies onto bedrolls to get what sleep they could, only to be wakened much too early and do it all over again, day after dreary day.

Four other ranchers had gathered a herd and mixed it in with the Lazy B-J bunch, making almost three thousand head. Each owner furnished supplies and a crew for his herd. Spit-So-Far and his Indians were in charge of the remuda and had started early in order to be at the spot where the herd would noon and the riders would change horses. Nebraska gave each man a position to ride, telling them they would rotate every couple of hours—this would give them each a chance to eat the dust of the moving herd.

Rita observed the men as they ate breakfast. No greenhorns in this bunch. Only leathered cowpokes who knew what to do, what lay ahead, accepting the hard work as a way of life. Watching each man catch and saddle from the remuda, she respected the way the men brought order out of so much chaos. Each cowboy roped his horse, threw the saddle on, stepped into the stirrup, and was gone to the herd in a short time. Not seeing Dusty anywhere, she rode to where Nebraska sat at the point of the herd, and not wanting to appear too obvious in her quest, she asked if all the men had shown up.

Nebraska gave her a searching look. "All but Dusty. He told me he'd catch up to the herd after we bed down for the night."

Rita swung her horse to ride alongside Nebraska as the herd rippled to its feet. Bellowing and jostling, they began to move out at the urging of the cowboys. No time to talk now—the herd needed to be lined out and those steers that wanted to quit the bunch had to be driven back. Everyone worked hard as the morning passed. They would only cover about eight miles today, since they let the cattle graze as they moved them slowly along. If you drove cattle too fast and they didn't get a chance to graze along the way, they would be skin and bones in the first week. Some range bosses made this mistake—they got in a hurry and when the railhead was reached, the cattle brought a poor price because of the shape they were in. Nebraska and the seasoned cowboys would never be guilty of that mistake.

At lunchtime the cowboys took shifts, going to the chuck wagon that had been pulled ahead of the herd. Rita helped Cookie prepare chuck for all the men. While they were working, she wondered aloud where Dusty was. Cookie gave her the same answer as Nebraska. It had seemed to her everyone knew Dusty's plans except her, and worry began to set in. What could be more important than this drive? She didn't like Nebraska being so secretive about Dusty not showing up for the start, and where had he been these last three weeks?

The drive had settled down to a nice leisurely pace by the time twilight arrived. The cowboys began to circle the cattle and bunch them into a compact group. While they continued to circle and sing softly to the cattle, a gentle easiness spread over the herd. The lead steer lay down, and as if on signal, the others bedded down and began to chew their cud. Four cowboys were left to nighthawk the herd, while the others went to eat, then play a few hands of cards before turning in for the night. The lonesome wail of a harmonica cut through the evening chill, bringing diverse memories to the cowhands. They would be up before dawn tomorrow, catch and saddle, and start the herd moving as the sun came over the eastern horizon.

Rita watched patiently for Dusty to show up. When the last cowboy turned in, she cornered Nebraska, leading him a short way out from the camp. Sitting on a rock, she spoke her mind.

"Nebraska, is Dusty in trouble?" Before he could answer, she spoke again. "If it's something you're not supposed to tell me, okay. But Dusty hired on as a ranch hand, and I haven't seen him doing much ranch work. This is my cattle drive. If he isn't going to help, why keep him on the payroll?"

Nebraska studied his boots for a few moments. "I thought you wanted Dusty on the payroll. That's why I haven't said anything to you. When he hired on, I thought he'd be a lot of help, but he's only worked two days in three weeks. He always has an excuse to go somewhere, then doesn't come back for days on end. When he does come back, you can tell he's covered a lot of ground: he's tired and sleeps long hours before he gets up and goes again. I've tried to talk to him, but it doesn't do any good."

Rita sat, mulling over this problem. She had to admit she was taken by Dusty, and apparently Nebraska surmised as much, so hadn't fired him. Her mind was so wrapped up with this that she spoke before she knew what she was saying.

"He's the first man I've looked at twice since the Arizona Kid helped me the day of the train wreck."

Nebraska's eyes pinched down as he listened to her. "I figured that, and frankly I thought you were making a good choice. Now I'm not so sure. Dusty's been wild in his time, it shows by the way he handles himself. And he's definitely got guts: I think he'd walk into a pack of wolves if there was a good reason for him to do it. I'da staked my life on him, but I just don't know anymore." He sighed as though he were truly disappointed.

As they continued to sit in silence, Rita became curious about the Mexican. "The man who showed up on the ranch the same time Dusty did, I haven't seen him around since. Did he ride out?"

"He worked on the other ranch about a week, then disappeared, didn't even collect his pay. I haven't seen him since." He stopped speaking as something crossed his mind. "Do you think his disappearance has something to do with Dusty?"

"Why do you say that, Nebraska?"

Suddenly she was afraid: if the man from Mexico worked for Governor Albright, and the Kid's gang got wind of it, something terrible might happen to him. Surely Dusty wouldn't have anything to do with that—even the thought turned her stomach. She chewed on this point for a while, but her heart would not let her give that possibility even a slim chance. Dusty was not a murderer, she was sure of it, no matter how mysterious he acted.

Nebraska finally came to a conclusion and answered her question. "Well, the two of them were talking out behind the cook shack when I rode in that Sunday. They seemed to be in deep conversation. Not knowing who they were, I just went into the office, and a short time later Dusty came in." Here Nebraska paused for a moment, as if remembering something, then started again. "He struck up a conversation, then you came back and we got right to ranch business. I hadn't thought any more about it till now."

Deciding there were no answers to their questions, they called it a night and went back to camp and rolled into bed. Rita spent a restless night; her dreams were all jumbled up, with Dusty saving her life one time and an outlaw the next. She gave up on getting any rest and was sitting up in her bedroll about an hour before dawn when she heard a horse come into camp. Spit-So-Far came out of the night and took the horse's reins, leading it out to the remuda.

The rider stopped at the glowing embers of the fire and poured a cup of coffee. Rita recognized him when he stepped from the saddle. Making up her mind, she got up to go talk to him before he disappeared again.

Stepping to the other side of the smoldering ashes, she tried to keep her voice low and nonchalant. "You always show up at the most unexpected times, Dusty."

He looked at her with tired eyes as he apologized. "I'm sorry, Rita. Guess I do have some bad habits. I'll try to be more responsible from here on."

Rita's heart melted at the penitent look on his face. She was so glad just to hear his voice that the sharp retort she had prepared left her, and reaching across the dying fire to lay a warm hand on his arm she said instead: "You're so tired you could drop. Crawl under the bed wagon and sleep till Cookie breaks camp, then catch up to the herd so I can talk to you."

He mumbled his thanks. Heading right to the bed wagon, throwing a blanket under it, and lying down, he was instantly asleep. Rita watched him for a short time, then went back to her bedroll to wait for Cookie's call to rise and shout. She would hear Dusty's side when he caught up with the herd.

Only he didn't catch up with the herd. When she saw Cookie drive the chuck wagon around the west side of the cattle, without seeing Dusty, she road over to talk with Cookie. She found out that Dusty had slept soundly till just before Cookie was ready to leave, then there was the cry of a meadowlark from some junipers behind the camp. Dusty immediately woke up and walked quickly into the trees. Cookie mentioned to Rita that he'd never heard a meadowlark at that time of morning before. When Dusty came back, he hurriedly ate some bread and meat, stepped into the saddle left for him by Spit-So-Far, and lit out at a fast lope.

Rita was stunned. Someone had to have been calling Dusty, with a message so important that he left without delay. She rode alongside the chuck wagon wondering about this, and just as she lifted her horse to a trot, she looked west of the herd and saw a dust cloud a couple of miles away, headed toward them. She stopped and waited. You could just bet it wouldn't be good news. Shortly, Nebraska pulled up beside her.

"Can you make out who they are, Rita?" he asked.

Pulling her field glasses from their case, she focused on the riders.

"They're being led by Logan—I recognize the sorrel horse he rides. Don't seem to know any of the others." She passed the glasses to Nebraska.

Adjusting them, he watched the men approach. "I think the sheriff of Orderville is with the group. Must be trouble; looks like a posse to me. Wonder why Logan is with them?"

The two sat their horses waiting for the posse to come up. Recognizing them, Logan waved his hat and put his horse into a run with the others following. Sliding to a stop in front of them with the bit biting into the horse's mouth, he stated: "Hi, Rita. Sorry to interrupt your drive, but the coach from railhead to Pine Wood got robbed last night, driver and guard both killed. The bandits rode away with twenty thousand dollars destined for your bank."

Rita's heart sank; she felt old and defeated. Her mind was as active as a bowl of mush. All she could do was stare back at Logan.

Nebraska cut in. "Do you know who the robbers were?"

"Looks like the work of the Arizona Kid again. Not a sign of which way they went after the holdup. We just headed this way thinking they might be going to Hole-in-the-Rock, and we could pick up their trail."

"How did you get involved so quickly, Logan? I thought you were off on a trip," Rita asked.

Logan smiled at her. "I was just coming back from scouting north of the Utah line when I ran into the posse; when I heard what happened, I joined up. It was a Wells Fargo shipment they got. You haven't seen any riders headed this way, have you?"

Nebraska answered before Rita could speak. "The only riders we've seen are those working for us. All our riders were in camp this morning."

The sheriff sighed. "I guess it isn't much use continuing on in this direction." He took off his hat and slapped his leg, dust going everywhere. "That damn Arizona Kid just disappears into thin air! I've chased after him so many times I can't count 'em all, and never caught nothin' but a sore butt."

Logan changed the subject. "I see you started your drive while I was gone. Everything going all right?" Rita nodded her head, so he went on. "Well, we'll turn back. I need to get back to Pine Wood—been gone too long now. See you when you return."

He doffed his hat to Rita, and the posse turned to head back. Nebraska and Rita sat their saddles till Logan and the others were out of sight.

Nebraska said in a disgusted voice, "I saw Dusty asleep in camp this morning. What time did he get in last night?"

Rita caught her breath. "Do you really think he was in on the robbery?" And before he could answer, she added, "Thanks for what you told Logan about all our hands being in camp this morning."

Nebraska paused, then said, "I don't know what to think, Rita. That Dusty sure tries a man's patience. Where in hell did he say he'd been, when you talked to him earlier?"

"So you saw him come into camp. The problem is he wouldn't say where he'd been, just said he was sorry he had missed the start of the drive and that he would catch up to the herd this morning. He never did catch up—Cookie said someone signaled from the trees as he was breaking camp, and Dusty went out to meet them. Came back, jumped on his horse, and took off. It looks bad, doesn't it?"

"I'm afraid so, but let's keep this under our hat for the time being. When he shows up again, we'll question him about it." Nebraska turned his horse back towards the herd and Rita followed.

Fourteen

usty was not seen again for a full week. The herd moved north and was well broke to trail by now. Things were going so smoothly that Rita decided to ride on ahead to the night camp and help Cookie get set up for dinner. All the cowboys, except the first night guard, came in after bedding down the herd and started to eat. Rita expected to see Nebraska since he had the early morning shift with her and two others. When he didn't show after a time, she asked Slim where he was.

"Dusty showed up about a mile back, talked a bit with Nebraska, then the two of 'em galloped off to the east. Nebraska told Andy he'd see us in camp later." Slim got up to put his dishes in the washtub on the tailgate of the chuck wagon.

Rita walked away from camp, wondering what was up. She heard a horse coming fast as she turned to go back. Nebraska rode in on a lathered horse, slid to a dusty stop, then yelled, "Hit your saddles, men, we're about to get jumped by rustlers!"

The men dropped their dishes and raced out to the remuda to catch and saddle. There was no time to ask questions. Nebraska pulled up beside Rita and offered her a stirrup so she could ride out with him to catch her a horse and him a fresh one.

As they rode, he said: "Dusty came back. Before I had time to question him, he said a band of outlaws had made plans to stampede the herd tonight and drive off a bunch of cattle in the process. I rode with him a ways to see the area where they'll be coming from. If we bunch the cattle tight and set an ambush about two miles from the herd, we can stop them."

"Where's Dusty now, and how did he find out about the stampede?"

"He's holed up at the ambush point in case they arrive before our men get there. He'll hold them off as long as he can."

They reached the remuda and no further talk was possible as they set to the task of roping and saddling horses. It took only minutes for the cowboys to get ready. Nebraska split the men and detailed six to follow him and the others to bunch the herd and hold them.

He sprang into his saddle and was gone before Rita could ask again how Dusty knew of the rustlers' plan. She led the men assigned to watch the herd to the bed grounds. Riding carefully and singing to the cattle, they began to push those out on the flanks towards the middle of the herd. Guns began to sound from the direction in which Nebraska had ridden, and Rita and the men doubled their vigilance over the herd.

Nebraska with his six men were about two hundred yards from the place where he left Dusty when the first shot cracked out of the darkness. He and his men pulled down to a walk in order to come into the battle as quietly as possible. A deafening volley of gunfire erupted from beyond Dusty's position. Quickly dismounting and tying the horses in a grove of trees, the men proceeded on foot.

Dusty was firing steadily when Nebraska and his men crept up behind him. A bullet hole showed through the crown of his hat and one through his left shirt sleeve. Just as Nebraska spread his men out, the outlaws, thinking they were facing only one gun, charged Dusty's position. A wall of spitting flame and leaden messengers of death met them when the defenders opened up with saddle carbines. Twelve outlaws started the rush, but only four were left to turn tail and run as bullets sang around them. Seeing the rustlers hightail it, Dusty yelled, "To your horses—we'll show those boys they can't monkey with us."

All hands rushed to mount and give chase. They followed the sound of the outlaws' horses running before them. Nebraska and Dusty were riding side by side when they caught sight of their quarry ahead, in the moonlight. Bringing their guns up, they fired at the same time; one outlaw dropped from his saddle, rolling over and over in the dirt as the two men raced by.

The three remaining outlaws threw lead back at the pursuing cowboys. A sharp cry was heard above the pounding of hooves, and one cowboy slumped in his saddle. When his horse slowed, Nebraska motioned for one man to drop back with the wounded puncher.

Blazing bullets ripped hot furrows through the air as the outraged cowboys gained on the hated rustlers and charged up over a rise. Topping the hill, another unlucky outlaw slumped in his saddle and then, with the next two strides of his horse, slid down its left side, falling into a patch of beavertail. When the pursuers flew by they could tell from the way the outlaw lay with his head twisted back that his rustling days were over.

Charging down the other side of the rise, Dusty and Nebraska saw the two remaining outlaws quirting their horses viciously in order to escape the vengeful pursuers. Dusty slid his horse to a stop and calmly raised his rifle, sighted, and pulled the trigger. One of the outlaws ahead straightened in his saddle, then toppled backwards to fall behind his frightened horse. A fusillade of gunfire erupted from Nebraska and his men as they raced beyond Dusty. Shortly after, the remaining outlaw slipped from saddle leather, catching one foot in a stirrup. The frenzied horse tried wildly to get away from this dangling object at its side. It took several hundred yards to overtake the horse, grab its reins, and bring the shaking animal to a stop. One cowboy stepped from his saddle to lift the dead man's boot from its imprisonment.

The men sat their horses, staring down at the last outlaw

crumpled on the ground. Dusty shoved his thirty-thirty into its saddle boot and, with hands folded on the saddle horn, rode up. "You men arrived just in time—another minute and I'd be the one lying there eatin' dirt. You sure gave those attackers a surprise when you opened up beside me—they probably thought the Devil hisself was after 'em."

"Your ambush worked perfectly, Dusty. I don't think anyone else will rustle Lazy B-J stock once this night's work gets spread around," Nebraska crowed.

He detailed a couple of men to put the dead man on his horse and bring him back to camp. Other punchers dropped off to do the same thing as more outlaw's bodies came in sight. When they reached the area of the ambush, it took awhile to gather all the bodies, tie them to saddles, and line out for camp.

When they approached the campfire, the horses, were relieved of their gruesome burdens, which they hid from view in a clump of trees. Nebraska rode out to the herd to give the news to Rita and the others, while Dusty and the rest of the men turned all the horses into the remuda. Going to the fire, they squatted down to drink coffee and reflect on the night's excitement. The wounded cowboy was resting on a bedroll by the fire, bandages shone white around his left shoulder. Cookie had done a good job of caring for the wound, and Dusty complemented him on being as good as a doctor.

Rita had listened to the distant bursts of gunfire with apprehension, and then when the sound began to recede further into the distance, she knew a running battle had ensued, with the outlaws taking flight. Soon the shots could no longer be heard, and the cattle bedded back down and all had been quiet except for the soft singing of the cowboys. It seemed an eternity passed before she saw Nebraska riding towards them. Gigging her horse, she rode out to meet him. She was afraid to ask him about the fight, and Nebraska, knowing why she hesitated, quickly told her the outcome. "Josh is wounded, but no other casualties on our side—Dusty had 'em stopped by the time we got there. When we opened up on 'em, they turned tail and ran. We gave chase and got 'em all. They're all dead."

Rita sagged in her saddle after hearing the news, tension draining from her face. "Thanks to Dusty, our cattle are safe. We owe him a lot. It could just as easily have been the other way around if he'd not warned us."

"You got that right. We'd've been up crap crik without his help!" Nebraska exclaimed. Then, with a contemplative look, he sighed. "For the life of me, I don't know where to place that hombre. One minute I think he's in with the outlaws, the next he saves our bacon. There's just no figuring what's next."

"Well, let's get the men back to camp. It'll be a short night for them now. We can sleep on it, and maybe in time we'll have an answer," Rita said wearily as she gigged her horse towards the remuda.

The night passed uneventfully. The next morning Nebraska detailed one man to ride ahead to the next town, leading the outlaw horses, each carrying a body. He would turn them over to the Utah authorities and return to the drive.

The wind gusted hard, this morning, making it necessary for the cowhands to wear bandanas over their nose and lower face to keep out the dust.

With breakfast over, the men started the cattle moving; it was a bigger job than usual because the animals all wanted to turn tail into the wind. Working doggedly, the men finally got the herd lined out in the right direction. Rita was ridding on the right flank, heading back towards the drag, when she passed Dusty chasing a bunch-quitter back to the herd. Slowing Thunder to a walk, intending to thank Dusty, the words died in her throat. Her eyes widened and she froze, staring at him with the bandana over his face. She'd seen this exact picture before, the day the Arizona Kid helped her!

Dusty, watching the bunch-quitting steer, didn't notice the shocked look in Rita's eyes. With hard-won composure, she recovered quickly as he swung to face her.

"I sure hope this wind dies down before too long I'm not sure I can swallow any more dust without turning a sandy color." She managed to give a short laugh, clenching her hands tightly on the saddle horn.

"Any color would look good on you, Rita, so don't worry. These dust storms usually only last a couple of hours this time of year anyway."

"I hope you're right," Rita answered as she started her horse moving in the direction of the drag. Her mind was in turmoil: Dusty was the Arizona Kid! No mistaking that fact; those eyes above a bandana had been burned in her memory for too long not to know the startling truth. How could the Kid be here when the governor had assured her he was in Mexico on his own ranch? No wonder she had fallen so fast for Dusty when she first met him. Now she remembered that first meeting on the ranch—there'd been something vaguely familiar about him. She chalked it up to him resembling his father and thought no more about it. Her senses tried to alert her all along but she had ignored them. How could she have been so blind, and what should she do now?

Turning her horse to follow the herd, she consider her predicament. Having Dusty on her payroll would look mighty funny to others if they found out he was the Arizona Kid. Those diehards who believed the leader of the outlaws was located in Pine Wood would really have a field day. Rita knew her power on the Strip would be greatly limited if others discovered what she now knew. What if Logan found out? There would be a shootout and either Logan or Dusty would die. That must be prevented at all costs. Late in the morning, she turned back to camp. Seeking out Cookie as he loaded everything up to move to the noon stopping place, she fixed a sandwich and rode on the chuck wagon with him, hoping Nebraska would ride back to talk to her and provide an answer to her dilemma. She sat quietly, saying nothing till Cookie stopped to fix lunch.

"Everything all right, boss?" Cookie inquired as he got down. He worried over her silence.

"Just thinking about last night, Cookie," she sighed.

When the cowboys started coming in to eat, Rita and Cookie had everything ready. The wind had died down like Dusty predicted, and his bandana was back down around his neck when he rode up. The men's banter centered around the excitement of last night, and they proclaimed Dusty a hero. He took their ribbing good-naturedly, then picked up his plate of food and went over to sit on a rock by the chuck wagon, where Rita had to pass every time she needed something. He always grinned and made some comment when she passed.

"Damn!" she thought as she continued to help Cookie feed the cowboys. Why did life have to be so complicated? Why couldn't she and Dusty just get married like Jake and Marie, have kids, raise them on the ranch, and live happily ever after?

With the cowboys fed and Cookie loaded up and headed for the night's bedding ground, Rita caught Thunder from the remuda and rode out to talk with Nebraska. He was riding point with Dusty when she came up. How could she talk now with Dusty around?

"I see you two convinced the others it was their turn to ride the drag," she said, swinging Thunder alongside them.

"Nope, we figured you'd be along soon, Rita, and we didn't want you to eat any more dirt and turn brown," Dusty joked.

Nebraska looked from one to the other, then asked, "This a private joke between the two of you?"

"Dusty thinks I would look good in any color. He hasn't had much time to get to know any girls, so he doesn't realize that we want to look just right all the time so you men will fall all over us."

"You see how it is, Nebraska? I can't ever get the last word in with this young lady," Dusty complained, trying to look hurt.

The three continued riding, with Dusty and Nebraska talking about the drive and the cattle market. Rita listened, but her mind remained on how to handle the problem of Dusty. Finally she decided to spit it out and get it over with.

"Nebraska, why didn't you tell me Dusty was the Arizona Kid?" she asked point-blank. Her question met with complete silence as the two men looked at her in confusion, trying to form an answer.

Dusty spoke before Nebraska could recover from his surprise. "That's my fault, Rita. When he arrived at the ranch the first day I met you there, I asked him to keep it under his hat. We were reliving old times when you came back from your ride."

Rita rode a ways before speaking. "So you hired on in order to have a base of operation after rejoining your old gang? Governor Albright assured me you were in Mexico running your own cattle ranch. Oh why, for heaven's sake, did you leave that ranch, Dusty?" she asked with exasperation.

Dusty searched for an answer to give her, at last saying: "I guess the old habits just took over. I wanted to see my folks, since it had been several years. When I got back and they were gone, I looked up the old bunch, and I guess I just fell back in with them."

Nebraska spoke up in defense of Dusty. "Remember, Rita, if it hadn't been for Dusty's warning, you wouldn't have a herd now, and some of us would be dead."

"I know that, but why did he have to take up with the old

gang? He could have worked on the ranch, and no one would have known who he was but you. Governor Albright assured me he was going straight."

Dusty again entered the conversation. "You and the governor must be pretty close friends, Rita. Why would he be talking to you about my goings-on, or did you know I was the Arizona Kid when you talked to him?"

"I didn't know who you really were till I saw your bandana over your face this morning. When I saw you as the Arizona Kid before, you had a bandana covering your lower face." A shadow of distress crossed her face, and she stopped a moment, wondering why there couldn't be an easy answer to all of this. "Since your gang was causing so much trouble everywhere, I asked the governor about you when I went to Phoenix. He told me where you were. Now I don't know what to do. I'm in your debt twice now. I just wish Nebraska had told me when you hired on."

"I really did think he'd gone straight when he told me where he'd been and that he owned a large ranch in Mexico," Nebraska said to defend his actions. "I should have told you, but at that time I thought it wasn't necessary. If the Kid was straight, it would just cause needless trouble."

The three rode in dejected silence for a while, then, without even a wave goodbye, Rita reined her horse around, going back to the drag. Dusty and Nebraska rode on, subdued, for some time, each with his own thoughts on what to do next. Finally Dusty spoke, putting out his hand.

"Well, old friend, I guess this is it—I'm moving out. Let Rita know I'd never do anything to hurt her, and watch her close. She's a wonderful young lady, and I sure do wish things could've been different. Don't let anything happen to her."

Nebraska could see the sadness in Dusty's face. "I guess you and her have a feeling for each other that's hard to overlook, despite the problems. I'll do the best I can for Rita, but you take care of yourself, Kid. It would break her heart worse if something happened to you," he said seriously, shaking Dusty's hand.

Gigging his horse, Dusty rode over the next hill and vanished from sight. Nebraska felt lower than a snake's belly: here were the two people he admired most, who seemed to care about each other, and they lived two different lives. He knew Dusty only became an outlaw because of the excitement of the chase. When he rodded the gang there was never any killing, and he kept a tight rein on his men. If he had stayed, there would never have been the trouble there was now. Rita was left without a choice—her position in Pine Wood would make it impossible to associate with an outlaw. People used to respect the Arizona Kid, but not anymore.

As Rita approached the herd, she made up her mind. She would quit the drive, ride back to Pine Wood and telegraph the governor about her discovery. How could she have fallen so hard for Dusty when he had now joined his old gang? She felt her faith in him was shattered beyond repair.

Maybe Jake would be able to advise her—he'd always been the first to help when anything went wrong. Sighing, she stopped at the chuck wagon to tell Cookie to let Nebraska know she would see them all back at the ranch when the drive was over. Packing some jerky in her saddlebags and filling her canteen, she mounted Thunder and headed for Pine Wood. Jake would be surprised to see her.

Fifteen

Jake was playing cards in the saloon with Fuzzy two days later when a man wearing a Mexican hat came into the barroom. The man bellied up to the bar and asked for whisky. Pete complied, and when the man kept the bottle and threw down a five-dollar gold piece, Pete gave him change and went back to serve other customers. The heavily built man wore two crossed gunbelts on his hips. He had a two-day-old beard and his clothes told of a long dusty ride. Taking the bottle, he went to an empty table and began to drink steadily.

Dealing the next hand, Jake mentioned to Fuzzy, "That hombre looks mighty tough. Wonder where he's been?"

Fuzzy, glancing at the man, held his cards without looking at them. "Probably one a the Kid's gang. Figgers he kin get drunk here without no trouble 'cause no one knows him. I bet he was in on that last shindig over in Utah."

Jake contemplated his cards and threw a dollar in the pot. "Well, it's for sure Logan and that posse didn't have any luck retrieving the money. If a person could find where the gang caches all the money they've stolen, he'd be a rich man."

"Mebbe, mebbe not. Them boys probably spent ever last cent of it. I bet they don't have a pot to pee in by now."

The two laughed at this thought, then Jake became serious again. "If Logan doesn't do something, or those Rangers the governor promised Rita don't show up, that gang will get bold enough to take on Pine Wood again."

"Don't git yer knickers in a sweat. Sumbody here in town bosses that gang or we'da been hit a long time ago," Fuzzy opined.

"You really think that's true, Fuzzy?" Jake asked, doubt plain in his voice.

"Ya bet yer bottom dollar that's keerect," Fuzzy stated positively.

Shaking his head, Jake threw down his hand, saying he was through for the night. Getting up from the table and picking up what little money he had left, he started out of the saloon. Glancing back at the man in the Mexican sombrero, Jake saw him put down his glass and head for the batwings. Jake pushed on through and went towards his house—it would be nice to spend the rest of the evening with Marie.

Opening his front gate, he glanced back again and saw the man with the Mexican hat moving toward him. Checking his gun that rested in a shoulder holster, he turned and waited for the man to reach him.

The man stopped a couple of feet away from Jake, and drew a match from his pocket, lighting the cigarette hanging from his lips. In the flare of the match Jake could see a hard leathery face, darkened by many days in the sun. The man's cruel black eyes pierced the gloom, and a shudder went through Jake's body. He'd not like to tangle with this man, and he'd been in many a barroom brawl and always came out on top. This one, however, emanated power just by his steady stare and stance.

Words dripped furtively from the man's mouth, reaching only Jake's ears.

"This Wells Fargo man called Logan, where can I find him?"

Jake was startled by the question, and more so by the secretiveness of it. "Why should I tell you? I don't know you from the Arizona Kid."

At the mention of the Kid, the man's eyes pinched down, and Jake almost touched his gun butt. Thinking better of it, he waited for the man to leave or answer his question. The man took the cigarette from his mouth and blew smoke into the air.

"You run the bank. I'll be around tomorrow to make a deposit. I want to look the place over before trusting my money to you and Wells Fargo." With that, he turned on his heel and left a puzzled Jake behind.

When Jake approached the bank the next morning, he could see the man with the Mexican hat waiting at the front door. Nodding good morning to him, Jake opened the bank and went to his desk. Sitting down, he watched Mexican hat survey the bank, checking the door between it and the Wells Fargo office. He came back to Jake and threw ten twenty- dollar gold pieces on his desk. Jake took the money, drew out the necessary paperwork, and prepared to write.

"What name should I put on the account?"

The man's stony eyes bored into Jake. "Bill Smith," he said in a cold voice.

Jake wrote the name. "What address do you want on the account?"

"Golden Palace Saloon will do," Smith sneered.

Writing the information down, Jake considered the strange request. Smith looked like he could chew nails and spit them out like bullets. An involuntary chill went through Jake...was this one of the Kid's gang? Well, all he could do was take the money and open the account. Finishing the paperwork, he handed it to Smith to sign. Smith took the pen and boldly signed his name, in a sweeping scrawl. Tossing the pen onto the desk, he turned and marched out, almost bumping into Rita when she came through the front door.

Stepping aside, she let Smith pass, then came on into the bank, saying to Jake, "That's the man who was at the ranch the day Dusty came to see his folks. I haven't seen him around since then."

Jake got up from his chair, surprised. "You're back from the cattle drive already? You either moved faster than expected or there's trouble, which is it?"

Making sure the bank was empty, Rita told Jake about Dusty being the Arizona Kid and how he saved the herd, then of her decision to telegraph the governor. Jake listened patiently while she talked—he could tell there was more to it than what Rita said. As he watched her closely, he realized she was in love with Dusty, alias the Arizona Kid. Since the day of the train wreck the Kid had meant a lot to her—it was evident every time news arrived of the Kid's exploits. Now she was faced with the most difficult decision of her life, but knowing her, she would do the right thing, no matter what the personal cost.

"What does Nebraska say, Rita?" Jake asked when she finished talking.

"Nebraska is as discouraged as I am. He's known all along about Dusty but thought the Kid was on the level this time. He sure thinks an awful lot of him, since he used to ride with the gang."

Jake watched her face, his eyes thoughtful. Shaking his head, he stated: "You really don't have any choice. The governor needs to know what you've discovered. Maybe then he'll send the Rangers in."

Rita looked ill. "Jake I don't know what to do. I've fallen hard for Dusty, and even knowing he's the Arizona Kid I can't seem to lose faith in him. There is another problem, the governor's a friend of Dusty's folks, and he thinks the Kid's still in Mexico on his ranch."

"When you send the telegram, just say you know the identity of the Arizona Kid and are awaiting further instructions. That way no one'll know who you're talking about till the governor wires you back for more information. It may be he already has someone on the case here on the Strip," Jake mentioned as he pondered the problem.

Thinking of the man she had passed in the doorway, Rita knew such a person was here, but how could she approach him to let him know it when she had given her word to tell no one? What a pickled mess! Here she was in the middle of everything with no way to extract herself.

"Thanks, Jake, I knew you'd come up with an answer. I'll go down now and have Jim send the telegram; hopefully Albright will be in Phoenix and we'll receive a quick reply."

She hurried out of the bank, going directly to the newspaper office, where Jim managed the telegraph. Opening the door and stepping inside, she saw Jim bending over his printing press. Glancing toward the doorway, he saw her and his face lit up as he came towards her.

"Rita, what a pleasant surprise. You're back sooner than I expected. Did you sell the cattle for a good price?"

Smiling faintly at his adoring look, Rita answered, "I left the drive early. The Arizona Kid's gang tried to raid our herd, but Dusty saved the day by alerting us to the danger. All the outlaws were eliminated."

"I got the news over the wire yesterday, but it didn't mention anything about Dusty," Jim said with a faint touch of sarcasm.

Rita knew Jim was jealous of any man who helped her and no doubt wished Dusty had never come to town.

"He stumbled onto the plan somehow, but there was no time for me to inquire before the gang hit. Dusty, Nebraska, and six of our cowboys ambushed the gang; after that I rode here to telegraph the governor."

This was going to be a touchy affair—Jim would really want to know more when he found out the contents of her telegram. Jim pulled out a paper and prepared to write the message. Patiently, enjoying just looking at her, he waited for her to dictate.

"To Governor Albright, Phoenix, Ariz. Dusty Jacobs discovered the identity of the Arizona Kid. Please advise as to your actions. Signed, Rita Jackson."

This should hold Jim off for a while, she thought. Everyone would have to wait for Dusty to show up in order to find out what he knew.

Jim started the telegraph key humming, and when he finished, he waited for Rita to fill him in.

"That's all I know now, Jim. When the reply comes, get it to me at the Golden Palace, please." Smiling at him, she hurriedly left the building.

Fuzzy was happy to see her and followed her into the office to hear the latest news. "Sure musta been a scrap, missy. We heerd ya whittled the Arizona Kid's gang down a mite."

"Actually, I didn't do anything, Fuzzy. Nebraska, Dusty, and six of the men did the shooting. We were lucky to be alerted in time to stop the raid." She continued on, telling Fuzzy all about it, leaving out only her knowledge of who Dusty was.

When she finished, Fuzzy leaned back in his chair, musing: "I knowed Dusty was a rip snorter. That youngster kin shoot straighter and act faster than any man I seen."

Rita was brought up short in her thinking. "Why, Fuzzy, you never told me you knew Dusty."

"You never ast, little lady. Why one time he purely saved my life. Weren't for him, I'd be down below tryin' to spit out the flames, and you wouldn't be no Queen of the Strip," Fuzzy exclaimed with emphasis.

Rita tried hard not to show any emotion. She just sent a telegram to Governor Albright intending to tell him all about Dusty, and now she finds out she is further in debt to the Arizona Kid. Fuzzy went right on talking.

"Was three year or more back... I was prospectin' on the rim of a big canyon. One day I got a mite too close to the edge. The damned dirt caved in, and 'fore you could say Lord amighty, I was tangled in some bushes 'bout forty feet down, askin' God to save my sorry hide. Hadn't been for them bushes, I'da gone clean to the bottom. I was all tore up, with a bad ankle, askeered to even breathe fer fear I'd fall the rest of the way. I was clingin' to them thar bushes like a baby to its mammy's breast." He stopped talking briefly as memory had its way with him, then resumed.

"Musta been two, three hours 'fore I seed this hat poke over the rim with a smilin' face under it. 'Say, Fuzzy, you wouldn't be needin' any help, would you?' he ast, just as calm as all getout. I hollered up and said if it warn't too much trouble for a young inexperienced feller like him, he could toss me a rope." He paused again, recalling the events with a smile. "That face and hat disappeared, then the purtiest sight you ever seed come over that ledge: a rope with a loop in it. Didn't take long to grab onto that and slip it round my waist. Dusty and his horse pulled me right up over that there ledge, then stayed an' took keer of me till my ankle healed. Yep, I owe that youngun my life."

When Fuzzy stopped talking, Rita asked, "Where did you meet Dusty before that?"

"Hell, I'd meet up with him jist 'bout any ol' place: sometimes down southern Utaw, sometimes Coloradee. Last time I seed him was in Nevadee a week or so 'fore I come back to the Strip and met you at Pipe Springs. He was always travelin' somewhere, but always stopped to gab, and make sure I was doin' okay."

"Was he a traveling salesman, Fuzzy?" she asked, hoping he could shed some light on Dusty's previous life.

"Cain't say I ever knowed what he did fer a livin', but he always give me a few bucks when he seed me."

"Well, he sure came in handy on the cattle drive," Rita said, getting up from her chair and going to the window. It just didn't seem possible that Dusty could really be the Arizona Kid with all the good he'd done. But he hadn't denied it, and Nebraska hadn't either. What was she going to do when the governor answered her telegram?

As if in answer to her question, a knock sounded on the office door. When she opened it, Jim held a telegram in his hand.

He stood there and watched while she read. "Will catch tomorrow's stage for Pine Wood. Give Dusty this message if you run into him: Long record-BL-New York, Kansas, and Oklahoma." It was signed Charles Albright.

Rita couldn't understand it—all she knew was that he would be in Pine Wood four days from now. Why did he think she would see Dusty? Then she remembered that news of the attempted raid on her cattle had traveled everywhere—Dusty must've been mentioned in the news the governor got.

She handed the telegram to Fuzzy and told Jim she'd walk with him to the bank...she needed to let Jake see the telegram also. When Fuzzy finished reading, he handed it back and Rita left with Jim.

"I can't make heads or tails of that part about Dusty," Jim mentioned while they walked.

Thinking quickly, Rita said: "The governor is an old friend of the Jacobs, so he's known Dusty since he was born. The message is probably from Glen Jacobs telling Dusty something he needs to know."

Jim seemed satisfied with her answer, but she was still very puzzled—maybe Jake could decipher it. Turning into the bank, she told Jim goodbye and stepped inside. Jake was with another customer, so she waited till he was through, then handed him the telegram. He read it once, gave her a questioning look, then reread it.

"This part to Dusty must be from his parents. Didn't you tell me they were friends of the governor?" Jake inquired, handing the paper back to her.

"That's what I think too. It doesn't make any sense otherwise. Anyway, when Charles gets here we'll know what he meant."

Leaving the bank, Rita went back to the Golden Palace to catch up with her book work. She had lunch with the ladies in the kitchen, answering all their questions as best she could. They were all interested in Dusty.

"All I know," Amy sighed longingly, "is he'd make someone a nice catch."

"Hah! It'd be easier to catch a greased pig," came the scornful reply from Sally.

"Don't you know it!" agreed Emily, the prettiest one of them all. "I put on my best dress, fixed my hair perfect, acted real ladylike, and dripped charm. Nothing worked. I bet his horse gets more attention than any girl he's met."

Giving Emily a poke, Amy joked, "So next time stick hay in your hair and whinny."

Rita left them laughing and discussing Dusty and went back to her book work. Jake poked his head in the door several hours later and said dinner was being served at the hotel, asking if she wanted to go with him and Marie. She couldn't believe it was that late. Closing her books, she said she'd be right with them.

Leaving the saloon, they walked to the hotel dining room, with Marie chattering about Dusty all the way, saying how he was really something and how Rita should forget business and set her cap for him.

Rita tried to change the direction of conversation several times during dinner, but it always came back to Dusty and the raid on her cattle. She was glad when it was over. Bidding goodnight to her friends, she walked back to the Golden Palace. Rita visited with the men and bar girls while she worked her way back to the office, then opened the door and swung it shut with a backhanded push. Throwing her handbag on the desk, she sat down in the chair with a sigh of relief.

Suddenly she tensed, realizing she wasn't alone in the room. Her gaze picked up Dusty as he sauntered toward the desk from his place behind the door.

"Howdy. Didn't mean to startle you, but I need your help."

Without even thinking, Rita sprang from her chair and rushed into Dusty's arms. He caught her and pulled her tight against him. She was sobbing with her head pressed to his shoulder.

"Now settle down, sweetheart. There ain't nothing so serious we can't solve it," he murmured as he ran his fingers through her long hair. Then he put his hand under her chin and lifted it up; his head bent and her lips met his. She couldn't believe the sensation that went through her body. Pressing hard against him, she just wanted to melt her whole being with his and never let go. It seemed to her that Dusty felt the same way as his lips pressed harder against hers. She could feel his heartbeat matching her own.

Presently he pulled away and looked deep into her eyes. "Really hadn't expected such an exciting welcome, honey. Maybe I could go back outside and come in again so we could do it over. Not sure the first time was real."

"Oh, Dusty, I did the most terrible thing," she blurted out while he stood holding her. Then she rushed on. "I sent a telegram to the governor saying I knew the identity of the Arizona Kid. He wired back that he's leaving on tomorrow's stage for Pine Wood—he'll probably bring Rangers with him." She clung to him again and the sobs started back up.

"Shoot fire, honey, that's nothing to worry about. I can be gone long before he gets here," he murmured, trying to comfort her.

Reluctantly stepping away from him, she picked up her handbag and retrieved the telegram. Handing it to him, she watched while he read it. His eyes turned to agate and his stare bored into her when he looked up.

"So that clinches it," he said grimly. Then, squaring his hat, he kissed her and headed for the window. Crawling through, he said, "Tell Jake to meet me at the bank at seven tomorrow morning. Don't tell anyone else but him." Then he stopped halfway out the window. "Maybe you and Fuzzy should be there too." and he was gone, leaving Rita more mystified than ever.

She was sitting in her chair, thinking how nice it had been in Dusty's arms, when Jake knocked on the door and at her bidding came in and sat down. He watched her for some time before speaking, a baffled look on his face.

"Last time I saw you, just after dinner, you were sad and looked like the sky had fallen. Now you radiate happiness and the look in your eye tells me something else has happened."

She laughed and got up from the chair, striding over to the window where Dusty disappeared. Looking into the dark and then pulling the window closed, she said: "Dusty just left. He came to see..." She stopped in mid-sentence and a confused look came over her. "Actually, he said he needed my help. When I showed him the telegram, he suddenly got serious and left through the window."

Jake sat contemplating the news. "You sure that's all he did?" he asked in a curious tone.

Rita's face turned red at Jake's question. Starting to defend herself, she was stopped by Fuzzy poking his head in the door. Then he stepped into the room, closing the door behind him.

"Thought ya should know that feller with the Mexikin hat is

back... looks like he's rarin' fer some trouble. Mean as a hungry coyote, wantin' a bone to pick."

"Jake, let's go take a look. I don't want any trouble with this Bill Smith. After all, we don't know he's a bad man—he may be just acting a part," Rita said.

Fuzzy gave a snort at this suggestion. "Missy, I knows a mean'un when I sees him, and this'n jist crawled out from under a rock. All that's missin' is rattles on his tail. He's been sneakin' round town, askin' for Dusty, sayin' he's a old friend. But don't ya believe it...somethin' stinks in the barn or I ain't Fuzzy Martin."

Jake confirmed that by saying, "He's after Dusty for some reason. Maybe he's one of the Kid's gang and wants to settle with Dusty for stopping the raid on your cattle."

Rita was about to answer when the barroom went quiet. The piano stopped abruptly and not a shred of sound could be heard through the door. Jake bounded from his chair and reached the door at the same time as Rita. He pulled it open and held her back till he could assess the situation. Rita, looking under his arm, saw Dusty standing just inside the batwings with that devil- may-care look on his face. Facing him was the hard-eyed Bill Smith.

Fuzzy was pushing behind them, trying to see what was going on. Rita's hand dropped to her gun butt, but as the gun swung up, Fuzzy grabbed her arm.

"No, missy, let 'em be. This wuz bound to happen. Stick yer money on Dusty and don't fret."

Jake nodded acceptance of what Fuzzy said. "There's going to be a shootout. Best for us to just observe this one."

Rita consented by dropping her gun into its holster. Dusty's eyes never moved off Smith. They seemed to be boring into the man as if to cower him. Glancing at Smith, she caught the same look going out to Dusty. Again she felt helpless to interfere. One of them would die. The governor would be mad as all getout if it was Smith, and she would be devastated if it was Dusty. A moment before she'd been radiant and happy—now she was in the depths of despair, and all she could do was watch.

Smith spoke first, his voice rough: "Well, Kid, it's about time you showed your face so the good people of Pine Wood kin see what the Arizona Kid looks like."

A general inhaling of breath rushed through the room, and Sally, one of the bar girls, exclaimed, "Oh no!", her hand going to her mouth.

"Sawdust, I really didn't think you'd match guns with me," Dusty taunted as he stepped to the side of the door where his back would be to the wall. "Didn't bring any of the gang to back your play, did you?"

Jake whispered to Rita, "I knew I'd seen that Smith fellow before. Several years ago he matched lead with three tough hombres on the streets of Denver. Only one of them got off a shot before Smith...or Sawdust...killed them all. Each man was hit dead center." He shook his head sorrowfully. "Dusty ain't got a chance."

Fuzzy pushed a twenty-dollar bill into Rita's hand. "You're on, Jake. Twenty bucks says Dusty takes him."

Seeing Jake pull a twenty from his pocket, Rita couldn't believe her ears: her two best friends were betting on the outcome of a gunfight. Fuzzy saw her expression and commented, "Don't you fret none, missy. I seen Dusty draw many a time. He looks awful easygoin', but when he starts somethin', he finishes it."

Rita's eyes were glued to the scene, her heart in her throat. Sawdust glared hard at Dusty, trying to break him with his stare. Dusty stood easy with his hands at his sides and a smile on his face. Seeing that Dusty would not break, Sawdust made his move.

Dusty had been watching Sawdust's eyes; when he saw the lines appear at the corners, he drew and stepped slightly to the side at the same time. Both guns spit lead, and afterwards no one could say which gun blasted first—their draws were not visible. One moment they stood glaring at each other, the next instant the guns were spitting deadly flame and lead across the room.

Rita saw Dusty's shirt move and a hole appeared in the material between his left arm and his chest. A spiral of smoke issued from his gun barrel. Her glance swung to Sawdust as he took one step forward, then his gun sagged in his grasp, his knees buckled, and he slid to the floor with a spreading blood stain slightly to the left of center on his chest.

Dusty's gun slipped back into leather. Moving his eyes over the crowd, he said: "Show's over, folks. One less sidewinder to cause trouble." With that he swung around and shouldered through the batwings.

Pandemonium broke out in the barroom: everyone talked at once, and several men left the saloon to spread the word. Rita stepped back into her office and closed the door as Jake and Fuzzy went over to have the body of Sawdust removed. She leaned against the door with her heart still pounding and her body shaking.

The governor was due in three days, his undercover agent lay dead on her saloon floor, and Dusty, the man she loved with all her heart, was long gone. He would be hounded from pillar to post when his night's work became known. Charles would probably place an even larger reward on his head: Dead or Alive, it would read. Rita sank into her chair wondering what would happen next. She wouldn't be kept waiting long.

Sixteen

Rita woke from a restless sleep, suddenly remembering she'd forgotten to tell Jake about Dusty wanting to meet him at the bank. Looking out the window, she knew the time was already past for meeting Dusty. Hurriedly dressing, she strapped on her gun and headed for the bank.

When she went inside, Jake and Logan were in deep conversation. Jake glanced up when she entered and motioned her over. She took a chair beside Logan, and Jake told her they were discussing how to stop the robberies. The two men continued talking while Rita sat and listened. Logan felt that a posse should be sent out immediately to try and apprehend Dusty, alias the Arizona Kid. Jake was in favor of waiting for the governor to arrive.

As the argument continued, with neither man convincing the other of the best way to proceed, Rita put in her two cents.

"Logan, for two years you've scoured the whole West looking for the Arizona Kid's gang without success. What makes you think you can find them now?"

Logan became defensive. "I didn't know what the Kid looked like or who he was until now. With that knowledge, it should be easier to locate him. We can telegraph his description all over the country. Surely someone will spot him and tip us off, then we can move in on him."

Rita understood his point, but she still doubted its success. "The Kid isn't stupid. He'll know what you plan to do and lay low for a while before showing himself. I think like Jake does. We should wait till the governor arrives since he'll probably have

Rangers with him. After all, he promised us he would work on the problem of the Kid's gang."

Her words irritated Logan. "It'll be another two days before he gets here—by then the Kid could be in Mexico where the Rangers can't touch him."

"Maybe he'll stay there this time. With so many of his gang wiped out, he won't be as apt to stick around and cause trouble," Jake mentioned.

"I still say we need to get after him now," Logan stated positively.

"Logan, if you feel that strongly about it, then by all means, gather a posse and go after him." Rita pulled a twenty-dollar gold piece from her purse. "Here's twenty dollars that says you don't catch him."

Logan was surprised to see such opposition from Rita. "I'll just take that bet," he said, pulling out a twenty and handing it to Jake. "You hold the stakes, Jake." He stood up and said he would get right on it, then left them.

When Logan left, Jake, looking confused, asked, "How can he be so sure now when he's spent over two years looking for the Kid without success?"

Rita was afraid Logan might be right. "He has a point, Jake. With Dusty's description spread everywhere, he may just manage it. But I still think he should wait for the governor."

Their discussion continued for several minutes before Rita remembered she'd missed breakfast and left for the Golden Palace. She figured Pete would be feeding the late-rising bar girls, and when she entered the kitchen, she found she was right. Sitting down at the table with them, she listened to the chatter as Pete put a plate of steak and eggs in front of her.

"So what if he's the Arizona Kid," Emily exclaimed

indignantly. "That other outlaw said the Kid left the gang a long time ago, and I believe him."

Amy agreed. "All you have to do is look in those dreamy eyes and you just know he couldn't kill anyone."

They all nodded wisely: it was a well-known fact that a person's eyes told everything. Among them, Dusty's eyes, besides setting their hearts aflutter, proved his innocence.

Putting the final nail to it, Emily said in a no-nonsense voice: "Besides, that Smith fellow was probably lying. Who'd believe scum like him?"

Rita got the distinct impression that all the girls were on Dusty's side. When Emily stated emphatically that Sawdust was lying, it surprised Rita. The thought had never entered her mind because she already knew the truth. But it was probably a sentiment that would be shared by many people.

As she listened, Rita began to see that just because Sawdust named Dusty, not everyone would believe it, especially those on the Strip who knew Dusty's parents. Then she remembered that Logan hadn't even questioned the point. He seemed positive Dusty was the Arizona Kid. Did he have other proof Rita didn't know about? That may be why he was so sure of catching him this time.

Finishing her meal, Rita went to her office to ponder the fact. Where would Dusty go, and did Logan have information that would lead him right to Dusty? Now she was really uneasy, and couldn't let it go. All the worries rolled around in her mind, never settling on one solid fact. Finally she thought of Rosy; maybe she could shed some light on the subject. Picking up her handbag, she started for home, her mind full of the questions she was going to ask.

Changing into riding clothes, she saddled Thunder and set off for the ranch. Rosy was in the kitchen when Rita arrived. She greeted Rita and went on about her work. For a moment this bothered Rita since Rosy usually came forward and gave her a hug, saying she was glad to see her. Rita walked over to Rosy and gave her a hug anyway, saying she came to talk about Dusty. For some reason a look of anxiety flickered over Rosy's face.

Turning and going to the table to sit down, Rita fretted over Rosy's strange actions. She seemed nervous and upset about something.

"You heard about the shootout in the saloon last night?" she asked.

"Yes, that's all the cowboys were talking about this morning. They all think that Smith man lied about Dusty. Seems since Dusty helped you and worked for you, there was no way he could be the Kid," Rosy answered, feeling uneasy. "I just wish Nebraska was back so I could talk to him...he'd know for sure."

Pleased that her men had so much confidence in her, Rita dreaded the day they found out different. That must be the reason Rosy appeared anxious. Rosy would be no help with solving her problem; she'd have to wait till Nebraska arrived from the cattle drive, and that could be awhile.

Changing the subject, she talked with Rosy about how things were going at the ranch, asking if there was anything she needed. Rosy assured her all was well and said one of the ranch hands had been to town and purchased supplies three days ago. They continued to chatter for some time, then Rita decided she would go into the room she used when she was at the ranch and take a short rest before going back to town.

Opening the door to her room, she stepped inside and came to a complete stop. Dusty was just rising from her bed, a gun aimed directly at her.

"Ah! It's you, honey. I was sleeping so sound I didn't hear

you till the door opened. Guess I relaxed, thinking I was completely safe here," he admitted sleepily as he shoved the gun back to leather.

Quickly closing the door, Rita gasped: "What in the world are you doing here, Dusty? Logan is out with a posse looking for you."

Dusty chuckled. "Do you think he'll look here, sweetheart?"

Seeing the absurdity of this, Rita laughed with relief. "No, I don't really think he'll come into my bedroom looking for you. Fact is, I'm surprised you thought of coming here. After all, the reward for you will go up, darling, and I might be tempted," she said as she walked over to him and sat in his lap with her arms around him.

Dusty drew her close and their lips met for the second time. Rita could feel the longing spread through her body, but she knew now was not the time to let emotions get the best of her.

Pulling away from Dusty, she got up, saying: "What are you going to do? Logan is sending your description all over the West...everywhere you go there'll be men wanting to collect the reward."

Gazing at her fondly, Dusty commented, "Guess I'll just have to stay here in your room with you—that's the only way I'll be safe. Who'd believe the Arizona Kid would hide in the Queen of the Strip's bedroom?"

Stamping her foot, Rita exclaimed, "For heaven's sake, Dusty, be serious for once. Can't you see this is terrible? You'll be a target for every gun wherever you go."

Dusty's face sobered up. "Sorry, darlin', but I've dodged many a posse in my short life and don't think they'll have any more success now than before. Logan thinks he knows where I'll go, but when he gets there, all he'll find is one or two men and few stray cows."

Seeing the seriousness of Dusty's expression, Rita asked,

"Why do you think he knows where you'll be? He hasn't been able to locate you before."

"I imagine Sawdust told him. That's why he's so confident this time. But he's in for a surprise: when I checked, all the rustled cattle had been moved out and have probably been sold in Colorado by now. Logan will find the nest empty." Saying this, Dusty got up and walked to the window. "When do you expect Nebraska back?"

"It may be another week before he returns, depending on how the drive goes." Then she remembered what he'd said about Sawdust. "Seems like you knew Sawdust well; was he part of your gang?"

Dusty took a moment to shape his answer. "He took over the gang after I left for Mexico. A petty crook before that, he had the guts and meanness to step into my shoes and keep at least a semblance of order in the gang. His problem was that he liked to kill and was truly fast with his six-gun. When I came back, he got jealous, and that's why he went looking for me."

The new information left Rita bewildered: how could Mexican hat, alias Sawdust, alias Smith, be the leader of the gang and still be an undercover agent? It didn't make sense, but how could she tell that to Dusty when no one but her knew an undercover agent was in the area?

"Are you sure he was the leader of the gang?"

"No, I said that wrong. He was leading the gang when I arrived at the ranch that day. Since I'd ridden with them before, he took me back in the gang. But I was off scouting a lot and never joined in with what the gang did." Dusty hesitated again before finishing. "I knew there was a head guy somewhere, and I wanted to know who it was before taking control of the gang again, so I spent a lot of time following Sawdust to see if I could find out. He was pretty slick; just when I thought I had something, he'd give me the slip. When I warned you of the raid on your cattle, that washed me up with him."

"So that's why you had to face him down. If he remained alive, he'd be after you, and there was really no place you could go without him following you." Rita considered this new angle. "Now Logan is going where Sawdust told him you'd be, which is why he's so positive of getting you."

"Sounds right to me. Sawdust figured if Logan knew where I was and that I was the Arizona Kid, it would be easy to trap me. All Sawdust had to do was tip Logan off and then stay away from the hideout," Dusty stated. "Since Sawdust was looking for me in the saloon last night, I decided I might as well get it over with."

"But the gang will be there and Logan will wipe them out. That'll leave you without a gang;" Rita reasoned.

"There's not much of a gang left—between your men and the posses, there's only three or four outlaws. I figure what's left will take off when they hear Sawdust was killed," Dusty explained. "Logan will come up empty-handed."

Rita wondered what Dusty was planning now, with his gang gone and the knowledge of who he was spreading throughout the country. "So do you intend to stay in my bedroom the rest of your life?" she asked impishly.

Watching her with a knowing smile on his face, Dusty commented: "Sounds good to me. However, there's one more job to be done first."

Rita was appalled as the import of his statement sank in: Dusty planned one final job. Somehow this didn't fit with what she knew of him. Everyone defended him; surely he wouldn't let them down by pulling another holdup. An unwanted answer came to her. "You're not going to rob the bank in Pine Wood, are you, Dusty?"

Dusty ignored her question. "Only you and Rosy know I'm here. Governor Albright will be in Pine Wood day after tomorrow; the stage will arrive about ten in the evening." He was interrupted by Rita.

"So that's why Rosy was nervous...she knew you were in my room and was afraid of what I might do," Rita mused, not completely following Dusty's comment about the governor. Then she remembered what he'd told her when she last talked to him. "Oh, honey, I'm sorry I forgot to tell Jake and Fuzzy about the meeting at the bank. Was it very important?"

Although puzzled at the interruption, Dusty answered, "That's okay. After the gunfight, I had some other things I needed to do, so everything changed again. Now, sweetheart, I need you to do one more thing for me." He stopped, making sure she was listening to him instead of thinking of Rosy or the bank. "Meet the stage, and take the governor to the bank immediately after his arrival. Have Jake and Fuzzy with you. Try not to forget this time, okay?"

Her thinking was brought up short—maybe Dusty was going to turn himself in.

"So you're giving yourself up to the governor and not planning to rob the bank," Rita stated with relief.

Smiling at the happiness showing on her face, Dusty teased: "Well, if I rob the bank and take the governor hostage, we should be able to get clean away."

Startled for just a moment, Rita smiled. "No, Dusty, I wouldn't go with you then. Besides, I know you wouldn't do that. Now's the time for you to go straight. The governor knows you were on a ranch in Mexico, and since your return here, you say you haven't been involved in any of the robberies, so just turn yourself in and I'm sure he'll be lenient with you."

"And you'll visit me every day in prison till I've served my time," Dusty laughed.

Hitting him lightly on the shoulder, she said: "Be serious. Governor Albright is a fair man."

Dusty studied her a moment. What a woman! He thought. What an interesting life they'd have after they were married.

"So you'll meet the stage and take the governor to the bank?"

Putting her arms around his neck, she murmured: "Only if you promise to give yourself up, darling."

Dusty consented and Rita left the room, finding Rosy just outside the door waiting for the fireworks. "Rosy, thanks for believing in Dusty. Take good care of him while he's here."

Heaving a big sigh of relief, Rosy said, "You can count on me. I knew Dusty wasn't the Arizona Kid."

Saying goodbye, Rita mounted Thunder and rode back to town. How would she present all this to Jake and Fuzzy? Maybe she could just tell them she wanted to talk with the governor in the bank where it would be private. Then she realized she'd have to tell them the truth before that; they'd been with her through all her problems so far, and she couldn't deceive them even a little.

Seventeen

When Jake entered the Golden Palace after closing the bank that night, Rita and Fuzzy were in the office talking over business. Jake came directly to the office and took a chair, saying: "There's a lot of talk around town about Dusty. Before he left with his posse, Logan stated positively that Dusty was the Kid. Most don't believe it, but there are a few who think he may be right."

"Ain't no way Dusty's a killer," Fuzzy stated emphatically. "Oh, I know he was purty wild a few years back, but he ain't never killed a man din't need killin'."

"I agree with you, Fuzzy," Jake said. "Besides, we have it from the robber we hung that the real Arizona Kid quit rodding the gang after that train wreck. So even if Dusty was involved then, he hasn't been with them since."

Rita watched her two friends, hating to tell them what she knew. Sighing, she announced, "I'm afraid he is the Arizona Kid; I've known it since the raid on my cattle. That's how he knew the gang would raid us. He was with them when the plans were made." Watching their stunned faces, she said the rest: "After he helped Nebraska fight them off, there was no way he could go back to the gang. The governor told me the Arizona Kid owned a ranch in Mexico and had been there for two or three years."

Then she told them how she had met the Kid on the train, and what he'd done after the wreck, and how she was sure he left the gang at that time and stayed in Mexico until he showed up at the ranch looking for his parents. She also told them of him meeting Sawdust and joining the gang again and of Sawdust's jealousy, which precipitated the gunfight.

Fuzzy sat thinking about what Rita said. His face a study of pain and confusion, he finally blurted out: "You're wrong, missy. Ain't no way Dusty took up with them killers to rob and steal."

"I know, Fuzzy, I feel the same way—he's not a killer. My heart tells me this, but the facts seem to indicate otherwise."

Jake added: "He's mighty fast with a gun. I told you what Sawdust had done in the past, and Dusty shaded him. Still, Dusty never struck me as an outlaw. I tend to agree; he may have been wild years ago, but not now."

Rita listened to her two friends, happy that they had faith in Dusty. She wanted so much to have them believe the way she did; it seemed that the Dusty she knew and loved could not possibly be a killer.

"It seems we all feel the same about Dusty, but if he's the Arizona Kid and going straight, why didn't he stay in Mexico?"

No answer was given to her question, so she relayed Dusty's request and said he was going to give himself up to the governor but wanted it done privately at the bank. They broke up for the night, going their separate ways, but with one collective mind.

Fuzzy went out to play cards with some of the businessmen visiting town. Being a Friday night, a great crowd of people were in town for the show to be presented by Sam and Rita's girls. The game lasted far into the night, and the saloon was almost empty before it broke up. Jake had gone home earlier, not wanting his pregnant wife to be worried, so Fuzzy happily escorted Rita to her house.

Saturday night the stage from Phoenix arrived as scheduled. Rita, Jake, and Fuzzy, among others, were there to meet it. The coach came to a stop, and when the door opened, Governor Albright stepped down, holding his hand up to assist his wife. Rita came forward to give her a hug, while Jake shook Albright's hand. Fuzzy stood back watching the welcoming committee; he never felt comfortable around dignitaries.

Stepping away from Lila, Rita shook Albright's hand, saying: "Welcome to Pine Wood, Governor." Then her eyes widened as she saw Glen and Susan Jacobs getting out of the stagecoach.

"What in the world are you doing here?" she exclaimed over Albright's shoulder. Didn't they realize Dusty would be taken away in handcuffs? Surely Albright had told them. To withhold such information would be unbearably cruel. Perhaps they knew and simply wanted to comfort Dusty, to let him know they loved him no matter what.

Governor Albright saw all these emotions cross Rita's face and explained, "They received a letter from Dusty saying he was in Pine Wood, so since they were in Phoenix at the time I left, we traveled together."

Rita's heart sank when she considered what the consequences of their being here could entail. She went to Susan and took her hand, leading the Jacobs and Lila toward the hotel, saying to Jake: "You take the governor with you and Fuzzy—I'll meet you shortly."

Jake motioned to the governor, and Fuzzy followed them to the bank. Opening the door, they went into the darkened building and Jake lit a kerosene lamp, making sure the shades were drawn tight. Placing a chair for the governor, he and Fuzzy sat down in two others and began to discuss the trouble on the Strip.

"I thought Dusty Jacobs might be here to meet his folks since they wired him they were coming," Albright mentioned.

Fuzzy spoke up quickly: "He'll be along right soon. That young feller shows up at the darnedest times. Why, I kin tell ya how he plumb saved my life once."

Just then a firm knock sounded on the back door of the bank.

Jake got up to see who was there, and when he opened the door, Dusty slid through, quickly closing it behind him. Going over to Albright, he shook his hand.

"Thanks for getting here so quick, Governor. Matters are coming to a head fast now and it'll be easier to handle with you here."

Jake didn't understand Dusty's statement: it seemed as though Albright had been summoned by Dusty. Before he could say anything, Rita came through the front door and stopped short, staring at Dusty.

Albright spoke as Rita sent him a bewildered look. "Glad you got back to hear what Dusty has to say, Rita. Come on in and sit down—this may take a while."

When they were all seated, Dusty spoke. "Charles, the man you want is living here in Pine Wood. It was so simple—I don't know why we couldn't see it sooner. He's gone right now but will be back soon. I hope I have enough time to prove my case before he arrives. I stopped at the Golden Palace kitchen and told Pete to let us know if he shows up."

Rita couldn't believe her ears: what in the world was Dusty talking about? It sounded like he was handing the governor information he had expected.

"That's what I gathered from your last telegram, Kid," Albright said. Then, at the puzzled look on Rita's and Jake's faces, he started to speak again, when he was interrupted by Fuzzy getting up and dancing a jig.

"I knowed he wern't no killer," Fuzzy cackled as he stopped his dance. Rita wondered if she was dreaming again, surely both Charles and Fuzzy were crazy.

Albright continued his interrupted speech. "It seems that I owe you all an explanation. Do you remember I told you I had a secret agent who would solve the problems you were having here, Rita?"

"But he was killed three nights ago in the Golden Palace," Rita blurted out as her glance went from Dusty to Albright. "Wasn't he?"

Albright laughed at Rita's doubtful expression. "Well, if he was killed three nights ago, I guess there's something to this belief of a resurrection, since he's sitting in that chair where Dusty is right now."

"You mean Dusty isn't the Arizona Kid?" Jake commented.

"Oh, I'm the Arizona Kid, Jake, and Charles knows that. But when I robbed your train and met Rita, I decided then and there that if I was going to ask Rita to be my wife, I needed to change my ways. So I said goodbye to the gang and headed to Phoenix to see my folks' friend, Governor Albright." Dusty sat relaxed in his chair as he talked. "Charles has known me since I was born, so I figured I could get a soft sentence from him. Instead of that, he pinned a star on me and put me to work as an Arizona Ranger."

Dusty stooped over and pulled off his right boot. Taking his knife, he split the lining at the top and extracted a metal object, then tossed it on the desk for all to see: it was an Arizona Ranger's badge.

Albright took up the story. "When Dusty came to me, we were having big problems with gunrunners and rustlers, plus all sorts of difficulty getting the Mexican government to cooperate with us. Knowing how the Arizona Kid eluded every posse sent after him, I figured Dusty would be the right man to go into Mexico and work undercover." Albright paused, thinking of all the Kid had managed to accomplish. "When his job was over, I sent him up here to investigate his old gang. Since they knew him, it would be easy for him to rejoin them and tip me off, sending coded messages to his folks when a raid was planned. He did that, and consequently the gang's been whittled down to almost nothing."

Dusty added, "There's still one big job to do and that's to catch the brains behind the gang." Getting up from his chair, he went to the door leading into the Wells Fargo office. "Jake, do you ever go into this office?"

Jake was mystified. "No. Usually if Logan needs to talk to me, he comes in here; I don't think I've ever had reason to go in there." Glancing at Rita, he asked, "Have you, Rita?"

Rita sat with joy in her heart, not really hearing his question then when it sank in she began to get a funny feeling in her gut. "No, I haven't been in there since Logan took over."

Dusty motioned for them to follow him as he opened the door and stepped inside. When they were all in the room, he asked, "Jake, does this room look small to you when compared to your bank room?"

Jake looked around, then stepped back into the bank. "It's about four feet shorter in length."

"That's right. I knew the head man had to be operating out of Pine Wood. I followed Sawdust several times when he came to town but always lost track of him. Studying this problem, I decided the man I was seeking had to be able to come and go whenever he wanted, without any questions asked. Logan fit that picture, so I wired Charles to check Logan's background." He paused, looking at Rita. "You read the telegram he sent back. The BL meant Bert Logan. That clinched my suspicions. I broke in here last night to look for proof—here's what I found."

Going to the bookcase behind Logan's desk, he reached up to the top shelf and pulled a book onto its side. But it wasn't a book at all, it was a lever painted to look like a book, and when tipped on its side, it opened the door made to look like a bookcase. He swung the fake bookcase back and stepped into a small room. The others stood knotted in the doorway.

Fuzzy gulped and said, "Well bless my soul," as they all saw the coins, bills, gold, and silver bars stacked neatly on shelves.

Albright whistled when he stepped into the small room. "So he would bring the loot back here and keep it till he was ready to quit the game."

Rita could barely control her emotions— she wanted to throw herself into Dusty's arms and kiss him soundly. He wasn't a crook, he was a Ranger and had put a stop to Logan and his gang. No wonder Sawdust wanted to kill him so badly and Logan tried to make everyone believe Dusty was the Arizona Kid. If Logan had caught Dusty at the hideout, he would have killed him without giving him a chance to surrender.

Dusty started to explain his theory. "He gave the gang members just enough of the loot from each robbery to keep them happy, telling them that after the last big job, they would take all this and clear out of the country and live like kings. That's exactly what he intended to do if he caught me. By now he'd have it all to himself since there's no gang left."

A hard rap on the front door silenced Dusty. Jake went to see who was there, opening the door a crack to let Pete slip into the room. Seeing Dusty, he said, "Logan and four men are about a mile out of town—he always comes to the saloon first when he gets back."

"Thanks, Pete. Go back to the saloon. I'll be over shortly." Dusty slid his gun from the holster, checked the loads, and placed a live one in the empty chamber. Spinning the cylinder, his hand flashed and the gun nestled lightly in its leather.

Pete went to the door, then turned back and added, "The four men with Logan are strangers. My scout said they look awfully tough; he figures they're all gunslingers."

Rita, knowing for sure what Dusty had in mind, grabbed his arm when he started to follow Pete. "You can't face them alone, Dusty. That's five against one, and I've seen Logan in action. He used to go riding with me sometimes. He can draw and shoot a moving target unbelivably fast. I thought I was fast, but Logan would have his gun out before I even cleared leather." She pleaded with Dusty with her eyes. "If you go it alone you'll be killed— you may get one or two, but not all five."

"Rita's right. I'm going with you." Jake pulled his gun to check the loads.

Fuzzy swung out in front of Dusty, pulling his old peacemaker. "I ain't fast, boy, but I kin hit what I aim fer. You ain't leavin' me outta all the fun."

Rita was proud of her friends. "See, Dusty, with our three guns to help, Logan will be stopped."

"I can't let you face gunslingers, honey," Dusty stated, his heart in his throat.

"I've faced gunslingers before," she said grimly, showing her mettle, "and there's no way I'll risk losing my future husband without siding him. You've had all the fun so far, darling. It's our turn to help out now."

Albright wished he were better with guns. "She's right. If I were any kind of a shot I'd help, but I'd just be in your road. I've spent too many years in easy chairs, talking to politicians."

He truly regretted not being able to get at least one of those vicious killers.

Dusty finally consented, and they all walked to the Golden Palace and went directly to the bar. Since it was Saturday night, the place was packed and the noise deafening. Rita drew her gun and fired into the ceiling. When the barroom was quiet, she announced: "There's going to be a showdown very shortly with the gang that's been causing all the trouble around here, so open a lane between us and the door."   Smiling wryly at their confusion, she added: "And keep your heads down when the shooting starts."

The patrons were stunned for a moment, thinking it was some kind of joke. Then, seeing the serious look on Rita's face, they scrambled to get back out of the way. A path from the bar to the batwings quickly cleared. Breaths were held as everyone waited for the fireworks to start.

They heard the sound of horses' hooves coming close, then the creak of leather as men dismounted and tied to the hitching rack in front. Boots scraped on rough wood, causing shivers to run up the spines of the less courageous. Hands tightened on drinks and cards, and every eye in the saloon fixed on the swinging doors.

No one moved.

Suddenly the batwings burst inward, and a furious Logan strode into the room, followed by four villainous-looking outlaws. He took three steps before he felt the tension and heard the silence.

Stopping abruptly, his gaze swept over the nervous crowd and then locked onto Dusty standing at the bar. His eyes widened as they fell on the Arizona Rangers badge now pinned to Dusty's vest, then they pinched down and his body straightened. Recovering quickly, he forced a smile.

"Well I'll be damned! I didn't know you were a Ranger." He started forward, intending to shake Dusty's hand, but Dusty's steely voice knifed through the air and pinned his feet to the floor.

"You and your men are under arrest for robbery and murder, Logan."

When the words penetrated the onlookers, there was an audible gasp throughout the room.

"What in hell are you talking about, Dusty?" Logan snapped.

"I may have been mistaken in naming you as the Arizona Kid, but that son of a bitch Sawdust said you were."

Governor Albright spoke from the side of the bar. "Dusty located your hiding place for all the money you've stolen, Logan. It's been impounded as evidence against you."

One of the outlaws with Logan whispered savagely: "Boss, we kin take 'em! Hell, one of 'em's a woman, and the others don't look like no gunfighters."

Logan silenced him with a cold glance. "You haven't seen the Queen of the Strip shoot, Ferral. She could put a bullet in your left eye before you cleared leather."

Logan hesitated, wondering what to do next. The jig was up if Albright spoke the truth. It had been so perfect till Dusty poked his nose into things. Where in hell had he been these last years, and when did he get that Ranger badge? Logan realized he should have left the country sooner instead of waiting to rob the Pine Wood bank as well as Rita's safe. He'd had big plans on how to accomplish that and then skip out and no one would have known who did it. Damn Dusty anyway. He had stolen Logan's girl and now spoiled his plans. Hatred began to flame through his body. If it weren't for this man glaring hard-eyed at him, he'd have pulled it off.

As the tension increased, the two sides stood riveted, watching for any sign of movement. Suddenly Logan's rage blossomed and his hand flashed. The outlaw on Logan's far left let out a curse and went for his gun at the same time. No one noticed as Pete brought his scattergun up from under the bar and pointed it right at the man going for his gun. Pete pulled the trigger as the outlaw's gun cleared leather—the load caught him in the stomach, blowing a hole in him you could drive a mule through. He was carried back by the blast to strike the wall, then he slowly slid to the floor, blood pooling around him.

At the same instant of Pete's shotgun blast, Fuzzy triggered the old peacemaker he held in his hand. He knew he couldn't draw fast, so he had held the gun by his side. When the fireworks started, he just tipped it up and blasted the outlaw to Logan's far right. The shot was true—it hit the outlaw between the eyes, and as his nervous system ceased to exist, he crumpled to the floor.

Dusty, Rita, and Jake whipped guns from leather at Logan's first move. Jake's gun blast shaded the man on Logan's left, and he slammed back into a chair, entangling his feet and crashing into the bar. Rita's lightning-fast draw had been hampered by the action around her, and Ferral managed to get off a hurried shot that took Rita in the left shoulder. Her slug went dead center to the left eye of Ferral, and he toppled over backwards onto a table behind him. Dusty and Logan exploded into action at the same time, both guns blasting their flame and lead across the hate-filled space. Logan's bullet took Dusty in the right thigh, missing the bone and going on through to embed itself in the bar. Dusty's shot was accurate, striking Logan in the chest, exploding his heart and going on to smash his spine.

Logan's feet took him one step forward before the muscles lost their function. He slowly sank to the floor, the smoke from the barrel of his gun drifted upwards as his face met the raw wood, dead before he hit.

The powder smoke from Pete's shotgun, coupled with the smoke from Fuzzy's old peacemaker, covered Dusty's party till the guns' echoes fell silent.

When it cleared, Rita was clinging to Dusty with her uninjured arm around his neck, and Dusty's arms were around her waist, holding her close. Blood dripped from his wounded leg to the floor, while blood dripped from Rita's superficial shoulder wound to mix with his.

Rita leaned her head back, staring at Dusty's Ranger star; then her eyes slowly rose to meet his. He could see in them all that he had ever hoped for as her lips parted and words drifted softly through the quiet of the Golden Palace barroom.

"Well, I guess law and order has finally arrived on the Arizona Strip."

L Brooksby was born and raised on the Arizona Strip, and J Brooksby in Texas. A veterinarian, L punched cattle, trained aviation pilots, and both went to BYU. Retired, they now spend their time writing western fiction.